Kyler rushed over and grabbed her backpack from Dante. "It's. . ."

"Empty," he provided plainly.

Dante stretched an arm across the back of the divan and crossed his legs casually. He wore dark slacks and his unbuttoned white shirt revealed hard abs. . . that she had licked not hours earlier.

"You did this! You had this all planned out!"

"I performed no such trickery. You'll recall it was you who eagerly suggested we finish off the evening here."

"You were scheming. Hoping to get me alone so you could steal the egg from me. I can't believe I fell for that!"

He waved a hand, dismissing the comment. "Doesn't matter now. I've come to Venice to claim the Fabergé egg, and I won't leave without it."

"So you admit you used me—seduced me—to get what you wanted?"

He lifted a finger. "Seducing you was not my original intention. That was a fortuitous bonus."

A VENETIAN VAMPIRE

MICHELE HAUF

MILLS & BOON

First Published in Great Britain 2016
By Mills & Boon, an imprint of HarperCollins*Publishers*
1 London Bridge Street, London, SE1 9GF

© 2016 Michele Hauf

ISBN: 978-0-263-92994-2

89-0117

Michele Hauf has been writing romance, action-adventure and fantasy stories for more than twenty years. France, musketeers, vampires and faeries usually populate her stories. And if Michele followed the adage "write what you know," all her stories would have snow in them. Fortunately, she steps beyond her comfort zone and writes about countries and creatures she has never seen. Find her on Facebook, Twitter and at www.michelehauf.com.

To Chelle Olson, editor, friend, rockin' cool chick.
Index finger up, middle fingers down,
pinkie up, thumb in.

Chapter 1

Dante D'Arcangelo insinuated himself into the Cannaregio Casa d'Aste with an ease that had come from more than 160 years of existing along the edge of the shadows. No one paid any mind to the tall stranger as he walked the Venetian auction house's marble corridor to the back room, where key arrangements for the event were being performed. Tomorrow evening's gala auction would feature dozens of valuable art items on the block. It was being hyped with celebrity fanfare. A media blitz.

The star of the show was a Fabergé Imperial egg called the Nécessaire. It had officially gone missing in 1952, after the last known buyer had been recorded only as: A Stranger. A month ago, it had suddenly re-emerged in the art world. Dante intended to remove it from the auction house tonight. No hard feelings. It was just that the egg belonged to him. And the very fate of his kind—vampires—required he get it back.

As he took in the layout of the bustling auction house, the placement of the dinnerware stacked and ready for service in the grand ballroom where a celebratory dinner was to be held, counted the employees and marked their various uniforms, noted security cameras and entrance keypads, Dante noticed one woman stood out from them all.

Rather, she didn't quite fit in.

A woman of medium height and more than a few delicious curves, she stood apart from the workers possessed of blasé European disinterest, slender frames and suntanned skin. A tourist who had wandered in from the streets? Doubtful. Her actions were purposeful. She moved along the edge of the activity, which hummed like a busy office expecting the district manager to show up at any moment to fire one and all. She was dressed all in black, and over that she wore a snug maroon apron like those on the auction house employees. Her dark hair was pulled into a ponytail.

Waiters and others who most definitely belonged in the mix shuffled to and fro, intent on their specific duties. Some spoke into earpieces; others checked details on clipboards or iPads. A pair of lanky busboys hustled clattering cases of wine toward the bar area set up along one wall.

The woman with the dark hair and mysterious presence kept her head down, yet her kohl-lined eyes took in everything—*except* the people. She did not miss a creased seam where wall met wall, nor a crimped electrical cable running from a computer along the floor and into a dark, attached room. Near her thigh, her fingers moved as if counting, slowly. She was marking her footsteps across the room.

Dante smirked. Was she actually casing the place? Well, he knew she was because *he* was. Only he had much more stealth, despite the fact he wasn't a professional thief. Although his life experiences did tend to put him in larcenous situations from time to time. He picked up necessary skills with ease and interest. And he never hesitated to commit a criminal act when he knew it could ultimately serve the greater good.

Such as obtaining this particular bejeweled prize.

When his shoulder was bumped, he turned and offered apologies to a slender blonde woman holding a stack of bid cards and offered to help her carry them. She thanked him and in mellifluous Italian said she was capable. And then she smiled widely as she stared at his face—a few seconds too long.

Dante was accustomed to that dreamy look. And honestly? It gave him a visceral thrill. Women gave him a thrill. All of them. All shapes, sizes and colors. Could a man ever get enough? So he touched her cheek, brushing aside some strands of corn-silk gold hair over her ear. She blushed and looked to the cards clasped in both hands, then fluttered her lashes as if she couldn't decide whether to look back up at him or clutch those blank cards tighter.

He needn't exercise his vampiric persuasion on her. If he wanted her, he could have her. But flirting with an audience present was gauche. And he didn't want her. He simply enjoyed the triumph of knowing she would fall sighing into his arms should he give her the permission to do so.

Dante bowed, gesturing she had the right of way. That gentlemanly move stirred her from her adoring gaze. She cleared her throat, blushed even deeper and nodded quickly. As she passed, he inhaled her perfume. A note of freesia vied to rise above the alcohol base. He did not care for unnatural chemical scents. Still, he did admire the warmth that continued to redden her skin.

Enough distraction. Where had the mystery woman gone? *Ah, yes.*

He crossed the room to the hallway into which his suspected thief had entered with carefully placed—and counted—footsteps. Immediately he noticed an armed guard in front of a closed door at the far end of the hallway. A walkie-talkie was clipped to his chest pocket. No gun at his hip, but the gleam of a carbon nightstick flashed from the holster at his waist. A badge would be required to enter what Dante guessed was the room where the auction items were being prepared to go on the block.

Halfway down the hallway, between Dante and the guard, the woman in black suddenly checked her wristwatch and stopped. After turning, she backtracked. Dante dug out his pocket watch and bowed his head as she passed him. He picked up no perfume scent from her, though was that a hint of salty sweat? She was nervous? *Poor girl.* Had she not done this before? Such a pity she would fail. It was in his best interest to ensure she did.

He'd have to adjust his schedule for this evening. Didn't want to run into her bungling her way through a hopeless theft. And he'd hate to see the disappointment in her eyes when she arrived on the scene to find whatever she sought was missing. Had to be the egg. It was the only item on the auction list that could possibly attract a thief. Missing from circulation for almost seventy years, the Nécessaire Fabergé egg was a showstopper.

Yet, it had been missing from *his* care for only twenty-five years. He hated to admit to himself, but he'd let it slip through his hands some time before the turn of the century.

And then a thought occurred as he confidently stopped before the guard and allowed him to scan the badge he'd lifted upon entering the establishment half an hour earlier. *What if?*

Yes, what if?

"*Immettere.*" The guard granted him entry.

"*Grazie,*" Dante said and strolled inside.

Two men dusting a bronze statue of a dandelion looked up as he entered, and again Dante bowed his head over the 1790 pocket watch he'd been gifted as an eighteenth birthday present. Four silver skulls were situated in the center beneath the brilliant copper hands. He wouldn't dream of destroying the line of his suit with a cell phone.

He wasn't going to remain in this room long enough to be asked questions. And the cursory glance he'd taken had confirmed only one camera in the opposite corner. The far wall displayed a digital lock beside the door, same as near the door through which he had entered. Inadequate security, as his advance research had reported while on the jet to Venice. Not that he'd surfed the information highway himself. He knew people who knew far too much about technology and ways to infiltrate security systems.

This auction house was small, finding its feet after decades of near failure. The egg was to be its ticket out of the red. Pity it hadn't boosted security for its big show. If a thief could get past the security sensors on the first floor, the reward for making it that far would be in this simple room.

He put up a finger to gesture as if he'd forgotten something. "I'll be right back," he muttered and left the room, tucking away the watch. He offered a gracious *ciao* to the guard as he strolled back down the hallway.

He didn't see the woman in black again. Didn't need to. He'd marked her as no threat.

As Dante made his way toward the front of the building and stepped out into the fresh summer air, he returned to the what-if scenario. He might consider it a fortune that another thief was slinking about his turf. Would she go after the object he wanted? It was the most valuable and unique of the auction's offerings. There was always the risk she was not at all interested. Perhaps bronze dandelions were her thing?

"Foolish not to take the egg," he murmured. "And if she does?"

He smiled a wicked smile that had caused many a

woman to strip off her lace-and-silk unmentionables and beg him to take her.

"I'll let her take the egg for me. It'll be a great diversion."

He did enjoy diversions. Especially those involving a beautiful woman.

Many hours after her visit to case the art house, Kyler Cole again left the building, but this time, on the sly.

Nabbing the Nécessaire Imperial egg had been too easy. So easy, in fact, that Kyler kept rubbing her palm over the black nylon backpack in which she'd placed the egg to reassure herself she'd actually done it. She had snuck into the Cannaregio Casa d'Aste and absconded with a nineteenth-century artifact that was worth millions. *Go, girl!*

And why had she, a thief who had only ever stolen to survive, taken on such a task? Because hidden within the egg was a spell that promised eternity, and that would give her freedom from worry and fear.

It had been a harrowing adventure—and entirely new for her—but well worth the risk. Her body hummed and tittered as she walked swiftly through a dark alleyway and toward the buzz of a crowd mingling at an outdoor bar near the Grand Canal's sparkling waters. The Venetian nightlife bubbled with laughter and music from a live acoustic band. The air was rife with smells of salty seawater, fried seafood and sweet spices. Her mood compelled her toward the celebration.

Kyler's toes barely hit the ground, and she propelled herself so lightly she thought someone might see her lift off from the pavement and fly at any moment. But she remained grounded by keeping one eye out for the local police, whom, she had noted earlier, dressed in gorgeous black-and-white uniforms and, with the addition of crisp, clean white gloves, looked like fashion models. Yes, she had a wandering eye for a well-dressed man.

She'd not tripped any alarms while in the auction house. The security had been lax. As well, she'd spied an open window on the second floor. She avoided the risk of setting off the alarms on the first floor, and a leap had allowed her entrance. Such skills she possessed! And once perched upon the windowsill, an interior scan had assured her no cameras were in the room.

If her luck continued to play well, no one would discover the theft until the final inventory preceding tomorrow night's auction. She intended to leave Venice as soon as she got the call for the handoff, which she expected sometime tomorrow. The man she'd stolen the egg for would arrange for someone to meet her here in Venice to take it off her hands, but she didn't have the details yet.

Right now, she could use a glass of wine, perhaps even champagne. Yes, a celebration was due! It had been a long time since she'd felt so elated. So ready to embrace the possibilities life now offered her. And some well-deserved merriment would wipe the tarnish from the crime, yes? She'd committed petty theft before. A few swiped cosmetics when she was a teenager, and the obligatory bottle of wine from the liquor store while her friends distracted the cashier. Stupid stuff. Last year, she'd upped it to food and pharmaceuticals when caring for her dying mother. Funds had been low. She hadn't had any other choice.

The crime she'd committed this evening felt…not so terrible, now that it had been accomplished. What was contained within the egg would give a certain man the reassurance he needed—for her, as well.

She insinuated herself into the crowd of partiers milling about an ivy-draped patio and eyed the open-air bar. A few bar stools were empty, so…why not? Sliding onto a stool, she kept the backpack slung over a shoulder.

"Prosecco," she told the bartender, and the bearded drink-jockey winked before turning to pour her a goblet.

She didn't speak Italian, so she was thankful that a word here or there served to get by in this country. Born and raised in Iowa, her first trip overseas had been six months earlier. And she hadn't looked back since.

"Celebrating?"

Kyler took in the side profile of the man who'd asked her the question in English. Chiseled cheekbone and a thick black brow. A blade of a nose and the hint of stubble darkening his upper lip. His hair was cut short, hugging a perfectly shaped skull, and was the same inky color as hers. She'd taken hers out of the ponytail after exiting the auction house. It was one of her best assets, and she now swung the thick mane over a shoulder as her sensual instincts screamed for her to get the guy's attention—and keep it.

"Yes. I've had a good day." She sipped the chilled prosecco. Beaming from the high of her accomplishment, she tilted her glass toward him.

He tipped his glass against the thin crystal. "My

wine won't match your bubbly, but I toast you all the same. To good days."

"Most definitely. I feel great. Life could not be better at this moment."

"Ah? I feel your enthusiasm. It is written on your face and in your movements." His eyes glinted from a flash that carried from the overhead swag of Christmassy strands of white lights. And his European accent? Kyler felt the deep tones melt about her heart. "You visiting the city or a resident?"

"Just visiting."

Her leg bobbed beneath the bar, and she cautioned her sudden nervousness. Nix that. She wasn't nervous; she was exhilarated. And talking to a sexy stranger only heightened that amazing sensation.

Would it be ridiculous to consider a celebratory roll between the sheets? Not at all. She deserved a handsome man kissing her, whispering sweet nothings to her, tasting her…

"You?" she asked with a perkiness that felt false. She was trying not to lean too close to him. He might see her drool. Not that she'd ever drool. Oh, mercy, his voice.

"I live in the city," he said, "but not year-round. Just arrived in Venice for a few days' visit, actually."

"Me, too. I'm here for a few days, that is. Might try to do some sightseeing in the morning."

"You haven't been yet?"

"Uh…nope." She sipped again. Gotta watch what she said. She concentrated on the man's gorgeous blue eyes. *Wow.* They were unreal in color, and he looked directly at her. His intense scrutiny of her lit a fire in her core, and she straightened her shoulders, which lifted her breasts. Attention from an attractive man? *Go, Kyler.*

"Forgive my manners. An introduction is necessary. I'm Dante D'Arcangelo."

Really? If that wasn't a sexy name, Kyler didn't know what was. And the man certainly did resemble a delicious dark angel. *Mmm...*

He waited for her to respond.

"Oh, right. Me. Kyler Cole." She shook his proffered hand, and at the sudden, scintillating, electric shimmer that shot through her fingers and up her arm, she tugged away and gasped. "Oh." And then, as she settled into the realization of *what* the man who sat beside her was, she repeated her exclamation in a more sensual tone. "Oh."

That shimmery feeling that had raced over her skin? It occurred only when one vampire touched another. Now she was definitely on board with a hookup. Because really, she hadn't met many others like her in the few months she had been vampire.

"Oh, indeed," he echoed in an equally sensual tone.

He turned on the bar stool to face her with his body, his knee hugging her thigh. Enchantment twinkled in his eyes as he took her in with undisguised wonder. It was as though he had discovered a diamond sitting among common pebbles. Kyler could eat up his attention for breakfast, dinner and supper.

"A like soul," he said. "Refreshing to find another here in Venice. Shall we toast to one another?"

"Absolutely."

Kyler had a tendency to trust most people, but a sudden moment of uncertainty emerged. To have walked straight up to another vampire like this? It was weird. Or possibly coincidence. Had to be coincidence. He'd already been sitting at the bar when she had arrived. Wasn't like he'd been following her.

She sighed and sucked in her lower lip as she tapped a fingernail against the goblet stem. He seemed harmless. Too handsome, for sure. A man as sexy as he was would not be by himself. Not for long, at least. And yet the appeal of him being vampire could not be disregarded. She'd not been with another vampire, between the sheets, or to share blood. And she'd been wondered what both would be like.

"I'm sorry. I don't like to see a woman looking so distraught. Have I said something wrong?"

"Uh, no," she said quickly. *Distraught?* Try "making up her mind about whether or not to pursue her illicit wonderings." Tangled sheets and bloody bites? She didn't need to consider it long. *Yes, please!*

Tilting back another swallow of prosecco, she clutched her backpack strap, assessing the weight of its contents. Quite heavy for the silver and gemstones that made up the object. "I, uh…didn't expect…"

"It's a nice surprise when it happens," he offered casually.

"Yes, it is. I've just never met another…" She cast a glance aside. The bar's patrons were all chatting in Italian. "Another…*you know*, in such a casual manner. You startled me." She leaned forward and her thigh nudged his knee, but she kept herself from touching his leg with her hand. "But it was a good startle."

"Excellent. We understand one another from the get-go. No masks to wear. And don't worry—I'm not after anything. Though I would be lying if I didn't admit that I followed you since right about there." He pointed down the street. "At the corner by the flower shop. I couldn't stop myself from following you. You're gorgeous, Kyler. And your demeanor is so attractive. You walk as if on air."

A shiver of her previous excitement returned, and Kyler wiggly gaily on the bar stool. "Like I said, good day. Probably one of the best I've had in a while. What about you?"

"My best good day? Hmm, that was probably…"

She leaned forward in anticipation of his explanation. Abandoning her caution, she wanted the banter, some good conversation and another glass of prosecco. She indicated to the bartender to refill.

"My best day must have been when I met Pablo Picasso and got to shake his hand."

"That's awesome. Early twentieth century?"

"It was 1972, actually. He died a year later. I've been around a while." He shrugged in a manner that drew her eyes to his well-fitted suit. Tailored perfectly for his lean shape and broad shoulders. "But the years don't show on my face."

"You've a handsome face."

He bowed his head as he grinned, then tipped his glass to her refilled goblet. *"Salut!"*

"Salut!" And she tilted back the entire goblet. Then felt compelled to say, "This is exciting for me. Talking to another of my kind."

"Is that so? You don't associate with others of our

species?" He leaned toward her, and she scented not cologne but something primal and innate. His essence, perhaps. A warm, leathery scent.

"No, I haven't had opportunity. I just transformed six months ago."

"I see. New blood. Well, don't worry. I won't bite. Unless you want me to." He winked. "That's a tired joke, but I couldn't resist."

She smirked, which turned into a genuine chuckle. "You never know—I might like a bite."

She could seriously entertain the idea of wrapping her legs about his hips and sinking her fangs into his neck—

"What have you come to Venice for, Kyler?"

Tugged out of the fabulous fantasy of lapping at the man's neck, she gave him a blank look. What had he said?

"Vacation or work?" he asked.

"Oh, uh…a search and find actually. For a friend."

"And did you find what you were searching for?"

"Oh, yes. It was actually a piece of art. Pretty."

"Something famous?"

She shrugged. "Could be. I'm not much of an art enthusiast. I wouldn't recognize Picasso if he sat down before me with one of his works in hand. I prefer music."

"I do, as well. All sorts, but I am partial to jazz. Do you like to dance?" he asked.

"I do, but I don't know how. I've always wanted to learn something like the tango." She hooked her fingers on the backpack strap. The hardy weave and weight reminded her not to lose all caution. "I was on my way back to the hotel when I stopped for a quick drink. Not really dressed for dancing or partying. I'll take a rain check, though."

"Rain checks often go untended. How about another prosecco?"

"You'll get me drunk."

"Do you get drunk?"

"Not usually." Vamps could consume a lot of alcohol with little affect on their sobriety. "But whiskey, straight from the vein, does make me sick. I learned that one the hard way." She touched her chest. Never had she confessed such a personal detail about herself. It was too easy to be open in his presence. Relaxing into the conversation felt like stepping into his arms and settling in for a nice long snuggle.

"Vodka is my bête noire," he offered. "I can't stand a drunk bite. I prefer them healthy."

"Me, too," she agreed. "But I'm still learning, you know."

She straightened and slid her hands down her ribs and to her waist, a weird habit she'd developed after putting on thirty pounds following her mother's death. She still hadn't lost the weight, but she had learned to embrace her curves. And use them to her best advantage.

A glance at Dante confirmed he was studying her with those mesmerizing eyes. Interested? If only she'd worn something more revealing than the pedestrian black turtleneck shirt and black leggings. *Wow*. Did she totally look like a cat burglar? What had she been thinking? Should have brought along a bright red scarf to tie around her neck after the deed had been done.

"So, tell me more about you, Dante. You are Italian, but I think the words you just used were French?"

"I am both. Italian on my mother's side and my father was French. But I don't mind speaking English. It is an interesting language."

And her only option. "Where are you living?"

"I own a palazzo a short walk away, in the San Marco. It's a vacation home. I spend most of my time in Paris. Though at the moment I am homeless in the City of Light. Sold my barge and waiting for my property agent to send me some new and interesting finds."

"You lived on a barge? That sounds…actually, kind of smelly and wobbly."

"You get used to shifting with the waves. And the Seine doesn't smell that bad. It's the tourists peeking in the windows all the time that made me decide to sell. This time of year they are like patrons peering in at the lone captive animal."

Kyler laughed and leaned an elbow on the bar. Her body nudged closer to his. Their thighs hugged now. There was something electric about him, and it wasn't the shimmer she'd felt with their handshake. The man oozed confidence and élan. Physically, he wasn't her type. While muscular and seemingly strong, he was too pretty, too perfect. He could model for a top magazine, and women the world over would swoon.

She much preferred a man who looked average, acted average and wasn't concerned about what others thought of him. An average Joe. Probably because that was all she'd ever dated. She'd never thought a man as handsome as Dante would give her a second glance. Yet she'd never ruled out flirting with any and all men. It made her feel sensual and alive.

"How long did you live in Paris?" she asked.

"Are you fishing about for how old I am? You can simply ask."

She shrugged. "Okay. How old are you?"

"I was born in Paris in 1860. Well before Picasso."

She quickly did the math quickly—over 150 years old. "I find it fascinating that immortality ages a person so slowly. It's an amazing gift, isn't it?"

"It is."

"But immortality does not mean you—we—can never die."

"Yes, a healthy fear of stakes does serve a vampire a longer life. I am a youngster as far as living centuries goes. I love to experience everything. There are never days I would bemoan my existence."

"I agree. Vampirism rocks."

"There is so much to do in this world," he continued. "So many adventures to be had. So many women to love."

Of course, a man as attractive as him would not want for a girlfriend. But could he possibly be between lovers? "You have…many lovers?"

"At one time? Never. I am always exclusive. But if you are counting years, then of course I've had my share. I never kiss and tell, though. Each woman is a memory I forever cherish."

"Sounds like I've met Casanova in the flesh."

"Eh, he was too boisterous. Couldn't stop himself from writing about his sordid affairs and sharing them with anyone who would listen." He skated a finger around the rim of his glass, and Kyler sucked in a corner of her lip. The movement reminded her of a fingertip circling skin. "I'll keep my secrets, thank you."

Kyler was suddenly all about learning secrets. Or making new ones with a certain irresistibly sexy vampire. Her elbow slipped, and the backpack slid from her shoulder to the crook of her elbow.

"Shopping?" he said with a nod to the backpack.

"Sort of. Just a few trinkets."

When she made to slide the strap back up her arm, he touched her again, wanting to help, and hooked the wide black strap over her shoulder. "That's heavy for trinkets."

"I should probably go," she offered. Though the idea of walking away from such an intriguing man felt wrong. She enjoyed talking to him. But really, she shouldn't risk sitting around with a valuable piece of art in her backpack. Or have him ask more questions she wasn't willing to answer. "It's getting late."

"It's just past midnight. Do you sleep much?"

She shrugged. "A few hours a night. I still cling to some of the more satisfying human rituals."

"Six months you've been a biter?"

"Yes, though I've never heard it called that before. A biter?"

He shrugged. "A silly joke. It's better than longtooth, yes?"

"Sure." She'd heard that werewolves called vampires longtooth—a terrible slang word the vamps hated. She hadn't experienced the whole vampire milieu long enough to know if it bothered her or not. Just owning fangs had taken a few weeks to become comfortable. Bite her lower lip much?

He tapped the goblet stem and asked, "Are you American?"

"Yes." She turned on the stool, deciding to linger a little longer instead of the quick escape. "Is my accent that terrible?"

"The American accent is…quaint." He smiled and his eyes glinted, full of moonlight. For a moment Kyler had to stop herself from leaning closer to him, sniffing, seeking his scent along the edge of his square jaw. "You're a long way from home. Did your friend for whom you've gone on an art quest send you from the United States?"

"I've been living in Paris six months," she said.

"I see. You were transformed immediately upon arriving?"

"Uh, yes. I don't really want to talk about that." She had to keep the theft a secret and any details about her transformation would ultimately lead to why she was in Venice.

"Sorry. I'll change the subject. Have you taken a gondola ride?"

She glanced at the canal, which whispered by on the other side of a decorative iron railing laced with thick ivy. "It seems so touristy."

"It is, but this time of year it is exquisite around ten in the evening when the last rays of sun glitter on the lagoon. With a bottle of prosecco in hand and perhaps a lover by your side?"

She lifted the goblet before her in a proposed toast. With more purr than tease, she said, "Now you're making me wish I had a lover."

He tinged his glass against hers. "I'd be happy to oblige."

No tease in that statement. The man meant every word of it. And should she take him up on that offer, Kyler felt certain he would not disappoint.

Mercy, was her fantasy about to become reality?

"Kyler? I think I've said something wrong again. I tend to be direct. A woman deserves nothing less than truth, yes?"

"No. I mean, yes, I appreciate your directness." She placed a hand on the back of his, which toyed with the base of his glass. "I—" she lowered her lashes and looked up through them "—was considering your offer."

He turned up his hand to touch her fingers but didn't clasp her hand. "A delicious end to a very good day?"

"Is that a promise or advertising?"

"I don't need to advertise, *chérie*."

"You certainly do not." She laughed then because a giddy sort of surrender had settled into her muscles. She liked the man. Vampire. And there were so many things about him that made her want to get to know him. Much better.

He tilted a nod toward her. "Come closer, Kyler."

Without reluctance, she leaned in and he touched her cheek. The shimmer again hit her with a shock of recognition. None of the humans around them could know two vampires sat talking to each other. His finger traced her ear and curled her hair over it. And his eyes walked over her face, taking her in, consuming her. They were so gorgeous. Devastatingly clear and direct. A hint of green danced within the blue, like sea glass.

Kyler opened her mouth to say something, but nothing came out. She was enthralled. And she knew a vampire could not enthrall another vamp. Just wasn't possible. They could work a number on humans, though, making them forget they'd been bitten, and that perhaps what had been two fangs puncturing their skin had instead simply been a nasty bug bite.

"I renege on my offer, Kyler," he whispered.

It took her a few seconds to shake off the blissful daze his touch had led her into. "What?"

"About being a casual lover to celebrate your good day."

"Oh…okay." But then she felt her confidence and straightened. What was wrong with her? Not pretty enough? Too…quaint? "Why?"

"It would wound my pride to take you home and then know you would walk away the next day without a care to look over your shoulder."

"Oh." Was he implying he didn't want a hookup, but rather something more? *Interesting.* But she didn't know him, and she wasn't willing to make such a commitment. "Isn't that how Casanova does it? Love them and leave them?"

"It is. And truth be told, it is my modus operandi, as well."

"Then it's because you're not attracted to me. That's all right. I understand. It was nice talking to you—"

He clasped her hand and pulled it to his lips, where

he pressed a warm kiss that overwhelmed the silly shimmer they shared and coursed over her skin with a heady intensity that would not allow her to do anything but sigh.

"Oh, I am attracted to you, Kyler. I cannot look away from your bewitching blue eyes that are not so sure if they should fear me or trust me."

She looked aside. But then a bold twist of her head showed him she wasn't afraid to meet his gaze.

"Or perhaps devour me." He brushed the hair from her cheek. "You're not sure what you want. You've never been with a vampire before, so I sense fascination coached with caution. Perhaps not enough caution? I would never ask a woman to betray her moral compass."

Why bring morality into the mix? Couldn't he simply be her reward for a job well done? She tended to dive into things and think about them later. Life had always demanded she challenge herself. To be the best. To learn new things. To steal if needs must. To never be afraid.

To soar.

So she leaned in and spoke near his ear. "I am quite sure I want you, Dante."

"Why? Is it as I presume? Because I am vampire?"

"Yes, and…" He was a Casanova, and she'd fallen under his spell. And he was a challenge she wanted to leap for. "Because you compel me. And I don't think it's because of what we are. Sure, a bite would be nice. As you've guessed, I've never been with another vampire. But beyond that? I want to feel you." She pressed her hand against his chest. "On my skin."

A playful smile tugged at one corner of his perfect lips. "And here I thought I was the Casanova?"

"I'm not afraid of asking for what I want. Truth? I've never done anything like this before. But it feels right. Take me home with you, Dante." She pressed her mouth lightly to his and whispered, "Let's celebrate a good day."

Chapter 2

Dante's place was but a ten minute walk away. And while he wasn't averse to hotel rooms, he preferred the homey comfort of his palazzo when entertaining such an intriguing woman. Along the way, Kyler had clasped his hand, and together they had almost run through the gaily lit, bustling Venetian streets. It was an exhilarating night. The moon sat high in the chrome-blue sky, and the air was heavy with the promise of rain. Streetlights beamed golden ribbons across dark palazzo windows and striped emerald hedgerows with glossy gold bands.

The woman with the curvaceous frame and lush, black Audrey Hepburn hair had suggested they have sex. It was his charm that had enticed her. Yes, he had it in spades and wasn't afraid to wield it to get what he wanted.

And tonight? He wanted Kyler in his bed because that's how he needed things to go down to accomplish his task. The surprise fact she was vampire was not so much a bonus as a creative challenge to his well-honed art of seduction. He rarely slept with vampires.

And yet he wanted her as much as she seemed to want him. Was he the one being led to bed by a new vampiress curious for the sexual bite?

Well, that was the challenge. If he bit a woman while having sex, he never saw her again. It was the way he rolled. And generally the bitten was human, or some other species of the paranormal. He had only once bitten another vampire. Too much was involved with such a piercing, such as emotional bonding. He didn't need that kind of headache. Or the heartache.

Though he might like a taste of new blood. Just a little? Dare he break his decades-old rule of never indulging in vampire blood again? What could a sip hurt?

Ah! What was he thinking? He mentally walked five steps ahead of himself. This night must be carefully orchestrated. He mustn't lose focus on the goal. And he must ensure she did.

"I live here," he said with a tug at her hand to divert her from walking farther. The sidewalk was moist most of the time due to the proximity to the canal, and it gleamed black. He shoved the key in the lock on the palazzo door.

Kyler's body heat hugged his arm and leg as she snuggled in close, wrapping an arm across his chest. It was an easy closeness that he would normally attribute to a few glasses of prosecco. But she wasn't drunk. And he was glad for that.

"You smell great," she said. "Like a wild autumn night."

"And you curl about me like a kitty cat." He'd never cared for the feline species. Until now.

He opened the door, and before he could invite her inside, she kissed him there on the threshold. Bold, unexpected and only a little tentative. She was finding her way, not afraid to dive into the unknown. Could she handle him?

Perhaps he should wonder if he could handle her.

What was he thinking? Of course he could.

"You're not afraid of cats, are you?" she asked.

"Here, kitty, kitty," he murmured against her mouth. "Come in."

With the proper invite into his home, the vampiress crossed the threshold, and Dante lifted her. Chest to chest, she wrapped her legs about his hips and swung her backpack onto the eighteenth-century tufted jacquard divan pushed up against the wall. She sought his kiss hungrily.

Dante eyed the backpack as he closed the door. It would be fine there. However, he would not be fine until he'd stripped this woman bare and made a thorough exploration of every inch of her skin.

Dante carried Kyler to the top of the stairs and into the bedroom. Rain spattered the windows, shrouded by sheer white curtains. The palazzo was dark, but moonlight illuminated this room brightly. Kyler had time to notice a bed with a white comforter and a chair with gray fabric as he set her down on the bed and then stepped back.

He stood there looking at her, unabashed sex clothed in a stylish suit and classy red tie. *Drink me in with your eyes*, she thought. The darkness shadowed half his face, and while that made it easier to stand in front of his admiration, it also made her want to see all of him. To share the admiration.

"Kiss me," she said, fighting a nervous rise in her voice. She would not punk out on this opportunity. *Being a little nervous with a new lover was okay*, she told herself. She tapped her lips. "Come here, vampire."

"You don't like me looking at you?" He adjusted the tie knot, loosening it a bit.

"I do. But you can look much better with your fingers."

"True." He leaned over her and tangled his fingers into the ends of her hair. "Lush and soft. Like you. Alone in Venice on an art expedition. How I do want to discover what makes Kyler Cole tick. I'll start with unwrapping you."

He slid her turtleneck up her stomach and over her breasts. Her hair spilled in static snaps to her bare shoulders, and she was thankful she'd worn a lacy demi bra. The lace-trimmed edge danced just above her nipples, and the rosy buds hardened under Dante's warm and desirous gaze.

He leaned in, the red tie tickling her stomach, and when she thought he'd kiss her above her breasts—and she lifted them expectantly—he instead hushed an exhale over her skin. A breath of desire. A shiver of want tightened her nipples. At her sides, her fingers curled into wanting claws and then relaxed. Heartbeats quickened.

Dante's tongue lashed her skin a teasing three inches away from the lace bra. Her moan was unstoppable.

"You sound like the kitten you are," he said as he wrapped an arm across her back.

As he glided his fingers up her stomach and rib cage to the base of her bra, Kyler gripped the tie and pulled him closer. The silken weave of his suit playing across her skin made her wonder whether or not she wanted him to get naked or stay clothed. Suit against flesh was an exotic sensation that heightened her desire even more.

He kissed her on the mound of a breast and nuzzled his nose across her skin, taking in her perfume. Yet she wore none. Couldn't risk giving herself away tonight had she gotten close to human guards at the auction house.

The auction house. She'd abandoned the backpack downstairs without a care. She really should—

Kyler gasped as Dante's lips closed over her nipple, still covered by the black lace. The heat of him and the firm pressure as his tongue teasing through the lace undid her rational thought. Whatever she'd been worried about mattered less than falling into his attentive discovery.

One of his hands pushed down her black leggings, beneath which she did not wear panties. She'd been going for a seamless look. He growled his appreciation at that and then nudged down the lace bra cups to fully take her nipple into his mouth.

Mercy, if it didn't go any further than this, she'd be a happy woman. But tonight, happy had already been superseded by elation. So she was in it for the win. And an orgasm or two.

Hiking up one of her legs along his thigh, Dante grasped her ankle and held her there. He suckled at her nipple, lazing his tongue in circles and then sucking hard. He indulged in her. He'd likely had a lot of practice in pleasing women—*no!*

She wasn't going to think like that. It was just the two of them. And she intended to enjoy every moment of his attention.

Shoving the suit coat from his shoulders, Kyler was able to shimmy it down his arms even as he drew a wet, exploratory line to her other nipple. He managed to unhook her bra in the back, and it fell away. She was now completely naked, and he was still dressed.

Dante pulled back to look at her. A sexy, know-too-much smile curled his mouth, preceding a low, whispery growl. He had her right where he wanted her.

And she was good with that.

Kyler leaned up onto her elbows and crooked a finger, inviting him to join her. When he stepped forward, she waggled that finger in a naughty admonishment.

"First, you get naked, too," she said. "I want to look at you as you've been looking at me."

"I can do that. But you won't mind if I pick up my coat, will you?" He bent to retrieve the abandoned piece of clothing, then carefully folded it and placed it over the back of the tufted Louis XIV chair near the window. He turned, unbuttoning his cuffs. "I appreciate the lines of a well-tailored suit."

Kyler leaned her head against her palm. "I appreciate the lines of a well-honed male."

Pulling away the red tie with a fling, he relegated it to the top of the folded suit coat. A few expert flicks of buttons released the crisp white business shirt from protecting his sculpted lines and curves. Hard muscles pulsed with his movement, and the rise of prominent hip bones drew her eye to the angled muscles that arrowed toward his crotch.

Kyler murmured a satisfied coo. "Nice."

Dante paused, his fingers teasing at his trouser buttons. "If you're going to narrate my undressing I'm not sure I can continue."

"Really? You are the last person I would expect to be shy. But I can keep quiet." She drew pinched fingers across her lips.

Dante nodded, gifting her with the rest of the show. Beneath the trousers he wore briefs that hugged—oh, a nice-size package. And it, too, pulsed beneath the fabric, teasing her with what might be revealed.

"Wait," she said with more enthusiasm than his surprised look showed he was comfortable with. "Come here and let me help you with that."

She sat up as he approached. Gliding her palm down his chest, she reveled in the warmth of his skin and muscles. Hadn't she always thought vampires were supposed to be cold, dead creatures? Certainly she had not grown colder over the past half year. And being proven wrong once again was all right with her. Her fingers skimmed over Dante's abdomen, a six-pack of ridiculously hard muscle. Each ridge tensed at her touch, begging her to move slowly, enjoy the sensation.

And then she moved her fingers downward and cupped over his briefs, drawing a hiss of pleasure from him. A squeeze to the form beneath her palm tested its hardness and heat. As he grew more erect, his penis bulged out the waistline of his briefs, and Kyler was able to slide a hand inside. She slid her other hand down the back of his briefs, easing them slowly over his buttocks. The weight of his steely erection in her hand made her feel powerful. Sexy. Wanton.

She giggled and then, before he could protest, tilted up her head to meet his mouth with a kiss. Hard and demanding and needy. As she worked her hand up and down over his erection, summoning him, coaxing him, she fed her own needs by dancing her tongue against his.

Every part of her being hummed. Her core spun in an apprehensive, wanting coil of soon-to-come fireworks and just-hold-off-a-bit warning. So she pressed her thighs together, staying the orgasm that already cried out for release.

Dante crawled over her and onto the bed, and she followed his direction, lying back, yet not releasing his hard, tight cock. She needed to feel him inside her. With that delicious thought, the curiosity to also feel his fangs inside her emerged.

"Show me your fangs," she whispered.

"You're not ready for that, Kitten." A flash of lightning sparkled around the room brightly and blinked out, darkening Dante's gaze above her. "Let's do this slowly, shall we?"

And as a whimper of protest teased at the edge of her tongue, Kyler surrendered to his command. How could she not? His fingers slipped between her thighs, and as she noticed the first touch of his index finger to her clitoris, she was surprised by the overwhelming release of orgasm that rushed up in a gasping cry of joy. Her body shivered and shook beneath his.

And she forgot about the bite.

"You come like the lightning," he said against her ear. "And you smell like rain and prosecco. I will always remember you this way."

With the thought that this was the beginning to the end of what had been a very daring encounter on her part, Kyler pulled his hips to her and directed his cock inside her. He filled her, hot and hard and thrusting.

She'd known this night would be a hookup. In the morning, she'd walk away and never see him again. And she was fine with that.

But not really.

Kittens and cream, Dante thought as Kyler's moist warmth clasped tightly about his cock. He thrust inside her as she orgasmed, and her rhythmic, squeezing pressure lured him toward his own swift climax. Two strangers came together in an irresistible crush of skin, sighs and sexual fire. He couldn't argue the results.

Shouting out as the tremendous orgasm shook through his system, he bowed his head to Kyler's breast and kissed the firm, hot flesh. His fangs descended without his volition. *Damn.* As quickly, he willed them back up. He was less ready for the fang reveal than she seemed to be. And it wasn't necessary. He wasn't hungry for anything other than more of Kyler's exquisite body undulating and moaning beneath him.

He'd fucked bold women, many a time. Kyler wasn't as bold as she thought. Some parts of her skipped along for the good time while he suspected another part of her hadn't expected such an encounter. She hid her nervousness well, though. And right now, she completely surrendered to the moment.

So lush, lying beneath him as though she were a goddess demanding worship. And worship her he would.

Pulling out from her, he glided down her body, trailing his tongue from one breast to the other and then taking the time to study the full curve on the underside of each breast. At her belly, he tickled a circle around her navel, then moved quickly south to taste her sticky sweetness.

Her fingers skimmed over his scalp and down his neck, nails digging in when they reached his shoulder. *Yes, just a little deeper*—he tongued her as deeply as he desired to feel her nails in his skin. Kyler moaned and then the exquisite pain was gone as she grasped the bedsheets.

"Yes," she whispered in a purr.

Again Dante's fangs ached to descend, but he cautioned them to stay put. He wouldn't bite her. Not yet. He didn't even know this woman, and if all went well, come morning he would never see her again.

A bite would only complicate things.

* * *

Kyler slid out from the rumpled white sheets and glanced over at the man stretched across the bed like a fallen angel. Dante D'Arcangelo? *Oh, yes, indeed.* He was some kind of dark angel. And an amazing lover. *Whew!* She'd made a good choice in taking him home with her. Or rather, she was at his palazzo.

But she mustn't get lost in the feel-good vibrations. She'd gotten what she wanted: a night of celebratory sex with a handsome lover. A new day glimmered on the shiny rooftops across the canal. And she knew better than to believe she actually meant more to him than a hookup.

While he slept, she had to get out of Dodge. Gathering up her clothes from the floor, she headed toward the en suite bathroom. The sun shone on the canal beyond the sheer white curtains. It was still quite dark, but thanks to a skylight, she didn't bother to turn on the light to check her makeup in the mirror. That was one thing she missed about being human—her reflection. And while she'd never been a Narcissus, mirrors did come in handy when applying eyeliner.

After running water in the sink until it was warm, she splashed her face and found a hand towel in the linen closet. She wanted to look around, to satisfy her curiosity about the dark angel who was really a vampire, but there wasn't time. And she'd left her backpack down in the foyer, not wanting to seem overly concerned about it last night and prompt him to ask unanswerable questions.

Pulling up her black leggings and then the long-sleeved turtleneck, she again lamented her wardrobe choice.

"You do look like a cat burglar," she whispered. "Who do you think you are fooling?"

Apparently, one very sexy French-Italian vampire.

Carefully pulling open the door, she peered across the whitewashed hardwood floor over to the bed...

"Where is he?"

The bed was empty. And her flat, rubber-soled shoes designed for sneaking into locked buildings and up along windowsills sat at the foot of the bed. Had he gone looking for her? No, he must have heard her in the bathroom. Probably he'd headed down to—well, vampires didn't do breakfast. They didn't need to eat food.

Drinking blood was the only sustenance a vampire required for survival. Something she'd learned to relish after initially balking at the strong, meaty flavor. Quickly she'd learned to treat the taste like wine. So many appellations and flavor notes. Humans offered a cornucopia of tastes she'd never tire of experiencing.

And if all went well, soon she could claim that taste for an eternity.

She'd wanted to bite Dante last night.

He was so irresistible. Would a little bite have hurt? He'd insisted it wasn't something she was ready for. Why, though? Too intimate? Perhaps. Kyler guessed even though Dante claimed a mastery with women, intimacy was well out of his repertoire. So she'd have to live without a taste of her dark angel. This had been a one-night stand. A satisfying reward for a job well done. A memory to keep.

And now to make her escape without some drawn-out explanation or an awkward goodbye. Damn, she wished he'd still been sleeping.

After slipping on her flats, Kyler strolled down the hallway to the stairs. At the bottom of the stairs a worn fieldstone floor stretched to the right and into the foyer. The stones were as dark as the gray-painted walls. She'd not noticed the dark decor last night. She'd had her arms and legs wrapped around Dante. And her mouth on his. And, oh…his mouth all over her skin as they'd made fantastic love to each other. He had worshipped her body.

As she veered toward the divan where she'd dropped the backpack, the shadows receded into a beam of sub-dued morning light. With a startled gasp, she noticed Dante sat there. With the backpack dangling from his fingers.

And it was open.

Chapter 3

"What are you doing?" Kyler rushed over and grabbed her backpack. "You went through it? It's—"

"Empty," he provided plainly.

Dante stretched an arm across the back of the divan and crossed his legs casually. He wore dark slacks, and his unbuttoned white shirt revealed hard abs. That she had licked only hours earlier.

"You had the egg last night before we came here," he said. "I took note of the weight of the backpack." He pointed toward the front door, and she spun to see that it was open a crack. "Someone's been here."

Clutching the empty backpack to her chest, Kyler squeezed her eyes shut tight, then turned toward him to unleash her anger. "You liar! You did this! How did you know? Were you following me? I remember you confessed to following me. Then you had sex with me to distract—" With a heavy gasp, she managed, "You *used* me?"

"Kyler, sit." He patted the tufted cushion beside him. Entirely too calm, he infuriated her. But then he could afford to express casual disinterest. He now had the upper hand. "Raging at me is not going to solve the issue of the missing egg."

"You bastard! Of course. You should know. You took it. But how did you know *I* had it? You had to have been following me far longer than the few blocks near the flower shop. And then to trick me into coming here with you...you had this all planned out!"

"I performed no such trickery. You'll recall we shared a few drinks, and then it was *you* who eagerly suggested we finish off the evening here."

"After your suggestion you were open to having sex with me."

He lifted a finger. "A suggestion you took to with amorous enthusiasm."

"You were scheming. Hoping to get me alone so you could steal the egg from me. I can't believe I fell for that! I wanted a night to celebrate and have wild sex—"

He grinned deliciously. "It was a bit wild, wasn't it, Kitten?"

"Aggh! Where did you put it?"

Dante spread his arms out in dismay. "I haven't touched it. Though I admit I slipped down here while you were in the bathroom to do just that."

"Steal it?"

He nodded. "Truth? I'd hoped to take it into my charge after you'd done all the hard work."

Jaw dropping open, she gaped at him.

He shrugged. "I saw you yesterday afternoon in the auction house. Casing the place. I was there doing the same. Don't get me wrong. I am not a thief. It's simply my quest to acquire that specific Fabergé egg."

She lifted a brow.

"Doesn't require explanation." He waved it off with a flick of his fingers. "It occurred to me that you'd probably strike the night before the auction, as I had intended. And I had the notion to see if you could manage the theft and bring the prize to me. Which you did. After following you from the auction house, I positioned myself at the bar, hoping you'd walk that way. It was a series of remarkable coincidences."

"Bullshit." She slammed the backpack on the floor, which didn't produce as loud of a noise as she wished. Pacing the stone tiles, she ran her fingers through her hair. "What makes you believe someone stole it? We were awake all night. We would have heard a disturbance. No. I know you're lying. This is another scheme. Make me believe someone broke in by leaving the door open a crack, and then when I'm gone you've got the egg all to yourself."

"Just stop, Kyler. Stand still."

She swung toward him. "Why?"

"Close your eyes."

She shook her head in irritation and shook a fist at him.

A trace of the Casanova smile tickled his mouth. "Humor me?"

Why did the man have to be so pretty? She didn't want to punch him; she wanted to hug him. And lick him. And allow him to touch her all the ways he'd done last night.

With a huff, she slammed her hands to her hips and closed her eyes.

"Now," he said gently. "What do you smell?"

About to reply that she smelled a bastard, she inhaled deeply, vying for a modicum of calm. She had to figure this out, a way to deal with him, to bargain perhaps and get the egg back. As soon as she got the call to hand off the prize, she had to be ready. Or bye-bye eternity.

Wrinkling her nose, she took in the scents in the foyer. First being Dante's after-sex warmth and musk. Mercy, could she have seconds? And thirds?

Focus, Kyler!

Beyond that annoyingly attractive scent lingered the dry coolness of the floor stones, and then—she opened her eyes. "Wet dog?"

"Exactly. It was raining hard earlier this morning. We were awake but were focused on one another. A delicious focus, I might add. Easy enough for a were-wolf to break in and nab the item with the rain to muffle the noise."

"A werewolf? Oh, please. Don't you have security on this place?"

He nodded toward the door. "Just a simple lock with key access. An easy crack. I never keep anything of value here, and oftentimes in the winter months I'll leave the place open, available for friends to use."

"I cannot believe you are so lax with security!"

"Yes, well. I'm paying the price now, aren't I?"

"How so? It was *my* nab! And there's nothing you can say or do to change that. I did the work." She thumped her fist on her chest in frustration. "I stole the egg. It's mine."

"Do you have it in your hands?"

She huffed at his need to state the obvious.

"Then it's not yours, is it? Whoever holds it owns it. As I learned when it was originally stolen from me."

"What?"

He waved a hand, dismissing the comment. "Doesn't matter now. What does is that I've come to Venice to claim the Fabergé egg, and I won't leave without it."

"So you admit you used me—seduced me—to get what you wanted?"

He lifted a finger. "The sex was not my original intention. I had not planned to use intimacy to obtain the egg. That was a fortuitous bonus."

"Liar. You took me home, knowing I had the egg on me. Then you fucked me and planned to steal it while I was sleeping or in the bathroom."

"I did intend to steal the egg from you. I won't deny that. But the sex was completely separate from my larcenist goals. And I'll thank you not to combine the two. What we shared last night was intimate and sacred."

"Sacred? Yeah right. You are a classic womanizer."

"I am not a womanizer," he protested. "I love women. All of them."

She blew out a breath. Was there a difference? "I don't believe you," she said. "But it doesn't matter. Right now, I've got to find the smelly wolf who stole *my* egg. You really think it was a werewolf?"

"The scent is obvious. And the fact we can both still smell it means the culprit must have been here in the last hour or two."

"Then I need to track it."

She sniffed the air but couldn't quite pick up the salty-wet scent. It was quickly dissipating. How to track a wolf? She'd never even met a werewolf. She knew it was safer to talk with them in their un-shifted *were* form than when they were in their shifted half human, half wolf form. She'd figure it out.

But first. "Stand up. I want to search you."

Dante stood and raised his arms out from his sides. His shirt opened, and his abs flexed magnificently. Kyler spread her fingers before her, deciding where to touch him first. No place on his person to hide an egg the size of a skull. Had she counted those ridges last night? That was definitely more than a six-pack, now that she considered it. And she could smell his leather-and-musk heat wafting through the atmosphere, tempting, teasing—

"Forget it." She gazed about the foyer to distract her waning fortitude, and as she did Dante pulled her into his embrace. She struggled against him, but he wrangled her into compliance with ease. "Don't touch me. I don't want this from you. You didn't mean any of it last night."

"I meant it all, Kyler. I promise you that. I take intimacy with a woman very seriously. Look at me."

She wouldn't give him that satisfaction.

"Fine. And you're right. There's time later to argue

the semantics of our ill-timed love-making session. We need to track the wolf before the trail goes stale."

"We? I don't think so. The egg is mine. I am out of here."

"I'm right behind you!" Dante called.

Kyler didn't listen. With the backpack in hand, she slammed the front door behind her, then, thinking to look for a clue, she studied the door handle and sniffed. Yes, maybe a faint scent of wolf there. The sidewalk was still wet, so she couldn't see tracks or decide which way the trail led. Tracking people was not her forte. Just as thievery was not.

But falling for some scheming, too-pretty womanizer? Sign her right up. Apparently she was a professional when it came to being seduced.

"I can't believe last night happened."

But she'd do her damned best to forget about her lack of discretion now. To forget the scent of him on her skin and at her mouth and—

"Aggh! Focus, Kyler. You are a vampire. You've got skills. You can do this. And no," she muttered as she strode down the street, tugging down her shirt, "this is not a walk of shame. I am without shame. Really."

Mostly. At the very least she could be thankful her hair wasn't in a tangle and she wasn't wearing a spangled miniskirt and sky-high heels.

She sniffed the air again. Tracking werewolves had not been a part of her paltry Welcome to Vampirism 101 education. Because she'd never received that complete course. Her creator had been too busy, unwilling to divulge more than a handful of details, and—

"Uninterested," she said with a sigh. So why was she here in Venice now trying to help that very vampire out?

Because she did appreciate the gift of vampirism he had given her. And that was all there was to it. She owed him.

She walked slowly, trying to pick up clues, scents, anything. As she struggled to fix on a doglike scent, it became horribly obvious she'd never find the wolf unless it walked right up to her.

Dante quickly dressed. He kept the palazzo stocked with suits. Rarely did he wear leisure clothing such as jeans, though he could manage a relaxed élan that would blend him in with the tourists. He preferred a suit. A well-dressed man could get through most difficulties life flung at him. But he hadn't time for the whole attire. Clean, pressed trousers and a white dress shirt would have to serve. He left the red silk tie lying on the bed, grabbed his door key and rushed out of the palazzo. He locked the front door, but, as had been proven, it mattered little. He must look into having one of those newfangled digital locks installed. He struggled with new technologies.

Then again, as he'd said to Kyler, he kept no items of value in this palazzo, so did tight security really matter? He wasn't a man who collected *things*. What mattered most to him were experiences. Visceral, tangible moments that were fixed into his brain forever after. Such as having sex with Kyler. She had been a hot one, and he'd like to handle her again.

He rarely spent more than a night or two, sometimes

a week, with a woman. And he shouldn't risk another night of passion with a woman whom he, by all rights, should deem an enemy. Well, she had been when she'd held the egg.

Now that neither held the prize? He'd reserve judgment on labeling her as foe or ally.

It was early morning, and tourists had yet to flood the streets. Gondoliers were polishing their conveyances and sidewalk café staff washed tables and metal chairs. The sun was hidden behind clouds, for which he was thankful. He hadn't taken along a pair of sunglasses, and the sun was not his favorite star.

He didn't have to go far before he found Kyler walking slowly, her hands extended out at her sides as if to feel the air and her eyes closed as she strolled to a stop at a corner. Her silhouette reminded him of a 1940s pinup girl, rounded at the hips and breasts, and all that gorgeous hair swishing about in curls below her shoulders. The memory of her soft purrs against his skin last night made him smile.

He would have her again.

Quickening his pace, he grabbed her hand. Following the werewolf scent he was still able to track, he tugged her along to the left when he presumed she might have turned right.

She protested with a tug. A gentle one. "I told you I didn't want to see you again!"

"Quieter, please." He made show of looking about. "We are on a mission. You're a thief. You must know how to practice stealth?"

The look she gave him made him immediately question that suggestion. But really, she had to be experienced to have walked out of the Cannaregio Casa d'Aste with a priceless artifact in hand. But why so impudent? He should be the angry one—she'd stolen from him. For now he attributed her anger to their current estranged intimacy. He'd make amends. All night long.

"Like it or not," he said, "we are now a team. This way."

He veered toward the canal and then left alongside a brick building that boasted a narrow sidewalk between it and the still canal. The werewolf scent faded because the salty, stale water overwhelmed his senses, but with intense concentration Dante was able to keep his focus on a tendril of wolfish odor.

Pleased Kyler hadn't further protested their working together, he took selfish pride in the fact that he'd fucked her well last night. She may hate him, but she still wanted him. And she freely held his hand now, trailing behind him as they neared a diminutive metal bridge arching across the narrow canal.

The scent of wolf assaulted his nostrils like a rotten egg. The hairs on the back of his neck prickled. This was not a stale trail they followed.

Dante pressed Kyler to a stop. "They are close," he whispered. "Can you scent them?"

She nodded and closed her eyes.

And he was able to pick up voices…most likely belonging to the wolves.

"When do we leave Venice?"

"Tonight. We gotta get out of here before news of the

theft will make leaving the city difficult. And there's the full moon. You smell that?"

"Uh...oh, yeah. Like musk and...blood. Vamps!"

"Shit." Dante pushed Kyler toward the narrow stone steps that descended into the clear green canal under the bridge. "They've picked up our scent. Get in!"

"But—" She didn't continue the objection. Instead she stepped quickly down and sank under the surface, and he followed.

Kyler didn't utter a word as the cool waters tugged them downward and he directed her to swim under the bridge. Their movements were sinuous as they glided underwater. Vampires could breathe for extended periods underwater; werewolves had about as much skill with that as humans.

They resurfaced beneath the bridge. Treading water, Dante pressed his finger over her mouth. Her bright blue eyes held such trust, not a bit of worry. Why trust him? According to her previous reasoning, he was the guy who had tricked her and stolen the egg. Perhaps she was so far out of her element even she didn't know what or whom to trust. *Poor little girl.* He really would like to be that kind of man—the one a woman could trust—but it wasn't coded into his DNA. He'd never trusted women, so why shouldn't they return that favor?

They averted their eyes upward as footsteps gained the bridge, and the familiar scent of werewolf kept their cautious movements to tight hand swishes and steady kicks to keep their ears above water.

On the bridge a male said, "I thought I smelled vampires. I know I did."

"Yeah, but they're not this way. Maybe it was around that other corner? Doesn't matter. We should head back to the vampire's palazzo in San Marco. Have stakes. Will kill vamps."

"We were told not to kill anyone."

"You complain too much."

"And you think you smell vampires everywhere."

"Yeah, well, they are nasty bloodsucking longtooths. And who's going to know if we stake 'em?"

"I do feel an itch to dust a longtooth. Let's go."

The footsteps tromped off the bridge.

Dante's eyes traced Kyler's face from her crimped brows to her sucked-in lower lip. Now she sought reassurance in his gaze. He could offer false security, tug her into his arms and supply some hopeful words, but it always ended in seduction. And right now he wanted to get out of this smelly water and onto dry land.

After a few more minutes of treading water and listening, when he felt sure the wolf scent had faded, they swam to the opposite shore and he boosted her up out of the water and onto the narrow sidewalk.

Legs dangling over the edge and into the water, Kyler tilted her head against a metal plate riveted onto the side of a building and closed her eyes. "That was close. And did you hear? They want to stake us."

"Yes, and they are returning to my palazzo. Guess I'll be staying elsewhere for a few days until I can assure myself it's safe to return. Damn." He tugged off a leather shoe and emptied the water into the canal, then followed with the other. The trousers clung to his ankles. "This shirt is silk."

"Really? You're worried about a shirt when it could have been your heart at the point of a stake?"

"But it's Zegna."

He could sense Kyler rolled her eyes, so he laughed softly. "There are very few material goods I value in life beyond a well-tailored suit. I will survive, though. As you've said, it beats taking a stake. How do you fare?"

"Just cheap leggings and an ugly shirt I picked up for the job. I never wear black. Ugh. I need color."

"Don't you wear black on your other heists?"

"Uh…none of your business. So now what?"

Was that none of his business because she committed so many other heists she couldn't keep them straight, or because this particular thievery venture was new to her? Instinct told him to go with the latter. *Interesting.*

"Shall we make our way to your hotel for some dry clothes?" he asked.

"I don't think you'll find a change of clothing at my place."

"So you'd prefer I return home and walk in on two werewolves with stakes? You bruise me, Kyler. I thought the sex we shared was, at the least, spectacular."

"It was awesome. But it didn't make us besties."

"Fair enough. Though we are in this adventure together."

"But—"

Rain suddenly spattered the canal and the sidewalk where they sat, and Kyler burst out in laughter. Dante could not find the humor in being soaked even more. Had he been on his own he might have returned to his neighborhood, tracked the wolves from his palazzo to their hideout and found the egg. But having to protect a woman?

She most certainly could not do this on her own.

"Fine. We'll go to my hotel room," she said. "But don't get any ideas, Casanova."

"You think I've seduction in mind when I smell like the canal? Absolutely not. I want to regroup and then find that egg."

"As do I."

Dante was surprised Kyler offered to let him accompany her back to the hotel room. There was that blind trust again. But it worked for him. Perhaps it wasn't so much trust as an innate openness and willingness to try new things. He decided she was an adventurous woman striving for full-on boldness. But with the loss of her stolen prize, adventure had turned and snapped back at her.

They wandered into the hotel foyer, shoes squishing and clothing clinging to their skin. The rain had escalated to a downpour, so they hadn't needed to worry about explaining why they were soaked. Everyone was wet.

Kyler pointed to the elevator bay, but Dante veered toward reception. "Hang on." At the reception desk he took a piece of paper and a pen and wrote down his name and the name of his tailor. "What's your room number, Kitten?"

"Three twenty."

He wrote that down, as well, then handed it to the concierge. Fortunately he had a few folded bills in his trouser back pocket, but they were pitifully wet. He stretched out a fifty and handed it over. "Call Signore Galleti. Give him my name and tell him I'll need a complete suit and shoes. Quick as possible, *per cortesia.*"

"Very good, *signore.* I'll have someone bring it right up when it arrives."

"Grazie." He turned and led the way to the elevator, feeling Kyler follow behind him. He was accustomed to having things go his way, but a niggle at the back of his neck wanted her to walk beside him, not behind.

Once in the elevator, she said, "You have élan."

"I've had a good century and a half to practice."

"You were born with it," she decided.

"Furthest from the truth possible, that guess."

He wouldn't elaborate on his odd childhood spent among the courtesans and johns. Who would believe he'd learned everything about women from tidying rooms in the morning while the courtesans slept off their nightly efforts in rumpled bliss?

"Were you born, uh…vamp?" she asked.

"I was not transformed until my twenties." The doors opened, and this time he allowed her to walk out first, following her to her room. Once inside, he kicked off his soggy shoes.

"So, how were you made?" she asked, toeing off her flats. They did nothing for her shapely gams. He'd prefer to see her in stilettos.

Dante strolled into the small but tidy room and unbuttoned his shirt. It took some finesse to peel off the clinging fabric. He dropped it in a pile near his shoes. After pulling down his trousers and stepping out of those, he turned to stand in nothing but his boxer briefs, which were also soaked and clung to his cock, which quickly hardened when he noticed Kyler's eyes alight there like heat-seeking missiles.

"How was I made?" he posited, barely keeping amusement from his tone. "Same as you were. One long bite, the sharing of blood until my heart almost burst and voilà!"

"Yes, but, that's not exactly what I meant." She ran a palm up her neck and glanced away from his crotch. "You can keep your undies on. Maybe I'll hop in the shower while you…dry off. You can tell me the whole story when we're both dressed and dry."

"You don't like me wet?" he asked as innocently as he could manage. Anything to distract from her wanting to learn more about his transformation to vampire.

Kyler shook her head and chuckled. "You try all you like. Those chiseled abs are not going to make me fall to my knees again. I'm over you, you sneaky bastard."

"I don't think I like being called such a thing."

"Too bad. You earned it." She began to pull up her shirt as she strode into the bathroom. "Don't sit on my bed in those wet boxers. Here!"

A towel flew out from the bathroom and landed on the floor two feet away from him. The bathroom door closed, and muffled sounds from the fan came from within.

"A sneaky bastard, eh?" He peeled off his wet briefs and tossed them aside. He wrapped the towel about his hips. "I'll show her sneaky."

Scanning the room, he sought her suitcase and personal items. There were a few things hanging in the open closet. A pair of black pumps sat on the closet floor. *Nice.*

She had to keep a purse and passport somewhere. As the patter of the shower began, he eyed the safe inside the closet. A safe cracker he was not. Though if given the proper impetus he'd give anything a go.

He bent before the square safe and rubbed his fingers expectantly before the dial. But, no. He wasn't that convinced he'd find any damning information on Kyler Cole. She'd come to steal the Fabergé egg. For a friend? He could understand the monetary reward, but selling the thing would be a bitch. She didn't seem the sort who had such connections as a fence.

Yet he knew next to nothing about her. Save that when he suckled her nipples she arched her back and squirmed as if possessed by an exotic goddess. Mmm, he had to do that again.

No.

Yes?

Most certainly he would not avoid the temptation if offered again.

Pushing aside the sheer curtain, he looked out over Saint Mark's square and focused on the campanile, the bell tower that stretched more than three hundred feet into the sky. The hotel room offered an excellent view of the entire square, which now bustled with a rainbow of tourists and a mad feeding frenzy of pigeons. He liked a crowd, getting lost among humanity. All those warm bodies rubbing against one another, most never aware that a man who survived by drinking their blood lurked close by.

It had been a week since he'd had a drink of blood. He didn't need it any more often than every other week, but he indulged whenever he desired. And much as he could use a long drink of human blood, he would starve himself of that treat for the pleasure of Kyler's blood.

And what was that about? It had been a long time since he'd been with a vampiress. More than a century. And he seriously wanted to taste her. To hold her close and feel her heart beat against his chest as her blood slid across his tongue, imbuing that pounding pulse into his taste buds.

If only she were not vampire.

Drinking from his own kind was intimate, and some vampires bonded in doing so. It wasn't necessarily a rest-of-their-lives thing, but it did connect them deeply. And he was about as willing to make that connection with another vampire as he wanted to take another dip in the canal.

Unless he found the right woman.

Never going to happen. Dante D'Arcangelo give up all women to settle for merely one? He chuckled at the madness of that thought.

Pulling the curtain across the window softened the light in the room. He eyed the television remote but shook his head. Instead he sat on the bed and closed his eyes. It took a while, but eventually he could move his hearing beyond the bathroom fan and pick out the individual water droplets that pearled on Kyler's soft skin. They spattered from her head, dribbled down her glossy hair and then glided across her full and heavy breasts. He should be in there, licking them as if she were drenched with wine.

But he'd given her reason to distrust him when she'd caught him going through the empty backpack. Now, to earn back that trust, or simply play with her naivety for as long as was necessary until he got what he wanted?

Chapter 4

Kyler pulled on the oversize T-shirt that she'd tossed over the towel bar. She should have brought a change of clothing into the bathroom with her, but she'd wanted to get out of the main room as quickly as possible. The sight of Dante standing in wet briefs that clung to his hard-as-steel cock had almost undone her.

She had only to remind herself of the empty backpack sitting on the closet floor to lose all interest in the sexy bastard. Sneaky and sexy made a terrible combination, so she would remain on her toes. Because…damn. She'd made a promise to another man to bring the egg to him. She wouldn't renege. He'd given her so much. And he offered her so much more than Dante ever could.

Stepping out of the bathroom in a mist of steam, she found Dante sitting on the bed, a pillow supporting his back, his hands clasped behind his neck. The position beckoned her gaze to his chest and abs. Tight and hard, a landscape that demanded an assessment from her fingertips. And then she noticed the white towel had a gap right…there.

"Your turn," she said, walking briskly to the table by the window and trying to look busy by opening the room service folder. "I may have used all the hot water. I'm not sorry."

"That shirt," he said as he stood.

"What about it?" She tugged out the frayed hem from the thirty-year-old rock concert T-shirt she'd inherited from her mother. It was one of the very few things Kyler had kept after she had died.

"Def Leppard?" He shuddered. "I was around when they were in their prime, but I can't imagine you were even a thought in your parents' minds then."

"Trust me—I was a thought. What do you think inspired my parents to have the sex that produced me if not 'Pour Some Sugar on Me'? Got a problem with it?"

"I think they're an excellent band. But the thing is four sizes too big for you. It doesn't show off your attributes."

"Suck it, vampire."

He gaped at her, but too quickly that familiar smirk tugged a corner of his mouth. "I've said you're not ready for me to suck on you."

"No, I meant it as—" She gestured dismissively. Did the man not recognize an insult when he heard one? Probably had never been insulted in his lifetime. *Pretty bastard.* "Never mind. Go take a shower before that towel falls off."

He pulled the towel away to reveal an astute erection. Kyler's jaw dropped. And Dante swung his equipment around and strolled into the bathroom, his dimpled, tight buttocks mocking her as he went. She couldn't see his grin, but she knew it was there.

"You're back to sneaky!" she called as the door closed.

And she needed a drink of ice water.

And to check her messages. Sitting on the bed, she grabbed the cell phone she'd left on the nightstand and scrolled through messages. Nothing about a pickup meeting place. That was weird. The vampire who had sent her on this mission knew she was going to nab the egg last night. Wouldn't he have expected she'd have it in hand by now?

He had been explicit that she not call him. He was a busy man. He didn't take calls; he made them. She wasn't sure what his profession was exactly—beyond vampire—but she assumed it was stressful.

She should check the local news. See if the theft had been reported.

"This may be a good thing," she mused. Because she didn't have the egg in hand. She had to hurry and get it back. When the message finally did come through, she wanted to be able to move as quickly as possible.

"Werewolves," she said. A big sigh sifted through her lips as she pulled her fingers through her wet hair. "I have no experience with werewolves."

She was thankful Dante had suggested their dip in

the canal to dissuade the werewolves from their scent. That man thought on his feet and used his instincts as they were meant to be utilized. She could learn from him.

If she weren't trying to dodge him and keep him away from the prize.

Picking up the remote, she clicked on the TV and determined the scroll across the bottom of the screen, in Italian, was local news. She found the captioning and switched it to English. Weather. Museum times. Breaking news: Fabergé egg missing.

Missing?

"Not stolen? Weird." But no matter to her. What did matter was that the media knew. It wouldn't take long before such information reached Paris, where her contact waited. "Now the heat is on, and I have no idea where the egg is."

She had failed miserably. But she wasn't about to give up. As long as she had Dante on her side, she could use him, just as he had used her. Much as she hated to admit it, she needed him. He knew the city and werewolves.

Ten minutes later, he emerged in a cloud of jasmine-scented steam, wearing a towel tightly wrapped about his hips. After rubbing his hair with another towel, he then tossed that aside to his abandoned clothes pile. His short hair stuck up like bristles on his scalp, a dark cap that drew her eye directly to his face. His bone structure was something else. All lines and angles and exquisite shadows. Mmm, for one more taste of his sex-warm skin.

"Maybe housekeeping can dry and iron your shirt for you?" Kyler offered in an attempt to redirect her wandering lust.

She got up to sit in the armchair beside the TV. She'd forgotten to get dressed between fretting over werewolves and what she'd say to her friend if she didn't get the egg back.

"It's silk. It's ruined." Dante toed the heap of his wet clothing. "I'll leave it for the hotel to donate to charity. If anyone wants to bother with this disaster. The shower felt great after a swim in the canal. And the water was still hot, much as you may have wished otherwise. Though I abhor the shampoo scent. I smell like flowers. Ah. Still in the ugly shirt, I see."

"You are such a charmer. How did I ever see Casanova in you?"

"As I've said, I'm nothing at all like that roustabout."

He sat on the bed, leaning against the headboard and stretching out his legs, giving no indication he might consider getting dressed. Kyler wondered how long it would take the tailor to deliver a new suit. Depending on the length of their wait, it could prove good, bad and so, so…naughty.

"I should get dressed." She stood and wandered to the closet, selecting a snug pair of black capris and a red shirt. She nodded toward the muted TV. "Check out the news scroll."

Behind the closed bathroom door, she swiftly changed and then drew some eyeliner on and combed her hair. She rarely did blush and eye shadow because she never could get makeup right. Her skin was flawless, though, so she never missed a made-up face. She bet Dante dated glamour-pusses. Those who really knew how to put themselves together and who could wield a makeup brush like an artist.

"Just average," she said to her thoughts. A sigh felt necessary, but she did not.

What was wrong with enjoying an exciting affair with a sexy man? Beyond that he wanted to steal something from her. She needed him as much as he needed her. So she'd work with him. For now.

Back out in the main room, Dante observed the TV. "The media is not reporting it as theft, merely missing," he said. "Curious. They must be trying to keep it quiet."

"By broadcasting it on TV?"

"Can't prevent the reporters that feed on the sensational, I'm sure. We need to get out of Venice."

"Not without the egg. It's noon. Do you think we'll be able to pick up the werewolves' scent again?"

"So you are relying on me now to help you in your endeavors? I thought you had decided to hate me?"

"I do hate you. With a passion."

"Always be passionate about your endeavors, Kitten. It makes them tolerable, whether good or bad."

"Whatever. But you do seem to have the better nose. I'll follow it until it leads me to the prize."

"I will do my best. But there will be a struggle between the two of us at the end—I can assure you of that."

"I'm strong."

"Yes, I noticed that last night." He tilted forward a shoulder and looked over it. "The claw marks are no longer there, but you do like to dig in and hold on, don't you?"

"You loved it."

"Of course I did. You are exuberant and fiery when properly aroused. And wow. Red is really your color."

She blew out a breath and shook her head. He was baiting her, and she should not take the hook. Again. It was just another line in his Casanova script, she told herself. He probably said the same thing to every woman he fucked.

"What is your reason for stealing the egg, if you'll share with me?" he asked. "I would guess the monetary reward, but really, we both know fencing that thing will prove a bitch. It's too famous. A lost Fabergé egg?"

"It's worth millions," Kyler said. "Why *wouldn't* I want the thing?"

"So you're a professional thief, are you?"

No belief in that question whatsoever. She set back her shoulders with as much confidence as she could muster. "I am."

He eyed her soberly.

Kyler felt her bravado slip. The man could read her like a book. And that stare was 100 percent seduce and master.

She wandered to the end of the bed. "I'm not going to give details. In my profession, that's never wise."

"Of course not. So it's a profession for you? I'm so glad I stepped aside to allow the professional to handle the details."

"Damn right."

"So you've a fence or buyer lined up?"

"Maybe." She leaned against the wall and crossed her arms.

"And where does this friend come in? I thought you said you'd picked up a piece of art for him. Or was that a lie you made up when we met at the bar? It is a *him*, yes?"

"It is. And it wasn't a lie. But how can you know the art I told you about was the egg?"

"You've committed *two* heists since arriving in Venice?"

Kyler shook her head. The man was insufferable! "Just the one. What about you? You said you were casing the place the same time as me. You don't strike me as particularly in need of pin money."

"I am quite well off, thank you."

No kidding. The palazzo must be worth a fortune, and she bet the suits set him back a couple thousand per outfit. "And I recall you said you weren't a thief? I don't get it."

"There's nothing to get, Kyler. I wanted the Nécessaire egg. I devised a way to obtain it, via you."

"How'd that work out for you?"

"I can't argue the night ending on a high point with you pierced by my cock." He stroked his jaw. The move was so sensual Kyler's body heat rose a few degrees.

Neither could she make the argument. And just the sound of it—pierced by his cock—ooh, it gave her a good shiver.

"And I do love a good adventure. Such as werewolves," he continued. "They provide a challenge. Keeps an old vamp on his toes. And in this case, I've also the pleasurable challenge of dallying with a very pretty vampiress thief who wishes to thwart my mission."

"I've never thwarted anything. I'm not a thwarter. But I will win this one. I don't care why you want the egg. It was mine. I had my hands on it. And I will have it again."

"Do you know what the egg does?"

She shrugged. She had a good idea what the egg could make happen, and she understood it wasn't the actual egg, but something inside it. But she wasn't about to lay down all her cards before this guy.

"I thought it was a woman's cosmetic kit inside the Nécessaire egg?" she said. "That's what was advertised on the auction profile."

"Right. Filled with combs, nail files, a mirror and so on. But beyond what the public knows...let's say it is important I obtain the egg. For the safety of many."

Kyler rolled her eyes. "Too vague. You didn't win that argument."

Dante tilted his head back against the headboard and slid a hand down his abs. The action took her out of her cautious reluctance and into a wanting desire for what was not-so-cleverly hidden beneath the towel.

"Fine," he said. "We'll play this game of cat and mouse. I like games. Especially one matched against a beautiful woman."

"I never mix business with pleasure," Kyler said quickly.

"Too late," he said in a singsongy tone. "I've tasted your sweetness. Everywhere."

Her shoulders dropped. Yeah, tell her about it. She hated the man. But she also found him irresistible. And she hated herself for being interested in him. This was exhausting.

"So what will we do with ourselves until my clothes arrive?"

"I'm not waiting for clothes," she said. "Perhaps I'll step out and see if I can pick up the trail."

"That wouldn't be wise."

"You don't get to tell me what to do."

"I would only wish to do such when you are naked and wanting before me."

She bristled and turned her head quickly to hide the sigh that crossed her lips.

Dante leaned forward. "Have you experience with werewolves, Kyler? With fighting them? We do know the ones we heard on the bridge are armed with stakes. And they have our scents. How many times have you faced down the pointy tip of a stake?"

She'd forgotten about that. Her answer was never, and please, never let it happen anytime. Soon enough she wouldn't have to worry about a stake being her end. But if she wanted to maintain any sort of advantage in this game of Dante's, she couldn't let him see her bluff.

"And what is *your* experience with fending off wolves?" she countered. "Are you some kind of trained killer? A werewolf slayer?"

Dante chuckled and swung his legs off the bed. As he stood, he ran his fingers through his hair, which had already dried; the short strands stuck up ever so invitingly. "Over the decades I've picked up some defense skills. Werewolves may be strong, but they're slow. We vamps have speed and agility going for us. And I'd like to think we have the brains, as well. The dogs are stupid. But if they are part of a pack, then we have to be careful. Two or even three werewolves shouldn't present a problem. A whole pack? Then we've got issues."

"How do you know if they are with a pack?"

He shrugged. "That is something we probably won't know until it's too late."

Kyler scoffed at his lack of knowledge. "What about you? Are you in a tribe?" She knew vampires gathered in tribes. She remained independent—not for lack of wanting to be in a tribe but rather for not knowing how to approach one to join.

"Yes." He strolled around to the end of the bed and stood three feet from her. Kyler's neck heated. She could feel his electrically sensual draw prickle at her skin through the air. Her nipples hardened. She caught her breath before another exhale could escape. "Tribe Incroyables."

"Seriously? The Incredibles? That's kind of cocky, don't you think?"

"We are rather incredible," he said with all the boisterous pride such a statement demanded. "I didn't name the tribe. It's a tip of the hat to Dumas's musketeers. Our tribe leader, Christian De Bareaux, was a musketeer in the seventeenth century. He's a good man."

"How many are in your tribe?"

"About a dozen. But no women allowed. Johnny Santiago's sister wanted to join, and we wouldn't allow it."

"So an old boy's club, eh?"

"Exactly, and we like it that way. What about you?" He took her in, assessingly this time. "You are tribeless." He stated it as fact.

"I am, and I like it that way. I don't care to have vampires telling me what to do."

"What vampire has told you what to do?"

She met his gaze and felt his delving intrusion deep in her being. It felt as if he peeled her open to expose the center, the secret parts she tried desperately to keep concealed. She fiddled with the shirt hem as he stepped closer.

"No one," she said, looking away. And then, more testily, she argued, "None of your business."

"Ah. So someone has told you what to do, and you're rebelling against it ever happening again. Good for you, Kitten."

"He didn't tell me what to do. I want to do this for him. I owe him."

"Ah? For what, may I ask?"

"None of your business."

"But the *he* you mention is the same he you've stolen the egg for?"

"This conversation is over." She turned to pick up the backpack, and he placed a hand against the wall over her shoulder.

"Since we can't leave," Dante said, "and since we've dispensed with the get-to-know-you bullshit, and you've set a boundary on conversation topics, I'm of a mind to make a suggestion for a new activity."

She could make one guess what that activity was, but

she wouldn't—couldn't—succumb to his seductions. No matter that this was the first time she'd seen him in daylight and noticed how clear his sea glass eyes were. Cool and mysterious, like the Venetian lagoon.

"And what is your suggestion?" she asked before she could stop herself.

"We can either turn up the volume on the television and zone out on some idiotic talk show, or…" He leaned in until his nose brushed her wet hair above her ear. "Despite the fact you're fully dressed, I could nail you to the wall with this." The heavy weight of his cock beneath the towel thudded against her hip.

Kyler maintained a modicum of strength. "I thought you liked the red shirt?"

He nodded and nuzzled his nose aside her cheek. "I do. The color makes your skin glow. But it's a bit loose. It doesn't emphasize your assets as something tighter would. I like your curves, Kitten." He licked her skin. Shivers traced her spine. The vampiric shimmer sparkled into her belly. "All of them."

Dante's tongue had found her clavicle. And it had become less and less important to be strong when really, what would that get her but frustration?

"You're perfect. Lovely. I like a woman who is abundant. I also love big breasts. And yours are—" he breathed hotly and heavily against her neck "—so voluptuous."

Kyler sighed out her surrender. If he thought he could control her with sex and compliments—ah hell, she'd lost the battle.

After pulling up and off the too-loose shirt, she

tossed it aside. Dante's mouth landed on hers, and he lifted her by the thighs so she could wrap her legs about his hips.

"Good choice," he said against her mouth. "You smell like jasmine."

"You said you didn't like that smell."

"On me? No. On you? It is delectable." He bent to lick the top of her breast, while he managed to unhook her bra with a deft move and pull it away. "And you taste even better."

After spinning her around, he set her down gently on the bed, then tugged down her capris. He parted her legs and dove to kiss her there, where her curls began. His tongue traced the crease between her thigh and lower belly, slicking hotly. It was difficult not to squirm with delight.

Kyler threaded her fingers through his hair and pushed gently, indicating she wanted him to move lower, and he followed her silent command. A dash of tongue here, a long, luxurious lick there. And when he suckled at her clitoris a deep moan spilled from her mouth. The man didn't waste time in going directly for the prize. She appreciated his determination.

"Purr for me, Kitten," he said.

Kyler did. And her purrs vibrated through her being and coalesced with the spinning want and desire that had formed in her core. With Dante's tongue lashing her to hip-rocking anticipation, she gripped the bed-cover tightly as his fingers entered her and began their own teasing dance.

He'd mastered her so quickly, and with such ease,

that she couldn't manage to cling to calm and relax. And it didn't matter, because as she tensed and released her muscles, the act of doing so increased the pleasure and just as his tongue lashed her pulsing, swollen clitoris one more time…

Kyler surrendered to a shouting orgasm. "Yes!" And flung her arms above her head and stretched out her legs as the bone-tingling sensations wavered through her body. Had she been determined to keep the man off her? Silly kitten.

A knock on the door prompted Dante to grab the towel he'd discarded on the bed and wrap it about his hips. He glanced at her, panting, naked, uncaring who entered and saw her like that. Her cheeks felt flushed and rosy beneath a spray of dark hair.

"Sit tight," he said with a sexy smile. "That's probably my suit."

Indeed, the tailor had delivered. Dante had already tipped the concierge, so he took the garment bag and closed the door.

"We are back in action," he said, unzipping the bag. "Gray superfine wool. Single-breasted. Nice choice. And a calfskin loafer. Bless the man, he knows my style. You want to make another round of it before I pull on my clothes?"

Kyler laughed and shook her head. "I'm good. I'm back to hating you now."

"Ah. Well, I guess I can't get so lucky as to win you over with my charm and cock. What is it, exactly, that will impress you?"

"You placing the Fabergé egg in my hands," she said plainly.

"Unfortunate. I really do like you, Kyler. But I guess I'll have to live with your hate."

Chapter 5

Dante paused near a building, stepping into the shade, and waited for Kyler to catch up. She seemed to be doing a bit of sightseeing, her eyes falling across the facade of the Doge's Palace. The grand staircase never drew his eye. He tended to focus on the task at hand rather than zoning out on scenery, but Kyler's fascination reminded him that a few seconds to take things in was permissible. He'd stayed in Venice every summer for decades, and he'd rarely taken the time to glance at the tourist sites or even wander inside Saint Mark's cathedral.

He'd lived a life, yet had he noticed it? Weird thought to have.

His gaze swung 180 degrees. At the sight of a particular shop, he chided his lacking forethought to bring along a weapon. He signaled to Kyler he wanted to step into the antique weaponry shop, and she said she'd wait outside. Fine with him. He knew she wasn't going anywhere, because, indeed, he was the one with the nose to scent out werewolves. Once inside, he asked about silver and the shop owner shook his head, but then he lifted a finger and described a blade he kept behind the counter.

It was a fine blade, a little dull, but when thrusting to wound it wasn't necessary to have a supersharp edge. And while not a bargain, it was a weapon he needed should they face werewolves toe to—well, claw.

"I'll take it, and—" he gestured to a pair of Ray-Bans propped on a rack behind the counter "—those, as well." Dante handed over his credit card and minutes later, with his eyes properly shaded against the sun, he joined Kyler and led them toward the canal.

"The bridge where the wolves scented us is around the corner, so I suspect they might have a compound or hideout nearby. How are you?" He reached over to cup her cheek and studied her eyes. Bright and smiling. And yet…"You're hot."

"It's July, and the sun is high. I appreciate that you're walking in the shadows."

A thoughtful lover would have purchased her a pair of sunglasses, as well. *Bad vampire.* "You know how to lower your body temperature, yes?"

"Maybe? I don't use it much. Never really learned, I guess."

"Now would be a good time." Had she not been taught the ways of his kind? Then again, so many vampires came to the blood having been turned and left behind to fend for themselves. He knew this firsthand.

"If we can keep our bodies cool, the wolves won't be able to scent us so easily. Just a few degrees will do the trick. I'm already there." He pulled her hand up and pressed it to his cheek, and she nodded; indeed, he did feel cooler. "Your turn."

"Give me a second." Stepping into the shadows again, she closed her eyes and bowed her head. At her sides, her fingers wiggled and she shifted her hips, as if summoning up courage or…well, women tended to have a process for so many little things he'd stopped questioning decades ago.

It was a simple matter of focus for him. He hadn't had time to do it last night before the wolves had gotten too close. Today he would not be so foolish. It was Kyler. She distracted him. But he'd strive to keep that distraction in the bedroom and not out in the real world, where a moment of inattention could cost him his life.

Smoothing his fingers along her cheek, he sensed a small alteration in temperature but not enough. "More," he whispered.

"Seriously?" She pushed his hand away and flashed her gaze up at him. "You touching me is not helping."

"Ah. Right." With a smirk, he took a step back.

So she was hot for him? And yet she wanted to keep him at a distance. What was wrong with plunging in for the ride and letting the chips fall where they may? He loved a dangerous affair. And this one could prove to be just that.

On the other hand, perhaps she was the wiser of them when it came to getting involved. For the first time in ages, he was actually tempted to drink another vampire's blood. What made Kyler so intriguing to him?

"All right, I'm good," she said. Holding up her palm, she indicated he should high-five her.

So he did, and he held her fingers in a clasp for a few seconds. Yes, she was cool to the touch. *Good girl.* And she was eager to learn and prove herself. That's what he found fascinating about her. Strong, bold and not afraid of her shortcomings, which, he guessed, were few.

"Let's go this way." He strolled between two buildings that hugged a narrow passage. "Do you sense them? They are in one of these buildings. Let's try up on the rooftop. Can you make the leap?"

"Of course I can. I did nab the Fabergé egg by entering through a second-floor window. Unlatched. Their security was ridiculously lax."

"I noted that."

"Yeah. Seems to be something you're comfortable with. Standing back and observing while letting others do the work." With a few running steps, she leaped and disappeared onto the rooftop.

"Touché." Dante followed, landing lightly in a crouch on the flat roof, thankful it was not tiled and thus, not slippery. He motioned to Kyler to listen for sounds below. Again he grabbed her hand, confirming she was still cool. They should not be detected.

After a moment or two of silence between them, he was able to home in on a conversation directly below where they were positioned, perhaps separated by one floor.

"Not there. Probably out sucking some poor bastard's blood," one of them said.

"Or left the island."

"Without what they wanted? Doubt that. We'll keep an eye on the palazzo."

"Can you hear?" Dante asked Kyler.

She nodded. "They're the same two from earlier. I recognize the voices. And there is a new one."

He was impressed she'd sorted that out. She may have been vampire for only six months, but she possessed good control of her sensory skills. As she should. A vampire should always be aware of his or her surroundings, close up and far off. It could mean life or death.

"One of them said he was working a shift at the auction house," she whispered.

"I heard that. I wonder…" He pressed his palm to the rooftop, staring hard at the pebbled surface. He was not trying to see through it, simply focusing beyond the exterior sensations of the rough roof material. "I assumed the wolves were after the egg, as we are. But can they know what it does?"

Kyler shrugged, not giving him a clue whether or not she actually knew what it did. She couldn't know. Could she? He'd thought that information exclusive to but a few.

"Not many know," he continued. "Maybe they are simply seeking the financial reward it could bring? The one working at the auction house said he followed the thief—you—from the scene of the crime, and tracked you to the bar. Yet I followed you, as well. I can't believe I wasn't aware there was a werewolf on my ass last night. But how else would they have known to follow the thief to *my* palazzo?"

"Yes, they had to have tracked me. And yet they stood aside and waited while we—ahem. I feel sick about this. I was so sure I had everything under control. And all along not only were you following me but also werewolves?" She dropped her hands onto the roof and groaned. "I let the thrill of accomplishing the theft go to my head."

Dante rubbed her shoulder to reassure her. "The wolves could have been planning to steal it, too."

"Two vamps and a bunch of wolves all planning the same heist for the same night? Doubtful. It's remarkable that *our* plans coincided." She tilted her head to look at him. "Unless you're working with them?"

"With the dogs? I think not." He motioned with a finger to his lips for silence and again focused on the conversation below.

They were talking about someone they intended to hand the egg over to. A fence? In…Paris. It was obvious to Dante the wolves had no clue what was inside the egg, and they only marveled over the gemstones encrusting the outside and its rarity.

He lay on his stomach, putting his cheek to the roof. Mutters and a clattering noise echoed below him. Someone had shaken the egg. They were trying to open it. And then…more conversation. The handoff was indeed in Paris. And there was mention of the full moon.

One more night and the moon would be full. Dante knew the wolves liked to transform on that night, and on this little island city a hulking werewolf would certainly not go unnoticed. They couldn't remain in Venice. They had to leave as quickly as possible and seek the safety of forested land.

"We've got to get the egg before they leave the island," he said, getting to his feet. "Otherwise we may be forced to track them across Europe. Let's take them out now."

"What?" Kyler sat up as he offered a hand to pull her up. "Take them out? Do you have weapons? Silver?"

He drew out the silver blade. "I never shop without good reason, Kitten. And we've our cunning and agility, as I've explained."

Kyler winced.

"You're not up for fighting werewolves?" he asked.

"I'm a thief, not a fighter. What if you take out the wolves while I sneak in and grab the egg?"

"And then head off with the prize yourself?"

"That's a risk you'll have to take, Casanova. You can't slay wolves and grab the egg, can you? Hell, I'm willing to help, and that's far beyond anything I imagined I'd be doing here in Venice. Standing up to werewolves?"

He sensed her rising fear and body heat.

"Keep your temperature in check. We need the element of surprise."

He wielded the blade, and a peek of sunlight glinted through the clouds and onto the elegant weapon. The sound of a door opening and closing on the street below lured him to the roof's edge. He peered over and spied one of the wolves. Broad in shoulder and tall, he walked like a prizefighter, arms arced and meaty fingers curled and ready for fists. He wasn't carrying a bag or anything that would indicate he had the egg on him. No one followed him. He strolled down the narrow street toward the canal, where a row of touristy restaurants served midafternoon diners. Perhaps he was a scout sent out to guard the palazzo.

"This may be a bit of luck," Dante said. "One gone. Only two left inside. We move now."

Once the door to the room had been kicked open, Dante moved like lightning. Kyler pinpointed the two werewolves, in human form, standing across a long room outfitted with a desk and one office chair. Nothing on the desk except the egg, which sat on top of a black cloth.

Taken by surprise, the wolves reacted quickly but not fast enough for one of them to avoid taking the silver blade to his gut. Dante tugged out the knife and turned to the other wolf, defying him with a jerk of his chin and a blatant, "Come here, puppy."

Meanwhile, Kyler jumped over the werewolf on the floor, who groaned and clutched at his bleeding stomach. He caught her foot and she tumbled forward. She saved herself, catching her palms on the desktop. She swept her arm over the egg and grabbed the cloth when she realized it was a bag. Without looking back, she headed for the window, thankful it was open, and looked out over the narrow passageway below.

Dante's yelp signaled he must have taken a punch. She heard repeated thudding sounds as someone got pummeled, but Kyler was not compelled to look back. The important concern was saving her own ass.

After stepping up onto the windowsill, Kyler jumped and landed on both feet with an ease that she would never tire of marveling over. With a scan down each end of the alley, she decided to walk the opposite direction from which they had arrived. Also opposite the direction Dante had seen the other wolf walking in.

She heard glass shatter, and some rained down onto the sidewalk. She jumped and ran, avoiding the slicing shards. For a moment she considered rushing back inside, but—

Dante would be okay. He was a big boy.

Besides, it didn't matter what happened to him now. She had the egg. And this time around she wasn't going to let it out of her sight. She'd head back to the hotel and...

Why hadn't she gotten a call telling her where to hand it off? It didn't make sense. Should she call and check in? He'd told her not to. That he would handle everything.

Then they could both begin eternity. But not together. He'd made it clear to her they were not in a relationship. They weren't lovers, and she didn't need it to be that way.

But she could use a little communication on his part.

"I'll give him a few more hours," she whispered, turning a corner and orienting herself to where she stood. Her hotel was across the canal and south. She'd cross at the next bridge and head back and wait.

* * *

Dante stood up from the second slain werewolf. The silver blade dripped blood near his shoe. He bent and wiped it across the wolf's canvas pant leg. Werewolves did not dissolve to ash as demons and vampires did, but silver could bring on a quiet and burning implosion. He'd best grab Kyler and get out of here before the local authorities got wind of what was up. Or before wolf number three returned.

Cursing the fact that his scent would linger, he quickly lowered his body temperature and decided he'd take a detour through the canal again to shake the final wolf from his scent.

"Kyler?" he whispered, glancing about the room.

He didn't have to look too long before he realized she wasn't there. Nor was the egg. He'd seen her move toward the desk; then he'd taken an iron fist to the temple and had decided to focus on the fight.

"She's not stupid," he ground out through an achy jaw. "But she doesn't have that big of a head start."

Praying she would have the sense to lower her body temperature, he walked toward the fallen door. He scented a new wolf. The third had returned and was not far down the hallway.

Dante dashed for the window on the opposite side of the room. The frame was frilled with broken shards; he took a running leap and soared through without taking a cut. Airborne, he heard the wolf behind him curse.

The narrow alleyway loomed below the window. He landed on his feet, shoes crunching glass shards, then turned and ran toward the canal. With a leap, he stretched and arrowed his body toward the water and landed in a dive. He cut through the water with the blade still in hand and kicked to propel himself through the dark murk. When he surfaced to check his position, he heard the smacking impact of another body hitting the water.

Kicking away, he managed to turn and see the dark blur before the werewolf grabbed his leg. Water bubbled about him and, tugged into darkness, he found it difficult to orient himself. He slashed the blade backward, but it landed on nothing. A claw dug into his back, and Dante jerked back his head, smashing his skull against what he hoped was the werewolf's head. The claw dislodged, and Dante was able to twist and face his opponent just as the beast struck toward him in a rush of bubbling seawater.

Dante thrust the knife forward, and it landed in solid flesh. He couldn't be sure where in the wolf it had hit, but it didn't matter. The silver would serve its purpose. He kicked the wolf's thigh and pushed away. Red water spilled around them. He could smell the blood and tasted its sweet taint. Suddenly, he was jerked from behind by the shoulder. His body bent backward, veering toward the bottom of the canal. The werewolf's teeth brushed his forehead—and slipped away.

Dante kicked the lifeless body away from him and used the momentum to surface near a closed motor repair shop. He searched the water's surface but saw no rising air bubbles, no motion beneath. He didn't see any gondolas or stray tourists wandering down the sidewalk. He quickly levered himself up and, pressing his back to the wall, slid along the building until he reached the corner and could step into a secluded alleyway.

Wiping the water from his face, he moved to throw the knife into the canal—but at the last moment he didn't release it. He may not be finished with werewolves. And this was the only silver he had. Tucking the blade in his waistband, he then peeled off the heavy suit coat and dropped it in the canal.

"My tailor will be inordinately pleased," he muttered with little enthusiasm.

He wandered down the alley. He straightened and inhaled, shaking off the tendril of fear that had briefly taunted him with the notion he could have died in the water. And in that breath he tasted *her* at the back of his throat.

He wasn't finished with Kyler Cole. And he wasn't sure if that was a good or bad thing.

Chapter 6

Kyler was close to her hotel. She didn't know Venice, and it was difficult to navigate without her cell phone, which she had left at the hotel.

She held the egg under her shirt and looked a little pregnant as she swiftly walked by tourists and vendors calling after her to check out their scarves and cheap key chains. The hotel was to the left. Or maybe the right?

She paused and pressed a shoulder to a cool brick wall, taking a moment to settle and acclimate herself. Her job back at the werewolves' hideout had been easy-in, easy-out.

Dante, on the other hand…well.

Was she worried about Dante? He'd taken out one wolf, and she had been sure he'd win against the other when she'd slipped out the door with the prize. He'd be fine. Angry. But no worse for the wear. So no need to stress about leaving him behind.

But with a pissed vampire out there gunning for her hide, she had best not stand around. She glided her gaze 180 degrees, noting the buildings she remembered were all to the right. Turning that way, she was rewarded with the sight of her hotel.

Once in the lobby, she let a family of eight go first in the elevator, not wanting to share the cramped box while trying to keep the egg hidden from prying eyes. It wouldn't be wise to advertise she had the missing egg blasted across all the news stations.

The second elevator was empty. After the doors closed, she slipped the egg out from under her shirt and took a moment to admire the gold structure, embedded with sapphires, emeralds, rubies and diamonds. Before the theft, she'd briefly seen a drawing of it, and since taking it in hand—twice—hadn't had a chance to open it and peer inside at what should be a woman's cosmetics kit. But there was a trick to opening it, surely.

How *did* it work? What little she knew of the eggs created by Peter Carl Fabergé in the nineteenth century was that most opened to reveal an inner secret surprise. And regarding this particular egg, she knew there was something inside beyond combs and tweezers. But how to get that surprise out was another issue. The man for whom she was claiming this egg had not given her that information. She was merely the thief. And really, she didn't want to fuss with the valuable thing in case she broke it or did something that would hinder it from opening properly.

As soon as she handed this over to him she would finally feel as though she had paid him for the priceless gift of vampirism he had given her. It had been worth the risk of getting caught. She'd relied on her vampirism for quickness and the ability to hear low-decibel noises before security could have found her. The dalliance with Dante had been worth it, as well. Much as Kyler knew she should never again go near Dante. Not if she wanted to keep the egg.

Which meant she had to hightail it out of this hotel because he knew where she was staying. But she had to remain in Venice until she knew where and to whom to hand off the egg.

The elevator door slid open, and she dashed down the hallway and stuck her keycard in the lock. Once inside and with the door closed behind her, she let out a relieved breath and dropped her shoulders. She strode past the bathroom door and toward the main room where the end of the king-size bed thrust toward the TV.

An arm snapped around her throat, jerking her backward and off balance. She struggled with her free hand to loosen the arm, but the grip was tight—and wet—and she kicked her feet, only managing to stub a toe on the nearby dresser.

"I'm guessing you got lost," Dante said tightly. "Certainly, you wouldn't have left me and taken off with the prize."

Oh yeah?

She swung her arm backward, trying to hit him, but

realized too late it was the hand in which she held the egg. He gripped her wrist and smashed the back of her hand against the wall, which hurt so much she opened her fingers. As the egg dropped, so did Dante's pinching lock about her neck. He shoved her away, and she landed on the floor on her hands and knees. She twisted her head in time to see him deftly catch the egg before it hit the carpet.

"That's mine!" she said and rolled onto her feet. Kicking high, she managed a solid connection to her competitor's chest.

His hip hit the wall, and he growled at her. Fangs descending, he lunged for her and fit one hand about her neck while he clutched the egg to his chest, pushing her back down onto the carpet. "It has always been mine. I won't allow some inexperienced little girl to dash away with it to hand off as a trinket to her lover."

His thumb pressed against her voice box, but not so hard that she lost her breath. His knees pinned her forearms, making it impossible to struggle. She'd not seen his fangs when they had made love. Now they didn't so much frighten her as tantalize. And that scared her more than returning empty-handed to the man who had asked her to steal the egg.

"I do as I wish," she said firmly. "And I wish to give him this egg so he can have eternity."

Dante's grip relented. Stretching back, he set the egg on the carpet, then sat back on his haunches, straddling her but not putting all his weight on her hips. His hair dripped water onto her chin. And his shirt clung to his chest, defining the firm pecs. How had he gotten all wet again? And for the first time she noticed the blood on his forehead. A thin cut that was healing.

"Eternity? The egg has no such power," he said and stood. He strode to the end of the bed and began to unbutton the wet shirt. "Who is this friend? He wants eternity? Must be a fellow vampire."

She wouldn't give him the satisfaction of that correct guess so she merely shrugged.

"I see. What makes you believe that the egg will grant eternity?"

Kyler closed her eyes and remained on the floor. Toying with her beliefs? It was part of his plan to win what he'd lost and was now rightfully hers. "What's *inside* that egg has power. A code or spell to grant vampires eternity. Even a stake won't cause death."

Dante laughed, ending it with a devastatingly sexy stare. "If it's eternity you seek, then why give the egg to someone else?" He pulled off the wet shirt and tossed it aside. "Why not simply take what you want? Is this man your lover?"

Kyler pushed up and turned to sit against the wall. Her hair fell forward across her cheek. She had to admit she feared what Dante could do to her. He was strong and had decades of knowledge to wield against her.

"He's not my lover," she said softly. *Not anymore, anyway.* "I…owe him a favor."

"A favor? Theft is quite a large favor."

Out of the corner of her eye she spied the egg, lying before the closet. Rich and exquisite, set there without a care as if it were a child's abandoned toy. She leaned toward it…

"Don't touch it," Dante said sharply.

She sat back. She'd keep an eye on it for now.

He kicked off his shoes and pulled down his pants.

"Not this again," Kyler muttered.

"Yes, this again. I've a certain distaste for wearing the canal. Damn, I have always hated fish and their smell. You are costing me a fortune in bespoke silk and calfskin leather."

"It's not my fault you like to swim in the canal. What happened this time?"

"Perhaps you should have stuck around to see?"

"You really think that would have been wise?"

"No. I'm actually pleased you were able to get away unscathed. I, on the other hand, had to make a quick escape. And I was followed by wolf number three into the canal."

"He came back?"

"Yes. I dispatched him. And I'm fine, thanks for your concern."

The silver knife landed on the bed. Dante leaned over her in his wet briefs. "I'm going to shower. With the egg. When I come out, we are going to talk about who it is that has sent you after the egg. And why it is so important to you to have a spell that grants eternity to one who already possesses immortality."

Steam surrounded Dante after he'd gotten out of the shower and stepped onto the bath mat before the vanity. The mirror was fogged, but he couldn't see his reflection anyway. On occasion he caught glimpses of himself in street windows, possible because the clear glass was not backed in silver. After a half a century or so, a man had seen enough of himself and it mattered little to continue to look. He'd not aged since the day Zara Destry had pierced his carotid and changed him forever. And he would age so slowly that a glance in a window once a decade was more than enough to confirm immortality.

He didn't bother to dry off because he hadn't been able to shower fast enough. He needed to look at the egg. No sounds came from out in the room, but he knew Kyler would not have left. She wanted this egg because she thought it had special powers to grant eternity? The only special powers he knew that were attached to this egg were quite the opposite. And devastating at that.

But it wasn't the egg, exactly, that provided such magic.

"It's what's inside," he murmured as he bowed before the gorgeous object and turned it slowly.

It was affixed to a gold stand and secured with snapping hooks, a part of the original design. He'd appreciated that when he'd first received the egg. He tended to be a bit clumsy with the more delicate objets d'art. Zara had given it to him. He'd thought it was a token of her affection, and it had meant so much in those first moments when she'd revealed it to him. For he had loved her. Deeply.

Zara had then explained to him why she wanted him to have it. It contained a spell, and she didn't want to be the one to have to guard it. Certain others wanted it, and she was afraid of having to face one, in particular, of those others. She trusted Dante. He was honest and brave. A single kiss had sealed his agreement to take the egg.

And then she had left him. Forever.

Dante winced now as he remembered that morning she'd kissed him and said goodbye. Fleetingly. As if he were just another lover and she was on to the next. As if they had not spent a lovely week together, entwined and breathing in each other's skin, sex and blood. He was familiar now with the process of a quick escape from emotional attachment. But back then he'd been devastated. Heartbroken.

"Man up," he whispered to himself now. "You're over her, remember?" And he'd never love again thanks to Zara's cruel indifference.

Turning the exquisitely crafted egg slowly, he sought the front. The largest of dozens of sapphires sat above a curved indent, into which his forefinger fit perfectly. It had been well over half a century since he'd last handled this prize, for he'd taken it on in 1952. Would he remember how to operate it?

After wiping his wet fingers on a nearby towel, he tapped the indent on the trim. Another tap. A gentle touch to determine if he had the right panel. And then he pushed in and slid the panel up a millimeter.

Click.

The inner mechanism began to rotate. He smiled at the sound of gears, recalling this had been created around the time that the steam engine had been retired for the motor. The Fabergé eggs had been created for the Russian tsars Alexander III and Nicholas II as Easter gifts for their wives and mother. This was one from the Imperial collection. It had remained nicely oiled during its absence from his care.

Had someone already opened this? The thief who had originally stolen it from him? He wasn't so curious to learn who had stolen it now that he had it back. But might a curator at the auction house have figured out the motions to open it? They couldn't know the correct order and proper finger placement required. As far as he knew, only he and Zara had that knowledge. And who knew where that vampiress was now?

He'd like to know. No. He did not. He'd gotten over her. At least, that's what he told himself.

"Damn it, man, pull yourself together." The last thing he needed was to fall into melancholy over a lost love with Kyler around. He would never expose that weakness to her. Love was simply something he knew he must avoid. He did not consider it a possibility now.

The top half of the egg snapped up, exposing an equatorial view of the inner gears.

He bent to get a closer look and survey the various cosmetic items inside. His heart thudded. Where was it?

Ah. Tucked between a tiny mirror and a foldable comb.

"It's still in here. Excellent."

Kyler pulled her hair into a ponytail, squeezed tightly, then dropped it down her back. He was taking a long time in there. The shower had stopped five minutes ago. And he didn't have clothes in the bathroom with him. What was he doing? Was there a way out of the bathroom that she wasn't aware of? Maybe he was doing...personal stuff. Frustrated man stuff that was a direct result of—well, it wasn't as though she'd resisted his advances.

She was a wimp when it came to sea glass eyes and a seductive smirk.

She dashed over to the bathroom door and listened. She could sense his calm heartbeat on the other side of the door. After quickly making her way back to the bed, she sat on the end of it just as the door opened. A towel was wrapped about Dante's hips. His abs glistened with water droplets, as did his legs and shoulders.

But the only appealing thing she noticed was the egg in his hands.

Kyler stood. Dante nodded curtly that she sit, and she did. And then she got angry at herself for following his silent commands and stood again.

"Really?" He huffed out an exhale. He strode over to the table and set the egg down, then sat on the chair beside the table. He then nicely asked, "Will you please sit down, Kyler? And tell me about this mystery man for whom you've stolen the egg."

"I won't reveal his name. He's a friend." She walked over and sat in the chair on the other side of the table. They were both now an equal distance from the egg.

"Then you won't walk out of here today with this prize." He leaned back, resting his forearms on the chair arms. Unaware of the sexual energy he put out sitting in but a towel and with water-bedazzled muscles.

On the other hand, she sensed the man was always aware of every sensual move he made. His entire existence was an orchestration of seduction and charm. And Kyler would do well to ignore the insistent twinge of desire that hummed within when she thought about how delicious it was to feel his muscles gliding against her sex-hungry body. Or when his mouth brushed her skin…

"You believe that egg will grant a vampire eternity?" Dante asked.

She had to play him carefully. Not reveal too much. "Don't you? You have said that the egg was once yours. Don't you know things about it? Why did you have it in the first place? And how did you lose it? I don't believe this ever belonged to you."

"Kyler." He paused a moment, and in that pause she felt his struggle to remain calm. To not leap across the table and choke her. To not simply dash away with the egg. He could. He was the stronger of the two of them. "Let me tell you a little about this egg and the spell contained within."

"Please do." So it was a spell? *Good to know.*

"It was gifted to me in the 1950s by a woman—a vampiress—and I was asked to guard it well. To not let it fall into the wrong hands."

"Great job." If a thumbs-up could be sarcastic, she'd mastered it.

"Ahem. Simply put, I was to never let anyone near it. Because, as you've intimated, it does possess certain powers. Or at least, what is inside of it does. So I placed it in a vault room of a home I once owned in Austria. It was a secure vault for the time period. That is, before digital combinations and the high-tech mumbo jumbo came about."

She rolled her eyes. Was he really such a technology noob?

"I was once an art collector. And I traveled a lot. I tended to put things in the vault and then forget about them. Until the mid-1990s, when I decided a move to Paris was necessary. Just as well, I'd grown tired of collecting things. They are just *things* after all. So, I sold the Austrian property to a young couple who were excited to renovate the centuries-old castle."

"You lived in a castle?"

"For a time. It's not as romantic as it sounds. Rather drafty most of the time. Anyway, the vault was opened weeks before the move date. A brief visual inventory alerted me something was wrong. Someone had been inside. There was no sign of forced entry. But things were missing. A few Rembrandts. A Lalique ruby brooch. And the Fabergé egg. I have no idea *when* it was stolen. Or by whom. Only that it was gone."

"Perhaps one of your many nameless lovers took it?"

He inhaled through his nose, clutching the chair arm with tight fingers, and continued. "I marked it off as bad luck and have kept my eyes and ears open for the egg. I didn't hear a thing until a few days ago. I'm not sure who had the egg—the original thief, or if it had been sold immediately after it was stolen from me—or how it came to be brought to auction. But know this." He leaned across the table and tapped the top of the egg. "I will not let this out of my hands a second time. I was given it to guard its secret, and I will do so."

"Because you did such a fabulous job the first time around."

He'd been told to keep it safe? How could he have not known someone had robbed him? Of course, if he was a world traveler, the castle must have sat empty a lot. And nothing high-tech like digital security? A smart thief could have had a field day within the safe. But she still wanted to go with the idea of a disappointed lover stealing the thing. Or perhaps even a scheming lover who had used him specifically to get to the egg. Would serve Dante right after he'd turned the tables on her.

"Your story, if it's true, is a good one. But you've not softened my heart to your plight. You had a job to do. You failed." She hooked a finger about the base of the egg holder and slid it a few inches toward her across the table. "I've been charged to bring this back to King."

"King?" Dante's gaze grew fierce.

Shit. She hadn't intended to reveal the name of her creator.

"You mean *the* King?" he asked.

"Not the king of any country. I just... I shouldn't have said that. Would you stop looking at me? I can't think properly with your big sea glass eyes beaming onto me like that."

Dante smirked and leaned back again. "You like me, Kitten. I'd even go so far as to say you're smitten by me."

Kyler blew out a "Puh."

"You are attracted to me. You like having sex with me. You favor my kisses. You even enjoy my company. Admit it."

"None of the above."

He mocked a pout. "I recall those orgasms you had were genuine and quite loud."

"Just because you're capable of getting me off doesn't mean I have to fall in love with you and swoon at your feet."

"No. But you wouldn't mind another kiss, would you?"

"Will a kiss get me the egg?"

"No. But it may get you another orgasm."

Kyler glanced out the window, trying desperately to distract herself from the growing desire in her core. Hell yes, she would love him to give her another orgasm. To lean into his kiss and feel his hands at her breasts, his tongue moving down, down and down...

"What do you want from me for the egg?" she asked. "Do you want to fuck me again?"

He stood abruptly. The height of him, the lines and hard landscape of his muscles and body, his over-whelming masculinity, set Kyler back in the chair. Her heartbeat thundered as he gazed down at her. He took a few steps and stood over her. "This." He swept a hand toward the egg. "And this." He leaned down and kissed her.

He kissed her hard. He kissed her deeply. He stirred up a wanting moan from her as she leaned upward, seeking more, begging for him to take her, to want her, to need her. To own her.

He broke the kiss and said, "Are two very different things. Can we agree on that?"

"I don't know. I still feel like you used me."

"You're not that stupid, Kyler. No man could use

you sexually. You are a strong woman. You take what you want."

Again he gestured to the egg. Yes, she'd nabbed that damn thing. *Go, Kyler!*

"And you fuck who you want." He returned to the chair and sat.

Kyler exhaled, wishing he'd gathered her into his arms and tumbled onto the bed with her. She was out of her element. Stealing the egg had been a leap into risky and advanced thievery. And now with no contact from King, she felt unmoored. She wanted to feel safe, to fall into Dante's arms…

"No," she said firmly, shoving back her wimpy thoughts forcefully. "I've told you as much as I'm willing. Now let me have what I've rightfully earned."

"You mean what you rightfully stole. Big difference between earning something and stealing it. And let's discuss King. He is *not* your lover?"

"That's what I've told you."

"Right. Then please enlighten me as to why you, a vampiress, would want to give such a remarkable gift to a vampire hunter?"

"A—" Kyler huffed out a breath. *Vampire hunter?* "You're thinking of someone else. The man I'm talking about is a vampire."

Dante's jaw dropped open in intent wonder.

She'd said too much.

Chapter 7

Dante stood and walked to the window. What Kyler had just said made little sense. Of course, there could be another man out there who called himself King. Weird name to go by. Pompous. But the only King he was aware of had founded, and currently headed, the Order of the Stake, an ancient order of vampire hunters dedicated to eradicating his species.

He eyed Kyler over a shoulder. She studied the egg without touching it. It must kill her to have it sitting there, so close, and after she had done all that work to obtain it. Twice. If he were to play by the rule of thieves, he'd allow her the nab. But he wasn't a thief, and keeping the egg was necessary to the very safety of his species.

Should the spell contained within that egg fall into

the wrong hands, Dante would feel responsible for the destruction of so many. And if it were to fall into King's hands, a vampire hunter—he didn't want to think of it.

He turned, hands on hips, and tapped his foot.

When she finally deigned to look at him, she shook her head and splayed out a hand. "Do we have to do this with you in a towel?"

"I can take it off." He loosened the twist at his hip.

"No!" she rushed out.

Dante smiled. "Then that leaves you with a choice. Towel off? Or a discussion about King."

She gaped at him. "I choose door number three."

"And what is behind that door?"

At that moment a knock at the door sounded. Had she been a witch Dante would have been impressed. But she was not. And his tailor was gaining speed with practice.

"Saved by the knock," he said, turning to answer the door. When he returned with the garment bag, Kyler held the Fabergé egg. "Touch all you like. It's returning with me to Paris, where I've a storage locker to stow it until I can find a new place to live."

"And how are you planning to get it out of Venice? We've wasted time. The news this morning already announced the theft."

"Not a theft," he corrected. "Merely missing. Keep your facts straight, Kyler, We don't want to upset the masses."

She exhaled heavily. "Whatever. But as for leaving the island, don't you believe there will be police everywhere? Most likely checking bags as we attempt to board a taxi?"

The thought had occurred to him. "I've a private water taxi. And a private jet." But he wasn't stupid. Of course there would be police and security at the docks. Fortunately, he was a patient man. "I intend to take a stroll over to the docks right now. Scope things out."

"Fine. I'll watch the egg while you're gone."

"You'll come along. Egg snug as a bug in your backpack. I won't let either of you out of my sight."

"You'll have to force me. That'll cause a scene and bring the police to you faster than a wolf on your scent."

He leaned over her and closed his eyes as he sniffed, drawing in her sweet scent and the slightest salty hint of fear. "I can control you, Kitten, with one bite."

Her intake of breath pleased him. It hadn't been laced with fear but instead desire. He had her right where he needed her to be.

"Yeah? Maybe I can do the same to you? You ever been controlled by a woman, Dante? Oh, wait. You don't give them any more time than to come and then you leave. It's gotta be tough hanging around me for so long, eh?"

"Not at all. Your acerbic personality makes it easy enough to avoid any thought of sex." The ease of that lie surprised him.

"I hate you," she said tightly.

"And here I thought you were running over ways to get me back in your bed. Seduce me? Control me? And then run away with the prize?"

"I don't use sex to get what I want. Unlike you."

That cut hurt him more deeply than he would ever show on his face. Dante unzipped the garment bag.

"You should try it sometime. Might loosen up those frigid muscles that wrap so tightly about your heart and—" He stopped himself from saying something crude. She didn't deserve his anger just because she'd successfully matched him at his own game.

"You're an asshole," she shot at him.

He caught her by the arm as she rose to walk by. This argument would end now. On his terms.

She initially struggled when he kissed her, but he held her firmly by the biceps. There was no way he would let her go. She deserved a bruising punishment for her cruel words. And he would do so by ensuring she did not forget the feel of him against her mouth.

When he felt her push his chest with her hand, he gripped her wrist. With his other hand against her back, he pulled her in closer. She tried to twist her mouth away from him, and then she pushed him against the wall. The kiss unbroken, her breasts pressed against his chest as she sought the depths of their connection. Taking from him instead of resisting, she answered his teasing punishment with a surprising rebuttal.

So sweet she tasted, like an addictive sugar. His soft yet independent kitten; how he did enjoy quieting her rages.

Releasing his hold on her wrist, Dante relaxed against the wall. Kyler leaned into him, hugging his body with her wanting warmth. As her tongue danced with his, his erection tightened beneath the towel.

She whispered against his mouth, "I hate that I want you so much."

And he loved that she did. Made her a hell of a lot

more interesting than a woman who was attracted to him for purely self-serving sexual reasons. Because she'd confessed she needed him to find and keep the egg in hand. He liked her layers, and if it meant sticking around and sharing the Fabergé egg a few more days while ensuring the coast was clear, he intended to do so. He was going to stay as close to Kyler as her love/hate would allow.

Suddenly the towel fell away from his hips. She'd tugged it off? He really did enjoy all this emotional torment. She gripped his cock and gave his lip a biting kiss, tugging out his lower lip.

"Despise me all you like," he said as he lifted her by the thighs. She wrapped her legs about him. She ground herself against his bare cock. Mercy, but he could come if he were not more practiced in delaying an ejaculation. "If you really hate me—"

"I could bite you?"

Dante stopped just inches from kissing her. She associated hating him with biting him? Grasping Kyler's wrists, he held her away from him, making her slide her legs down and step back. Her eyes glided to his rigid cock, which ached for her body back against it, rubbing her moistness along the length.

"I don't know what it is about you," he said, "but I forget myself around you."

"You want me," she said with a purr. "Always."

"I do. Always. But I…don't want the bite."

"Oh." Her shoulders dropped, and she looked away but then right back at him with a hopeful smile. "You know we don't have to bond with the bite—if we make it short and sweet. I understand bonding would have to be a mutual agreement between us."

She tapped her kiss-reddened lips, and her eyelashes fluttered softly. A talented seductress despite her inner disbelief.

"I want to taste you, Dante, but I want to taste you on your knees, and begging for it. I want to know that I mean something to you. But I know that will never happen. Not with your record with women."

"The only time I go on my knees before a woman—"

She put up her palm. "Yeah, I get it. Casanova has returned. And I've lost my appetite for charm. But I am hungry. I'm going to head out for a bite." She shuffled into her shoes and strolled toward the door.

"And leave me like this?" Dante turned to display his erection, full-mast and up against his torso.

He knew he was pushing it, but really? Women didn't leave him high and dry. And he'd never left a woman that way, either. What was wrong with Kyler Cole that she could walk away from such opportunity? Such delicious pleasure?

"Just you and your hand, buddy," she said and opened the door. "I'll be back. I trust you won't go anywhere with the egg."

"How do you know that? I might have an emergency exit off the island. Friends in the know who can secret me out of the country."

She paused in the doorway and smirked. "I know, because you want me as much as I want that egg."

"Ah." He lifted a finger. "But I've already had you."

She strolled her fingers down a breast, which drew

his eye to the hard nipple beneath the thin red fabric. "You haven't had your fill. I know that as much as you do. And you're not about to walk away from the conquest of biting me. No matter what you tell yourself. I can see it in your eyes, and—hell, your cock doesn't lie."

The body part she'd mentioned performed a mutinous pulse that jerked it heavily against his abdomen. Dante lowered his palm to calm it down.

"We're not finished with one another," she said, winking sweetly. "See you soon, lover boy." She closed the door behind her.

Indeed, they were not finished with each other. But that she was enjoying the game as much as he, well... he had to admit he liked her enthusiasm.

Dante looked down at his softening erection. No time for self-pleasure now. He had a vampiress to stalk.

But first? The foolish vampiress had left him alone with the egg.

Kyler had needed to get out of that hotel room as quickly as humanly possible. Hell, she wasn't even human anymore. She should have been able to vacate the premises with vampiric speed. And yet seeing Dante standing there in the buff had taxed her every need to strip naked and be the one to bow before him.

On the other hand, she hadn't felt the least bit of defeat when kissing him. Or stroking his cock and bringing up a wanting moan from him. For a few precious and triumphant moments, she had owned that vampire. And she could do it again.

But did she want to control him? The man was an obstacle. Granted, he was a sexy obstacle. But also cunning and dangerous. She should be able to take the egg and walk away. But she couldn't, simply because she enjoyed playing against him. And she couldn't fathom ending it now when it had only begun.

She was letting emotions fall into the mix. The wanting, needy, romantic kinds of emotions that were perfectly fine at any other time. But right now, when she should be focused on the prize?

"Mercy," she muttered as she turned down a narrow, cobblestoned alley that was bracketed by three-story brick buildings. She stopped and leaned against a wall, putting a foot up on the opposite wall. Closing her eyes, she fought with her thoughts.

She could walk away. Tell King she hadn't found the egg. But he'd know that was a lie because the missing-egg story had already played on the news. He must realize she had it by now. Of course, she could still use the lie that another thief had taken it.

And another thief almost *had* taken the egg.

But no. King deserved it. And she wanted in on eternity. She wanted to live forever without worry of the stake. That had been her reason for asking for vampirism in the first place. She'd been motivated by her mother's death. She'd died so young. And the idea of gaining immortality with a few drinks of blood every now and then had been an easy fix for the heartbreak and grief Kyler had felt at the time.

But then to learn that immortality wasn't forever and that she needed eternity to make that wish so? Well, she'd been in for the transformation to vampire; she was in it to win it all now.

But why would Dante think King was a hunter? They'd avoided that discussion. He must be thinking of the wrong man. No vampire would become a hunter and slay his own kind. For what reason? Certainly Dante was wrong.

"Dante D'Arcangelo," she whispered, eyes still closed. Sounded adventurous and sensual, not dangerous or even a threat to her. Why did her opponent have to be so damned sexy and consistently determined to seduce her?

Kyler wasn't sure what she'd do if he managed to get her into his bed again.

On the other hand, there were plenty of things she could do. Kiss him. Fuck him. Come with him. Bite him.

She pressed her lips tightly together. She did want a taste of Dante. It would rocket up their intimacy. A taste would be fun, sexy, teasing. It was the longer drink that would give them a blood connection, and that he seemed to fear.

A connection just as she had with King. She could feel her creator when he was near, and he her. And sometimes she could sense his thoughts. She expected King knew more about her because he was old and experienced. But because they hadn't had a relationship beyond that one night of sex they were not as intimately connected as she suspected others—lovers—could be.

She'd never feared King. Dante had no clue what he was talking about.

A noise at the end of the alleyway pulled Kyler from her thoughts. A young man smiled and swaggered toward her in the cool shadows. He wore a blue-and-white-striped shirt. Probably a gondolier on a break. He was tan, and his curly dark hair spilled over one eye.

Kyler turned toward him with a Cheshire cat smile. A crook of her finger quickened his steps to her. She didn't like to chat with her bites. Or kiss them, if that could be avoided. The whole sexual intimacy line was not something she crossed, because she considered her donors simply a meal. She reserved her sensual energy for real sex and relationships.

He bowed his head toward her and said something in a mix of English and Italian so quickly she could only make out "pretty" and "hungry." Yes, she was hungrier than she'd realized. She needed blood. Now.

Tilting onto her tiptoes, she glided a palm up the front of his shirt. His heartbeat thundered. He thought he was going to get lucky. And he would. The swoon the vampire's victim experienced with the bite was an erotic thing, oftentimes close to orgasm. Enough to leave them smiling and dazed with the pleasure they thought they had received.

Acting quickly, she stroked a finger up his neck and pushed aside his soft brown hair. She lunged for him, fangs descending. He expected a kiss as he wrapped his arms around her, his hands straying down to her ass. Such an uninvited touch was frequent, and it annoyed her, but she would endure it for the blood.

After pricking him deeply, she drew out her fangs and sucked in the hot, thick blood that tasted of wine, oregano and the salty sea. A sweet blend that enticed her to take more than a few sips—

"Hey! *Ciao!*"

Pulling away from the man's neck, Kyler shoved him off her. She had the forethought to enthrall him, even as another stranger approached from down the alleyway. As his knees bent, his body gently fell and he crumpled into a semiconscious heap against the brick. He would be deeply immersed in the swoon for a few more minutes. The bite would heal quickly. By tomorrow evening it would but be a memory.

"What about me?" the man asked as he walked up to her, arms splayed out in demand. "You are kissing men in the shadows?"

Asshole. She didn't need this. But she didn't want him to see the other man's neck. She hadn't gotten more than a tiny taste! It wasn't enough to satisfy her hunger. And she'd forgotten to lick the wound, a necessity to heal and prevent the victim from transforming to vampire.

Unsure what to do, she acted instinctively and crooked a finger at him to step right up. He quickly moved to grab her, wrapping a hand across her back. He smelled like cigarettes and wine, and he wasn't a tourist; she sensed that. He clutched her tightly, one hand groping up under her shirt at her back.

Kyler suddenly had the urge to extricate herself from this mess. Forget about the blood. This had been an ill-prepared quest. When he dove to kiss her, she punched him under the jaw. Remarkable, the strength she had gained with vampirism. The punch sent him stumbling backward against the wall to land in a sprawl.

He'd passed out? *Nice.* Diving to the other victim, Kyler quickly dragged her tongue over the wound to seal it.

Standing, she wiped her mouth with the back of her hand and shook her head. "Still so much to learn," she said with a sigh. Taking bites in public places, no matter how private she thought they might be, was best exercised with much more caution.

Stepping over the second man, who groaned, she exited the alleyway and turned onto a main street. Ten paces ahead, a tall shadow stood beneath a froth of pink roses climbing a wrought iron fence.

"Have a good bite?" Dante said. "Your collection skills are sketchy, Kyler. You could get into trouble one day, pushing a donor up against a wall so close to where tourists wander."

Chapter 8

"Collection?" Kyler laughed as she strode past Dante. "Maybe I like the quickies. And the danger of *collecting* so close to others."

He didn't reach out for her. That was a disappointment. To be tugged into the handsome vampire's arms and then ravished with his kisses? *Oh yeah.*

Then again, she was frustrated, having missed out on a chance to thoroughly feed, so his charm did little more than annoy her.

Dante matched her pace as she veered toward the docks where visitors arrived from the mainland. "You lie to yourself a lot, Kyler. Why is that?"

Did she? Why lie about wanting some fast and fun sex? Such pleasure was a woman's right. As for that other lie, though…fine, she'd had to embellish about the quickie back in the alley. She'd not gotten enough blood and was still hungry. But the last person she wanted to confess her fuckup to was Signore Casanova.

"Maybe it's just you I feel the need to lie to," she shot back.

"I don't understand that. I've been straightforward with you. We both want the same thing. And I am quite sure I was clear that the intimacies we've shared are completely separate from the challenge of winning the egg. I'm not using you. I don't use women."

"Oh please, Dante, you've used every woman who has ever walked into your life."

"I protest."

"I remain firm."

"How so?"

She stopped walking and faced him. His eyes entreated, and yet she thought she noticed a glint of sadness. She wanted to hug him, pat him on the head and tell him it was all going to be—damn it! He was doing it again. Making her feel for him when it was all a manipulative act.

"You claim to admire women—"

"Always. I love women."

"You love to play with them. To control them. To move them about on your game board. Satisfying a woman sexually isn't loving them, Dante. It's exerting your control."

"I don't—why are you so afraid of being controlled? It's King, isn't it? What's he holding over you? Is he controlling you?"

She turned and swiftly walked onward, brushing past

a gaggle of teenagers snapping selfies before a bronze statue of some saint she didn't have time for. Why did he have to guess it on the first try? Not that it was an aggressive or even forceful control. It was that she felt she owed King. And what was so wrong with that? The man had given her so much.

She wanted to be right about Dante being a bastard who used women to build up his self-esteem. And yet she wasn't sure about that summation. She was too screwed up herself to be diagnosing other people's habits. But since becoming a vampire, her life was growing clearer. At least, she hoped it was. She knew what she wanted. She had taken steps to get it.

Now to hand over the prize and earn her eternity.

"I can help you get away from him," he said as he gained her side. He didn't look at her. They both walked quickly forward through the bustle of tourists that edged Saint Mark's square. "If you want that."

"That sounds a little too generous for your love-them-and-leave-them act. Or do you play a long game with your lovers?"

"Truth?" He slid a hand into hers and pulled her to a stop. He didn't push her against a wall or forcefully grasp her wrist, and Kyler almost missed that dominant control. Almost.

"I've never been in a committed relationship," he said, "and most affairs never last more than a few days. A few weeks is a possibility but a rarity. I said I love women, Kyler. I didn't say I loved being tied down. How can a man love all women if he's connected to only one for his lifetime?"

"You really are Casanova. Sure you weren't born in the eighteenth century?"

"I don't see the problem with that. I am vampire. I will live for centuries. Millennia, if I avoid the stake. Could you imagine being attached to one lover for so long? Be honest."

"No, I couldn't," she said without thinking. "I'd eventually want to see what else was out there, even if I was in love. Can love last for centuries? I'm not sure. But I'm not talking about commitment and relationships. I'm saying that you are more dangerous to the women you come in contact with than a mere bite. It hurts to be swept off our feet and into a lie."

Now he put his hands on her shoulders. "The contact I have with woman is never a lie, Kyler." But she sensed his sudden wince told more of the truth than he did. "If I didn't want to kiss you, I would not. If I didn't want to make love to you, I would not. It's not a game, or a notch on the bedpost. It's—" he exhaled and shook his head "—what I need."

"A new challenge? Someone prettier, younger, more sexually talented every time?"

He kissed her then, and Kyler shoved him off her so hard his shoulders hit the rose-festooned fence three feet behind him.

"I'm not going to feed your addiction," she said, striding on. "And I'm not being controlled by King. Trust me on that one." She quickened her pace, knowing he would follow like the hungry, touch-starved Lothario he was.

That was it. She could believe it wasn't a challenge or

the notch thing for him. The man was simply addicted to women. New ones, pretty ones, brief encounters or longer, as he'd said. The man needed a woman to feel alive. Perhaps even more than he needed blood.

It was sad in ways she couldn't quite sort out. But Kyler knew she didn't want to be Dante D'Arcangelo's latest drug, despite the overwhelming attraction between the two of them. She needed more from a man. Respect. Trust. And honesty he could share with her as much as with himself.

"What happened to you?" she said over her shoulder.

"What do you mean?" He joined her, the tall, model-perfect gentleman in a suit and tie juxtaposing the oh-so-touristy-looking failed thief.

"What in your life made you seek women for the quick fling? To, in your mind, love them, but only from a distance? Never with your heart. Is it Mommy issues?"

He chuckled. "I'll thank you not to make guesses about my relationship with my mother, may she rest in eternal peace."

"I'm sorry." Of course, his mother must have died in the nineteenth century. If he was a created vampire, his mother had probably been merely human. "I'm being defensive. That was mean."

"Not mean, just—you're trying to match me in this stupid game." Now he tugged her to a stop again and took both her hands in his. "Let's not do this anymore. I don't need to win arguments with you. I want you to shine, Kyler. You can win them all from now on. Abuse me with your words if you must."

"I don't want to abuse you with words or in any other way."

He was right. They were reacting in ways that were not moving their partnership forward and only making every little thing an issue. Smoothing a hand down his cheek, she took a moment to connect with his crestfallen gaze. "Sorry again about your mother. I know how that feels, losing your mom."

He nodded. "My mother was young. So lovely. And…now is not the time or the place to get into this personal stuff."

Right, because his personal stuff was off-limits to those women he "loved." It was too intimate, she guessed. It would force him to move beyond the surface and into things he'd probably never experienced before. Things like trust and respect and, perhaps, even love.

"But will you share that part of your life with me?" she asked, genuinely wanting more of him, one more piece of the real Dante D'Arcangelo. "Sometime?"

He nodded. "We'll see. For now…" He stretched his gaze over the hoards of tourists bustling about the open square.

Ahead loomed the dock that boarded passengers on the vaporetti that transported them to the main continent. While a person could hop a water taxi and disembark the island virtually anywhere, this was the main arrival point.

They both observed what appeared to be a long line waiting to go through a security checkpoint. Not the usual security. This one was checking all bags, suitcases and purses, and doing pat-downs.

"Local *polizia*," Dante said. "They must to be looking for the Fabergé egg."

"Now what?" she asked quietly. "Can we hop a taxi and get off this chunk of rock someplace else?"

"Possibly." He rubbed his chin. "You see down there?" He pointed toward a dock where private taxis parked. It was closed, and she could guess the sign, written in Italian, had something to do with going to the main landing for a security check. "We may have to wait them out."

"We?" She wasn't sure why she questioned that. Wasn't like he was going to give up the egg, and he'd already said they were a team of sorts. And she certainly knew she wasn't going to sneak it away from him unless she seduced him into a freakin' coma. "Right. We. I guess we should call it an evening, eh?"

Maybe then she could slip away from him and satisfy her unquenched need for blood.

"Indeed." His gaze stripped her bare, and Kyler shivered to imagine his mouth right there, at her breast, licking slowly. "The night is young," he said. "Do you really want to go back to the hotel room with me and sit in close proximity while we try to avoid the obvious?"

The obvious being that they wanted to rip off one another's clothing.

Kyler asked, "What then?"

"This way." He headed toward the canal.

Kyler was curious to learn what he had in mind for them now. When they arrived at a gondola dock on the Grand Canal and Dante handed over some cash to the gondolier, she knew exactly what he had planned. Not an escape from the island, or a touristy sail down the canal, but rather a romantic cruise under the moonlight.

"I thought we had agreed to avoid exactly this scenario?" she asked as he waited for her.

"You think I have seduction in mind?" He shrugged. "It's a beautiful evening. The moon is full. And I've asked for a route that will take us near all the major and minor docks off the island." He tapped his temple and flashed her a sexy grin. "Casing the island, yes?"

"Good call." But she knew it was a ruse, all the same.

Sighing heavily, Kyler looked over her shoulder. She could walk back to the hotel herself. Had he left the egg there? It had been a good twenty minutes between her leaving the room and him finding her in the alley with her disastrously botched snack. Enough time for him to stash it elsewhere. Which meant she wasn't about to let him out of her sight.

The blood could wait. Right now she would suffer the romance. He might talk a good game about casing the docks, but she knew what his ultimate goal was.

She turned to find him standing in the gondola, holding his hand out to her, silently entreating her to step forward. Take a chance. Enter his wickedly seductive game. Because he wasn't ever going to stop playing. She knew that. He couldn't. He didn't know how.

"Casanova has returned," she said as she took his hand and stepped onto the gondola. There was only one seat at the back, which fit two comfortably.

"It's what I do," Dante said as he sat beside her. He didn't leave any space between the two of them, nudging his thigh against hers. "And I do it well. Time to pull Kyler out of uptight mode and settle into relaxation. There's nothing we can do until the heat goes away and we can leave the city."

"I could get another hotel room."

"And leave me alone with the egg? If you wish it."

"Even without the egg in hand, you'd follow me. I know you would. Like I said, you won't be satisfied until you've completely mastered me. And that means biting me. Much as you think you don't want to? You do."

His sigh was inexplicable. Had he not commented because she was right or because she was so, so wrong? She wanted to be right. She would be.

The gondolier pushed off, and they sailed smoothly down the quiet waters, which were almost as crowded as the streets. The canal glittered madly with moonlight, alchemizing into liquid mercury. Dante put on a good show for a while, noting the docks, which were shut down with signs redirecting travelers to the main dock. But he eventually clasped her hand and pulled it to his mouth to kiss her knuckles. Slowly, one by one, savoring a treat. His breath whispered over her skin as if an enchanted breeze.

And before Kyler could succumb to the inner meltdown of desire, she tugged slightly, jarring him from his erotic focus.

He blinked and nodded. "Right. All business?"

"You did say we should stop it."

"I suggested we stop trying to berate and argue with one another. I said nothing of the sort regarding a cease and desist to our intimate play. Come, Kyler, I can hardly keep up the indifferent ruse. You are an ir-resistible woman."

Kyler caught her breath. She hadn't ever been told that. She had always been average in every way. But she didn't need the flattery from Dante. Really.

Maybe.

Who was she kidding? It felt great.

"Can I have a bite?" she asked, testing his reaction.

"Right here?" Smoothing a hand down his shirtfront, he cast his gaze across the waters away from her.

"Of course not," she said. "Later, in the hotel room. I'm curious about being bitten, and biting, another vam-pire."

"Is that so?" He leaned in close to her ear, keeping their conversation quiet. The gondolier was humming and had on earbuds anyway. "You've never been bit-ten by another?"

"I was bitten for the transformation," she explained. "And I've not been with a vampire since. So yes, I'm very curious about the bite in a non-transformational way. Just for kicks. Can we do that and *not* have sex?"

"What's so terrible about having sex with me?"

"Have you not been following the conversation? It's your means of controlling me."

"If only I had such power. As I've said before, Kyler, you are a strong woman. You'll not allow any man to control you. Unless of course, you feel you owe him something. Is that it? And you believe the egg grants a vampire eternity. King wants this supposed eternity?"

"It's not for you to know. I've already told you too much. We were just talking about an agreement between the two of us. We agree to a bite without sex. And winner takes all when the coast is clear and we're finally able to leave with the egg. Whoever leaves Venice with it in hand is the winner. Yes?"

"No sex. All the blood. Winner takes all. Hmm…" He leaned in and nudged his nose along her ear.

"Do you bite every woman you've ever had? I mean the vampires. Do you let them bite you?"

"No," he said softly. "No vampires…"

And Kyler knew then that he must be afraid of the bite from another of his kind. Why? They didn't have to bond. Or did he believe they would?

"I may give it a try," he said slowly. His eyes glanced fleetingly into hers. He lifted her hand to his lips again and held it there. "There's a lot you don't know about me."

"Like your reasons for pursuing women as if they were precious objects without a heart and soul?"

"That's cruel, even for you, Kyler."

"But it's the truth, and I think you know it." She turned his head so he faced her. A glint of steel pierced his gaze, the moonlight a deadly ally with his soul. "Trust me, Dante. I won't judge. I'll tell you anything you like about myself. My mother died of cancer a year ago. It turned my world upside down with grief."

He leaned his head against hers. The soft, leathery scent of him melted into her senses, and she wanted to kiss him. She sensed his vulnerability right now, though, so she would follow his lead. He deserved her patience and respect.

"My mother killed herself," he said quietly.

"Oh, Dante, I'm so sorry."

"She was…" He inhaled and exhaled deeply. He sat back on the cushion. Kyler leaned against his shoulder, placing a hand over his chest. Again he took her hand and kissed it. "My mother, Angelique D'Arcangelo, was a courtesan. A very famous and lovely courtesan who serviced many royals, actors and artists in her prime. During my teen years, my mother's home was a brothel. I grew up in a household teeming with women who had no shame about their bodies and who often walked about in all states of undress. I learned a lot." He smirked at that memory.

Kyler could imagine what his sexual education must have been like. That alone could forever alter a man's perception of women. But for good or for otherwise, she wasn't sure.

"It seeded my love for women," he continued. "But a courtesan's career is short, and her competition can be catty and vicious. Age tends to lessen a woman's value, and her fellow courtesans tend to boldly remind her of that at every new wrinkle, every age spot. After a particularly horrible argument with a younger friend who had taken over her clients, Angelique killed herself. It was her fiftieth birthday."

He closed his eyes and tilted his head back. Kyler didn't know what to say. What a strange and interesting childhood he must have had. But his poor mother. She bet he'd asked for vampirism for the very reason she had: to avoid death after watching it swiftly draw in their mothers.

"Is that what you wanted to know, then?" he asked, opening his eyes to gaze skyward.

She understood a bit more about his obsession with women now, knowing he'd grown up surrounded by prostitutes. What he must have learned. And then to have lost his mother because of one of those women he may have trusted?

But she wouldn't push any more. He didn't deserve her scorn, only acceptance and understanding.

"Thank you." She kissed his jaw softly. "For sharing that with me. It means more than you can imagine. I will keep your confidence. And I'm not saying that as another ploy in the stupid game we've been playing."

He nodded and pulled her in closer to hug up against his chest. "That game is over, Kitten."

Yes, the emotional subterfuge game was over. But there was still the physical prize that she must not overlook. How to mark herself the winner if it was over? She would not leave Venice without that egg. But for now she was content to set that worry aside and simply hug Dante. He needed her.

For the next half hour, they sailed the narrow canals under the moonlight, not speaking a word. Yet their hearts beat as one, and their fingers entwined in an embrace. Words weren't necessary. Their synched heartbeats said it all. They'd settled into a certain acceptance of one another.

When the gondola dock loomed into view and Kyler had to shake herself out of almost falling asleep against Dante's slow, rhythmic heartbeats, she remembered that all was not well, and that she had yet to figure out a plan to get the egg out of the city.

How easily snuggling in Dante's arms could sway her focus.

"Where is it, by the way?" she asked as she sat up and fluffed out her hair.

"The egg? In a safe place."

"In the hotel? If you put it in the safe—"

"My palazzo. I stopped there before finding you after your bite."

"What? The very place that was easily broken into by creepy werewolves? I thought you were smarter than that."

"I do have security in the office. I have simply never used it until now. Besides, the wolves must have left the island." He nodded toward the moon. "It's not safe to be trapped on a small island when you shift to a monster."

"We can hope. What if they don't shift?"

"It's safe, Kyler. All werewolves shift under the full moon."

"I need to see for myself. Tell the gondolier to take us to your palazzo."

"For a kiss."

She kissed him quickly, feeling his disappointment as she sat back in the seat and gestured for him to do as she'd requested. He gave the gondolier the directions in Italian.

Damn him! This push and pull of want and need and trust and mistrust for the man would prove her greatest challenge.

Chapter 9

Kyler flew toward Dante's palazzo. She'd wanted to race ahead, but she'd had to rely on him to find the place. Now she recognized the brick-red door. "Open the door."

He stuck a key in the lock and pushed the door open. Kyler dashed inside and across the stone floor. The foyer's welcome coolness swept over her face and shoulders with a greeting. She smiled and then immediately frowned. "Where is the safe?"

"In my office to the right," he offered casually.

She found the carved rosewood door and pushed it open. The room was dark save for the moonlight streaming through the white sheer curtains, which fronted the windows that looked over the canal. The wall opposite the door was lined with shelves, occupied by books and artifacts. A seashell here, an odd bronze statuette there. It smelled old and dusty. *The way a vampire's lair should smell*, she thought briefly. A massive wood desk dominated the room, but no papers or supplies sat on top, save for a slim silver laptop, closed.

"Where's the safe?" She spun to find Dante poised in the doorway, one shoulder tilted against the frame and a hand at his hip. He always looked so cool and together. That suit was his damsel-seducing armor.

"Come on, James Bond. That egg is mine. You can't take it as you please."

"I thought it was finder's keepers? We agreed to that stipulation while on the gondola, yes?"

"Don't you do this to me. You promised we would sit it out together until the authorities removed the checkpoints."

"I made no such promise. Although if we were in this together, why the concern about the egg? It's in a safe place. Don't you trust me?"

Just when she'd thought they'd come to terms with each other. And, well, hadn't they gotten closer on the gondola ride? He'd opened himself to her about his mother. Had it been a ruse to gain her sympathy?

Of course it had been. Every move the man made was calculated. And she continued to fall for such trickery.

With a heavy sigh, she said, "Just show it to me."

Dante strode in and at the bookshelf he tugged out a book with a red spine. That activated a mechanism that slid back a row of shelves populated by dusty books to the right. Behind it, fitted into the wall, appeared a small twelve inch by twelve inch safe, on which was centered a combination dial. Without need of the moonlight, which was blocked by the position of his back to the window, he spun it right, left and right again. The door swung open with a creak, and inside sat the egg, filling the small space. Nothing more.

"Satisfied?" he asked as she studied the dark interior.

"Take it out. If it's in there, it's yours. Out here, it's ours."

He lifted a brow, studying her. She hated him more than dirt right now because, once again, he had the upper hand. And she could still taste their kiss—quick as it had been—on her lips. And recall his sad confession. His mother…

Okay, so she didn't hate him. How could she after learning what his early years had been like? Though a mild dislike was permissible.

"I'll give you the combination," he said, quickly closing the safe door on the egg. He strode to the desk and opened a drawer, pulling out a pen and paper. His hands illuminated by a stream of moonlight, he scribbled down some numbers and then handed the paper to her.

So she could open the safe at any time? She could deal with that. Kyler stuck the paper in a back pocket, then glanced at the book he'd pulled out and that still stuck out. A red spine with no writing on it. The rest of the books were darker colors and dusty.

"Will that suffice?" he asked.

"I'll need a key to the palazzo."

"You are a demanding woman, Kitten." He sat on the desk chair and pulled open another drawer. After shuffling about inside, he produced a thin silver key tied with a frayed bit of red velvet and handed it to her. "I'll want that returned before you leave Venice."

"Why is that? Don't you want me stopping by in the future for a booty call?"

He gave it some consideration. "Keep it then." He sat back, putting his hands behind his head in a stretch. "It's late. I'm not tired. You're all hyped up on a power tirade. What *shall* we do with ourselves?"

"If you want me to tell you what you can do with yourself…"

"Why don't we finish the conversation we never started at the hotel? About King." He gave her a look that said, "I told you my stuff, now it's time you did the same."

"There's nothing to tell about King," Kyler said dismissively. "He asked me to get the egg for him, and I am."

"What's he holding over you to make you do such a thing?"

"As I've said, I want to do this for him."

He assessed her calmly. Even in the darkness, those eyes of his permeated her skin and tasted her doubt and fear. It felt more intimate than if he had pierced her with a fang.

"You're not a good liar, Kyler. The man is holding something over you. You don't want to tell me. Fine. Let's move on to the fact you're working for a vampire hunter. I don't get that. I can only guess that once he has what he wants from you he'll whip out the stake and ash you."

"You have no idea who I'm talking about. He's certainly not a vampire hunter."

"King is not a common name. Rather a narcissistic moniker, if you ask me. But really, I'm quite sure we are discussing the same man. Tall, sandy-brown hair, built like a dancer with muscles."

"He's tall and built, but I'm sure there's more than one guy named King who has brown hair."

"If I recall the one time I saw him he's got a sort of Christian Bale thing going on. Not an unattractive man."

Kyler sucked in the corner of her mouth. She had indeed thought King looked similar to the actor, perhaps taller and always with a fierce look in his eye. She could never tell what was going on behind that intense gaze. Maybe they *were* talking about the same man?

But still.

She shook her head and thought about laughing to throw him off, but it didn't feel right. He had set her off her game, and she felt unmoored. Propping up a thigh on the corner of the desk, she leaned forward, meeting his gaze through a slash of moonlight.

"King—the King I know—is a vampire."

"Can't be. The man I know has killed hundreds, perhaps even thousands of vampires over the centuries."

"I know he's a vampire because he's the one who transformed me."

At that announcement, Dante leaned his forearms on the desk and peered deeply into her eyes. "You're fucking with me."

She shook her head. "You must be thinking of another King." She paused, considering. *Could it be?*

"Your silence tells me I'm thinking of the same man you've been dealing with," Dante said.

"He's a friend!"

"Kyler, seriously? King is the one who made you vampire?"

She nodded, the unmoored feeling pushing her further out to drift. She wanted to reach out and cling to him for safety. Because she'd not had that help after King had changed her. He'd scooted her out of his life and on her merry way to fly solo. "Best way to learn," he'd said with indifference.

She'd asked for vampirism because she'd wanted the fantasy of living forever and gaining freedom over life and death. King had sweet-talked her into his embrace, and she had fallen, willingly. That first night he had probably only expected to bite yet another donor and leave her in a thrall. But she'd pleaded with him. And two days later he'd found her and taken her to his home. The bite had been painful but blessedly welcome. Immortality had been hers.

When leaving his home the morning after the transformation, she had seen notes on his table about an eternity spell along with a diagram of the Nécessaire egg. He'd told her it was a valued family heirloom that had been stolen. He'd been searching for it for decades and was getting closer to finding it. She'd asked him about the spell, and he'd explained the difference between immortality and eternity. The definition of *immortality* had been an eye-opener to her. She'd thought she'd gotten forever with his bite, but she hadn't.

When King had told her how determined he was to have eternity, she had eagerly reminded him she was a thief and, should he ever need her assistance, she could help him. It had been a desperate ploy to keep his interest. He'd told her he would come for her if the egg ever emerged on the scene.

Dante sat back in the chair, crossing an ankle over his knee. He rapped the desktop and then rubbed his chin. "Well, well. King is a vamp? Valuable information. Though, mind you, I'm still not going to believe you one hundred percent. It makes little sense."

"Why do you think King is some kind of hunter?" Kyler leaned onto her palm. "A vampire wouldn't kill his own kind."

"King is the founder of the Order of the Stake. You've heard of it, yes?"

She nodded. King had, almost as an afterthought, told her to beware hunters with stakes, among others such as werewolves and angels, and even faery dust. But she couldn't believe King was allied with vampire hunters. The founder of such a vile organization? Doubtful. As Dante had said, it made so little sense.

"In the mid-twentieth century one of his knights slayed a friend of mine," Dante said. "While King stood watching. I assumed it was an initiation of sorts. Rook was there, too. He ever mention that man's name to you?"

King hadn't talked about much that first night they'd had sex, other than to offhandedly suggest she might lose a little weight. And when he'd returned to offer vampirism…their encounter had been depressingly businesslike. She'd wanted more from him but had cautioned her crushed heart to be thankful for what he was giving her.

Though, maybe…he'd taken a phone call as she'd lain in his bed, feeling her heartbeat race with the delicious new future she'd been granted. He'd spoken the caller's name. Yes, because she recalled thinking how crazy it was that a man named King had a friend named Rook.

"He did mention him," Dante guessed. "Rook is vampire, too?"

She shrugged. "I don't know. I only heard the name once. And that was spoken casually to someone on the phone as he was walking around picking up my clothes." In an effort to get her to leave. But that detail wasn't necessary for Dante to understand. "The Order of the Stake? Impossible."

"As far as I know, the Order has been around since the sixteenth century. Founded by, as rumor tells it, King. I've never given consideration over what he was, beyond immortal, for he's been around for centuries. Yet everything makes perfect sense if the man is vampire. Immortality and all that. But why kill his own kind?"

"He's not a killer. I was with him—"

She couldn't confess she'd been the man's lover but once. Hardly enough time to get to know him. She should have gotten the hell out of there the moment her still-mortal self had found out he was vampire. Instead, she'd followed him. Because of desire for what he could give her.

"So you are King's lover? He's not going to like hearing that you've slept with me."

"I'm no man's lover. I sleep with whom I want, when I want." And Dante didn't need to know she and King were not currently lovers. Need to know, baby.

"If you insist. Let me get this straight, then." Dante sat forward. As he spoke, he gestured firmly with both hands before him. "King bit you and then tricked you, I take it?"

"He's never tricked me. I asked for vampirism."

"I got that. But what I want to know is when did King come out and ask you to get him the Fabergé egg?"

"Well…after I saw some notes on his desk. But he just contacted me a week ago. The egg hadn't appeared until then. I had actually forgotten about seeing the notes and telling him I could do him a favor."

"Ah."

"Ah? Would you ask whatever it is you really want to ask?"

"So King knew you were a thief before changing you to vampire? He had to. He's calculating."

"Well, no, I just—when we first met, it was at a coffee shop. Just a casual bumping into one another over the cream and sugar, and we ended up chatting for over an hour. I was attracted to him, and sensed he was to me, as well, so it turned into flirting. I did offhandedly mention I had a thing for stealing to him. But I never said I was an art thief."

"Because you are not."

"Because…" Kyler exhaled. Was it that obvious? On the other hand, she *had* pulled off the heist. "You think he transformed me just so he could get me to steal the egg?" She had mentioned she could steal the egg if it ever turned up merely as a means to impress him. Had she been so desperately smitten? Oh, the idiot things a woman did when in lust. "That can't be right. He hadn't even found the egg when he transformed me."

"Possible. But he knew he would require a thief eventually. So you told him at your first meeting, and then he transformed you two days later. The man probably laid out the notes on the egg expecting you'd see them. He took you to his home to transform you, yes? And after the deed had been done, you casually happened to notice those notes lying within eyesight? It's the only explanation for the situation you are in now. Unless you are on his side and you're playing the fool to me. Are *you* a vampire hunter, Kyler?"

"Don't be ridiculous. I may be a thief, but I'm no murderer. You're wrong about King heading the Order. You have to be."

But she couldn't convince herself of it. This information was startling. If King were a vampire hunter, why would he want an item that granted vampires eternity?

Did he *really* kill his own kind? It was difficult to wrap her head around it all.

Dante stood and ran a fingertip along the desk until he landed at her leg. "Why did you ask for vampirism, Kyler?"

Hadn't she told him already? He'd told her—ah, no, she hadn't. She hadn't wanted to take away from his sadness by jumping in with her sad tale.

She had already given him too much. She should

take the damned egg and run. Take her chances passing through security at the docks. She could bite the policemen, enthrall them and be gone with the prize.

"Talk to me, Kyler. I told you why I asked for it. It was because I wanted immortality, to live life. Forever."

"It was because you feared death. Because of your mother," she said on a whisper.

"It was."

"Me, too." She bowed her head and wrapped her arms across her chest. "Do I really need to do this right now?"

He tilted up her chin and held her gaze with soulful, understanding eyes. "Please."

She sighed. "My mother died of breast cancer over a year ago. It was a terrible time. I quit college—I started late, after a failed attempt at a homemade jewelry venture—to move back in and take care of her. She died slowly, an agonizing death made all the worse, I'm sure, by the chemicals the doctors pumped into her system."

Kyler flinched when Dante tried to embrace her. He put up his hands in deference, yet remained close. His leg against hers felt warm, reassuring. So she spilled all.

"I was angry and scared after she died. Alone. Unsure. I wanted to die and then I did not. I wanted to be bulletproof. To never fear death. My mother had made me promise, as she was dying, that I would use the trip to Paris she had gifted me for my birthday. We'd planned to go together—this summer, actually. I didn't want to go without her, but then I decided it would be a great remembrance of her if I did go. She loved

Paris. Had been there half a dozen times. So I used the vacation.

"A week into it I met King. At a coffee shop, as I mentioned. He charmed me. And I took him home with me, and he bit me. He was going to leave it at that, get dressed and slip out in the early morning hours, but in a moment of desperation, or maybe pure determination, I asked him to make me like him."

"Then you would never have to fear death," Dante said quietly. "A son or daughter should never have to watch their mother die at such a young age."

She nodded. "Never. There's still the chance of death for me. Stakes and all. But I have a future ahead of me now that I was unsure about before. I want this life, to never fear cancer or disease, to fear suffering as my mother did."

Tears dropped from her eyes and now she did let Dante hug her. She fell against his chest and dropped her head onto his shoulder, clinging as he rubbed her back. He really did understand her, even if his grief had been long ago. She felt he was a kindred soul, and that she could tell him anything. And she needed to because he was the first person who offered her quiet understanding.

"I was going to school for fashion design when my mother was diagnosed," she said with dreamy reverence. "I had the world in my hands. I was pretty and sexy. But then, when I moved in with Mom, I started eating my stress. During her hospice I put on thirty pounds and started doing desperate things. Stealing items we needed like drugs and food. I'm not a professional thief by any means, but I told King I could handle a heist. I wanted to impress him. It's stupid stuff we women do when we are flirting with a handsome man and want him to notice us. So when King contacted me a week ago, all the feelings I'd had for him reemerged, and I thought maybe we had a chance at getting together."

Dante looked up at her. His gaze asked her so much.

She nodded. "I'm not good with letting go. And when a handsome man calls me…" She sighed, thinking that her current relationship with a handsome man could very well mirror the one with King.

No. It was different with Dante. He'd not asked anything of her. Just the egg.

"Anyway, once I got to his place I realized that all my pining for him was in vain. He was the consummate businessman. Offered me a glass of water and pushed the notes about the egg toward me. It had surfaced in Venice, he told me, and if I wished to honor what I'd promised him six months ago, I could give it a go. Get the egg for him."

"I see." Dante pulled away enough to meet her gaze. He took a moment, nodding, perhaps running what she'd said over in his thoughts. With a stroke of his thumb along her lower lip, he said, "I'm sorry about your mother. But that you were there for her must have meant everything to her." He kissed her forehead. "No one should have to experience such suffering."

"Thank you. We share that same grief. You must still think about your mother?"

"At times. She was so beautiful, Kyler. I can't believe

she succumbed to the vicious taunts from her younger workmates." He kissed her cheek. "Never believe you are not beautiful."

She bowed her head against his and took the moment to accept the compliment and not deny it, as was easy to do at times. He meant it, and she felt his regard infuse her all the way to her soul.

"Thank you. But look at me. I took the easy route. A way out of death."

"As did I. But vampirism is never easy or an escape from death. Only it does afford the luxury of time. I can understand you wanting that. We are alike in that desire and our fears. You must never feel badly for asking for such a gift."

"I don't."

"You do, else you wouldn't feel the need to assuage your guilt by giving King such a gift. You said you believe the spell contained in the egg grants a vampire eternity?"

She nodded.

"This information about King troubles me. What to do with it?" He strode past her out of the office.

Kyler glanced down the moonlit hallway but didn't see Dante. Troubled by a vampire who wished for eternity? It hadn't bothered her at all to learn such a thing. Yet what she knew now about King...

Vampires, by nature, were secretive and manipulative. Or at least, that was what she had believed from the media and fiction. Now that she thought about it, King had spoken oddly about the vampire species. Mentioning that those who killed deserved the hunter's stake.

She shivered and brushed her upper arms with her palms. Could she truly have been created by a vampire who was also a vampire hunter?

Dante tugged off his shirt and tossed it over the back of the tufted Louis XIV chair sitting in the corner of the white-walled bedroom. He paced before the open windows. There were no screens, and the sheer curtains billowed softly with the salted breeze. He kicked off his shoes and shoved them against the wall.

He fisted a hand and punched the air. This man Kyler wanted to hand the egg over to was the furthest thing from a friend Dante could possibly imagine. They were talking about the same man: King, the founder of the Order of the Stake.

Was he truly also vampire?

Of course he was. He had transformed Kyler.

What must he do with this information? The Council should know. How could they not know? *Did* they know? No, they couldn't possibly, because they would never condone such genocide at the hands of one of their own. Maybe. The Council was the overseeing governing body for all paranormals, and it was notorious for watching but never acting. On the Council sat a few dozen members who represented various species. They didn't make laws, but they did try to keep things in order within the mortal realm.

Dante was unsure about how to approach them. But to ignore the information about a man who headed an organization designed to take out vampires when he was a vampire himself?

What had he stumbled onto?

Dante had come to Venice in the hope to get the all-important spell back and again safely secure it away. The task should have been simple. Take back what had once been entrusted to him. Lock it away. Go on with his life.

But now...

That spell must be kept out of the wrong hands. Especially King's hands. When Zara had given him ownership of the spell she had specifically said King wanted it and mustn't have it. Dante hadn't given the man much thought after putting the egg in the safe at the Austrian castle. He'd thought all was well.

But now it was not. Because although Kyler believed the spell granted a vampire eternity, Dante knew it did otherwise.

Could King possibly know the truth? It made much more sense to Dante if the man did. He must, if he and Zara had struggled over ownership of it so many decades earlier. And if King had not revealed he was a vampire hunter to Kyler, of course he would not tell her the truth about the spell.

Kyler had introduced a twist. And much as Dante should walk away with the egg in hand, he couldn't help but wonder what would happen to her should she not obtain the egg for King. She thought she was doing a friend a favor. Should she not hand over the egg, would he slay her?

The truth about the egg's power would serve the Order of the Stake far more than the lie King had told Kyler would.

She was caught in something much bigger than she could possibly imagine. Should he tell her the truth? It would force her to see King for what he was. A manipulator who was only using her.

And the spell, if enacted, may end up killing her. And Dante.

Chapter 10

"Come to me," Dante's voice called from the bedroom.

Kyler had been pacing in the foyer. Glancing into the office and catching sight of the red book on the shelf. Then a few paces took her to the front door. *Open it and run.* And back down the foyer to stand before the open office door. *Pull the book out and use the combination he gave you.*

But what would she be running to now? She'd gotten out her cell phone to call King and then remembered she didn't have his number. He'd kept her on a need-to-know basis. Strange, now that she considered it. Why hadn't he called her? Surely he'd seen the news and wanted to get the egg.

She sighed and glanced up the stairs. She knew what Dante wanted from her. He was a man. And when men got what they wanted? They tossed her aside and forgot she ever existed.

Yet Dante already had what he wanted. He'd claimed her as a notch. He had the egg in his possession—mostly. He could toss her aside with ease. But that he'd given her the safe combination proved he either trusted her or he was a raging egomaniac who believed no one would ever undermine him.

He was a bit of both. A handsome egomaniac. With an enchanting kiss and devastating eyes. And a broken heart that had pressed him to seek immortality from the vampire's bite, just as she had.

She wanted him again, damn her. She wanted to glide her hands along his skin and feel his muscles pulse under her palms. To share his intimate pain. To taste his salt and musk. To feed on his blood and satisfy a craving she'd not realized she had until she'd met him.

"Kyler?"

She shook her head. She didn't need more heartache. She was only just rising from the sadness over her mother's death. Dante had had a long time to recover from that equal pain. And yet…there was so much more to her and him than mere sex.

She knew that. But did he?

She glanced up the stairway. Could Dante protect her from King? Did she *need* protection? All that she believed about King could be a lie. Of course she needed protection.

Kyler padded up the stairs, pulling off her shirt and dropping it in her wake. She unbuttoned her pants and slid them down as she entered the cool bedroom. Dante sat on the open windowsill, shirtless, the moon dancing in his eyes.

She wanted him. And she would have him. On her terms.

"So you want me again?" She unhooked her bra and dropped it at her feet as Dante looked from her bare breasts to her face.

"I do."

"Then kneel, vampire."

A tiny smile curled the corner of his mouth as he glanced out the window. The waters were calm and yet glittered with moonlight. Scents of the city wafted in. Salt, seaweed, limestone and motor oil from passing boats. She could sense his increased heartbeat. The seductive perfume of his want. The heat of his presence.

"As you wish." The darkly seductive vampire slid onto the floor in a sinuous move, kneeling but inches from her legs. The room grew smaller, and Kyler could hear every breath he made, every slip of fabric over his skin. Her heart thundered in response to the desperate ache of wanting. Before he touched her, he paused and looked up into her eyes. "Please?"

Kyler shivered with the immensity of her position. Of her control over this exquisite man. "Yes."

The first touch of his lips to her thigh shimmered through her. Two vampires touching. A signal of recognition. Always that brief, telling electricity. Yet the shimmer swiftly changed to desire, needy and intense. His hands glided over her skin, tracing her bare hips and around to cup her ass. A hot breath warmed her bare mons, and his nose nudged the uppermost part of her labia. A tease that held so much promise.

When he glanced upward and his eyes fixed to hers in a quiet plea, she wanted to gasp out, "Please hurry—do it now." But Kyler resisted. She was the one in control. So she slid her hands through his hair and, gripping it, pulled his head back from her heat. She leaned down. "If you want to taste me there, you must also taste my blood."

Moving her fingers down to trace his hairline, she landed them on his mouth and teased open his lips. She asked a lot of him. He avoided the bite as he avoided true and genuine intimacy. But she needed it from him to prove that she was more than just one of the many women he'd loved.

She tapped the tip of one of his fangs. To linger on that hard incisor would give him an incredible orgasmic sensation, so she did not. With a moan, he licked her fingers and gently bit the forefinger. He took her hand, kissed the palm of it, then set it free as he nuzzled his mouth to her clit and pierced her hot wetness with his tongue.

Kyler moaned and let her head fall back. Her hair spilled across her back, and her fingers grasped for his shoulders to keep balance. She wanted to lift her leg and wrap it across his shoulder, but she'd lose her balance and she didn't want to lose him there, so deeply indulging himself within and without her.

She'd failed at keeping Casanova at a distance. His tongue tickled and toyed with her, tracing along her labia and where her clitoris hugged both sides of her opening. The intense humming in her loins floated into her core and fizzled through her being. She felt him in her bones.

And when he entered her with his fingers and curled them forward to nudge at her ridged inner space, Kyler's gasp escaped unbidden. She swung her arms backward, catching her palms at the edge of the bed. Dante pulled her to him, burying himself in her, finding her sweetest spot and painting it with his wet, wanting heat.

Her body tingled. Pants and moans beckoned he continue. His fingers curled and thrust, moving in harmony with his tongue. He devoured her. He worshipped her. He gave her exactly what she wanted, and so much more.

He'd exposed his heartache to her. Could he know how much that had meant to her? They shared equal fears. They were alike. And she wanted him both in body and blood.

Kyler shouted out as the orgasm enveloped her being and shook her hips. Dante pressed her back, and she landed on the bed, gripping the sheets as her body answered his expert ministrations.

She heard him mutter, "Again," and felt his tongue lash at her clit. Even as she still rode the incredible orgasm, he deigned to bring her to yet another climax, and it arrived swiftly, crashing into the previous and bursting from her throat in a deep and delicious cry of joy.

After rapidly stripping away his clothing, Dante hilted his cock inside Kyler's hot, lush body. She hugged him tightly as he thrust in and out, gorging himself on her exquisite heat. She felt so good. He never wanted to leave the haven of her.

He bowed his head to her breasts, so full and firm, and sucked in a nipple. She squirmed and ran her fingernails lightly down his back then dug in at his spine, which only deepened his pleasure. She grabbed his ass and pushed him in deeper with each thrust. She wanted so much. A greedy little kitten. And he loved it.

And when he felt his cock was so hard he could release, he pulled out a bit, delaying satisfaction.

"Harder," she whimpered. "Dante, please don't deny me."

Mercy, but he wanted to give her everything she asked for. He did not deny a woman anything—save his heart. But now? He wasn't sure what he offered Kyler, but he wanted to give it. All of it.

He slid in deeper, and as he did so he glided up to kiss under her jaw. His fangs descended, and he teased the tip of one along her carotid. Musk and heat urged him to press the fang against her skin. It would be so easy to have all of her.

"Yes," she gasped. "Bite me."

He'd never bitten another vampire since sharing blood with his creator. He'd known when meeting Kyler and discovering she was vampire that to bite her would only complicate things. Yet now his heart ignored that caution. Nor did he give a second thought to the wisdom of such an act. He desired a taste of Kyler. More than a taste, *all* of her. And he would have it.

Allowing the pressure to increase, his fang sunk in with ease, piercing the vein and spurting sweet blood onto his tongue and palate. Licking the fountain of life, at her hips he pumped harder, faster. She squirmed with the sweet torture of it. The wicked energy of taking her life and feeling it infuse him with vigor only made him harder, hornier, more wanting. He felt as though he could pump inside her for an eternity and never need the climax, for at his mouth was the real prize.

"That's…so good. Yes, take from me. I want to bite you, too," Kyler whimpered. "Yes?"

Her biting him? What wicked alchemy could that bring? Bonding, a deeper connection, something he'd never wanted with any woman. The intimacy frightened him. And yet as long as they didn't sate their thirsts and took only sips, he was confident they would not establish such a connection.

"Please?" came her soft, gasping whisper.

Dante shifted onto his hip, bringing her body over the top of him as he rolled to his back. Rocking on his cock, which was still embedded within her, Kyler cupped her breasts. She sat like a divine goddess upon him. Curvaceous and confident, she was so much woman, he wasn't sure he could ever learn all of her.

But he wanted more of that delicious red cocktail spilling from her vein. "Here." He tapped his mouth, and she obeyed, bowing over him and pressing her neck against his lips. He bit her again, drawing up the blood flow faster, more freely.

Her nails dug in at his shoulder, and he growled at the fantastic pain. Swallowing and pulling away from her neck so he wouldn't be tempted to take too much, he turned his head to the side, exposing his vein to her. "As you wish," he said.

"Oh, hell yes."

The puncture from her fangs blasted into his head with a myriad of colors and sensations and sounds. It was a heady trip. He'd forgotten the mad ecstasy of being bitten. The exquisite pain amplified through pleasure. Slamming his hands out to his sides to seize the bed, he groaned as Kyler's tongue lapped at his blood. Every dash along his skin felt as if she'd stroked his cock, and combined with the squeezing thrusts presently working his cock he could no longer withstand holding back.

As Kyler's body shook above his, and his blood dripped from her crimson lips onto his chest, Dante succumbed to the shared orgasm. A wicked cohesion of body and blood. He'd never experienced such pleasure.

Never.

Hearing Dante's soft snores, Kyler got out of bed, picked up her clothes and headed down the stairs, dressing as she did so. Her body felt…used. Deliciously used. Completely and utterly satisfied. Perfect in every way. And she could still taste Dante's blood slipping across her tongue. In his veins flowed mead. She was so glad she'd gotten a taste. She wanted more and more and more.

But would that be wise? If she had indulged and taken more, they may have bonded. She didn't want that. And she knew he did not want that.

"Don't think about it," she muttered. Right now she

wanted only to indulge in the heady afterglow of a being well fucked and bitten.

Reaching the office doorway, she paused to pull up her pants. Just because she was a well-pleasured woman didn't mean she wasn't also a smart one. Tugging out the slip of paper from the pants pocket on which Dante had written the safe combination, she wandered through the darkness to the bookshelf. Outside the windows, a rose-orange glimmer painted the sky with the promise of imminent sunrise.

Pulling out the red book with no words on the spine, she was relieved when the false wall slid to the side with little noise. She dialed the three-number combination and opened the door, then drew out the Fabergé egg.

It was a solid piece and probably weighed about three pounds. It had been through a lot of joggling, but the base was still attached. She should be more careful with it. If it was capable of doing what King said it was, she could not risk damaging some inner part.

As soon as she gave it to King she would feel as though her debt to him had been paid.

But had Dante been right? The lure of eternity was great. Who wouldn't desire the guarantee of imperviousness to death? Had King used her? He had known she was a thief before transforming her. Why had she given that fact no consideration until now?

And what about King as a vampire hunter? Crazy to even think it. Why kill your own kind while also desiring eternity? So he could continue to slay vamps without fear of death? It made weird sense.

What would keep him from staking her after she'd handed over the prize?

Dante wanted this valuable bit of gold and jewels because he'd been told to protect it long ago. To guard it with his life. And he'd failed. He didn't need it because he sought eternity. If he had, he could have used the spell long ago.

She had more reason to walk away with it. And she would.

Kyler strode to the front door. When she paused to slip the egg into the backpack she'd dropped on the divan, she couldn't set it down. Her fingernail traced a curling line of tiny diamonds set about the circumference.

Dante had trusted her by giving her the safe combination.

Or was he testing her?

Her heartbeat pounded in her ears. If she walked away now, that would be the end of whatever they had begun. She'd never see Dante again. Unless, of course, he pursued her. But if he were forced to pursue her, that would only cement their sides: enemies. And after making love with him—and sharing blood—she couldn't embrace that label for the two of them.

"Never enemies," she whispered. *Always lovers?*

He interested her. He compelled her. Hell, he did things to her no other man had. He embraced and indulged in her voluptuous figure. No man had ever made her feel so sexy. So desired. And beyond his attraction and the sensual allure that kept her returning to his kisses even though she strived to hate him, there was a wistful longing embracing his soul she wanted to learn more about. Sure, he was an innate charmer. But sadness lurked inside him. Something that called to her and begged her to discover more. To give to him that which he didn't even realize he needed—love.

The memory of his fangs sinking into her neck increased her heartbeat, and her breath came faster. A swirling hum in her core revisited the delicious orgasms he'd given her earlier.

She was enamored by the man. In lust with him.

The thought that it probably happened to every woman he slept with—and he knew it—was what saved her from running up the stairs and jumping his bones again right then and there.

Despite her best efforts, she had yet to remain cautious around him.

What if Dante was right about King? To what purpose would it serve Dante to make up such an odd detail about King?

She needed to know more. She needed to make sure she had all the right people in all the right places. And that if she allowed anyone to stand on her side, it was someone she could trust.

With a decisive nod, Kyler took the egg back to the open safe and set it inside. A regretful sigh was necessary as she closed the door and then returned the red book to its normal position. The false wall slid shut.

Plucking up her backpack, and undressing along the way, she climbed the stairway and padded into the bedroom. Slipping into the bed and snuggling up to the warmth of her lover's body, she smiled as his arm slid across her stomach and he hugged her close.

Dante nuzzled Kyler's slick black hair and inhaled her sweet scent. Her blood scent that he'd sipped with lacking caution earlier. No regrets. Never. Yet he'd known when she'd gotten out of bed that she intended to take the egg and leave.

So her return to the bed? She'd thrown him off his game. And, while unanticipated, he liked it.

Chapter 11

After shutting off the shower, Kyler heard her phone ring. She stepped out of the tub, dripping onto the rug, and picked up the cell phone tucked in the pocket of her folded pants. It was King.

"You are still in Venice," he said. A statement, not a question.

She pulled the bathroom door open an inch. Dante had gone down to collect the paper, he'd said as she'd gone in to take a shower, and she could find him out on the patio.

"I've been waiting for your call," she said. "For the handoff?"

"Right. But did you actually steal the egg?"

"Uh, yes? Hasn't it been on the news in Paris? You sound as though you don't believe I actually went through with it. I told you I could do it, and I did."

"I never doubted you, Kyler. I've had some issues with the party I was going to have you hand the egg over to. Can you bring it to Paris?"

"Yes. But I'm not sure I can get out of the city today. They have increased security at the docks."

"Is that so?"

He didn't sound convinced. A heavy sigh preceded, "Don't take your eyes off that thing, Kyler. It means the world to me."

"I know that. Don't worry, I—" Dare she ask him for the truth? If he was really a vampire hunter?

"You've proven exceedingly skillful," he said. "I trust you. You've my number now. Text me when you've left Venice."

"I—"

The phone clicked off, and she almost dropped it. While King was a stern man of few words that meant volumes, she suddenly felt as though he had *assigned* her to do this, and if she failed he would punish her. Weird.

If Dante were right about King being a vampire hunter, what had she gotten herself into? She could hardly walk up to King now, hand over the egg and not expect a stake to the heart. Had she signed her own death warrant the moment she'd looked into the man's big brown eyes and asked him for vampirism? He could have been plotting for her to be his instrument of ac-quisition the moment she'd told him she was a thief.

The more she thought about it, she realized it was feasible.

Had she been that stupid?

Tugging on her pants and a blue top she'd hastily shoved in the backpack, Kyler then pulled out her makeup case and drew on eyeliner. No blush necessary. When she'd finished her lips, she straightened the bathroom a bit because she didn't like to leave behind clutter.

Of course she'd head back to Paris. It was where she lived. If not, King would find her.

She had to go to him and learn the truth. But could she do that by herself?

A fine mist dusted Dante's bare shoulder. He reclined on a wicker chair on the narrow patio with his bare feet up on the wrought iron railing. The local newspaper lay unopened on the small round iron tabletop. Pale green paint flaked from the railing and into the canal. He should see to some freshening repairs on the exterior before winter.

The drizzle was coming from the opposite side of the palazzo, so it didn't touch the patio. And the cool mist felt nice on his skin—he'd not pulled on a shirt this cloudy noon—so he wasn't inclined to move as Kyler strode out and leaned her elbows on the railing. She wore slim black pants and a fitted blue top that was cut low to reveal her deep cleavage. Color really was her thing. He wished she'd burn the awful 80's band T-shirt; it had been an insult to her beauty.

Mmm, the taste of her lingered on his tongue. While on the gondola, she had said she was going to resist sex with him. Allow a bite, sure, but she'd been determined not to continue the sex part of their relationship. He'd never agreed to that. And of course, her resistance had been futile. But even as he sensed her need to pull away from their intimacies, he wanted to pull her closer.

What was up with that? And really, what was up with him? He'd told her about his childhood and his mother's death. And then he'd ignored his caution against biting another vampire. Perhaps it had simply been a relief to share that painful memory with someone who offered him understanding. Sharing blood had, in a manner, sealed their trust for each other.

Crazy, but…he wouldn't question it too much.

Indeed, they were alike. Both had sought vampirism as a means to erase the terrible memories from their pasts.

"Cloudy day," he said. And to avoid all thoughts of relationships and sharing emotions, he tried for a mundane topic. "We should go museum hopping."

The look she delivered him arched up her brow and the corner of her mouth. She wore dark eyeliner and her lips were a matte red. So sexy. Yet blatantly all business.

"Have you ever seen the museums in Venice?" he offered.

"No."

"Very well. Then after we can indulge in a bit of shopping."

"I hardly feel vacation mode is proper considering what we're involved in right now."

"Then what did you have planned? To sit vigil in my office, eyes affixed to the safe? We can't do anything until the security checkpoints are closed. I've checked the news. They are still operating full force. I give them another day, and then we'll make the attempt to bring the thing off the island via a private taxi."

"I have to get out of this city today, Dante. For my own sanity. Of course, I expect you'll follow. You'll be lurking in the shadows somewhere."

"Really? I'm not much of a lurker."

"I find that hard to believe. What about when you go after a bite?"

"I welcome my donors into my arms."

"Of course. Do you always bite women?" She turned and, crossing her arms over her chest, eyed him with an insulting look.

"No. I seek all sorts to feed my hunger. Depends on my appetite. Men tend to have denser, saltier blood. A woman's blood is sweeter. Less iron, too. I hate that metallic taste."

"Such a connoisseur."

"You'll develop a palate as the years pass and the decades turn into centuries." He stretched his arms behind his head and clasped his hands behind his neck.

Kyler's eyes took in his abs, but she quickly looked away. "I suppose."

"You really want eternity, Kyler? Isn't immortality enough? It's a long time no matter how you toss the coin."

"A stake will prove that statement wrong."

He sighed. To tell her the truth about the spell or not? She'd hate him for lying all this time. He couldn't fathom why King would tell her the lie unless he also did not know the real truth of the spell. In which case he may need to keep Kyler in the dark until he stood toe to toe with the vampire hunter. He could no longer tuck away the egg and hope everything would go back to the way it had been. King was involved. He had been looking for the spell since the 1950s when Zara had betrayed him and stolen it—he sure as hell wasn't going to relent now.

Kyler leaned her thighs against the railing and crossed her arms under her breasts. The blue fabric caressed them and screamed out an invitation to Dante. He'd take it, but he wasn't feeling the love from her this dull and misty noon.

"What's going on between the two of us now?" she asked.

He shook his head. "What do you mean? I thought we were cautiously guarding our dash for the prize?"

"We are, but…we shared blood last night. And it was the most amazing thing I've ever experienced."

Same for him. But confessing that shared intimacy didn't feel natural to Dante. Putting his emotions in the fore. Exposing himself like that. He had to stifle a visible shudder. "You think we're like boyfriend and girlfriend now?"

"Oh, no, never."

His jaw muscles clenched at that quick response. *Really?* What was so terrible about being his girlfriend? Did she despise him so much then?

Not that he wanted a girlfriend.

Did he?

Seriously, what was going on with him that he was struggling with his rules about women and how often he fucked them and then how quickly he left them?

"Uncommitted sex," she said. "I'm very cool with that. And the bite didn't bond us. Right?"

"No. We didn't take enough from one another. Never," he replied. "Wouldn't dream of attaching myself to one person."

"Of course not. You'll walk through the centuries alone and ever hungry."

He was not alone. He enjoyed his bachelorhood, thank you very much. As for hungry? "You know, drinking from another vampire doesn't satisfy the innate need for sustenance."

She nodded and stroked her neck. Oh, such a sensual move. His cock hardened, and he didn't bother to cross his legs to hide that fact.

"I realized that as I was walking out onto the patio," she said. "I'm hungry. When you found me yesterday I didn't have a chance to take more than a sip from my donor. Another curious idiot showed up, and I had to take him out."

"Take him out?" Dante gaped.

"Not kill him. I punched him out." She rubbed her fist appreciatively. "I've developed some awesome skills. Anyway, I need blood. From a human donor who can satisfy my thirst. I should head out. I'll be back in a bit."

She left the balcony. He heard her slip on her shoes out in the foyer, and then the front door closed.

Dante stepped inside to run upstairs and pull on a shirt. He wore casual jeans today because he didn't want to risk another dip in the canal in a suit. He didn't own a T-shirt, so a button-up Hermès shirt would do.

A pair of bespoke leather shoes sat on the floor of his bare closet, which he stepped into.

She'd not taken the egg with her, so he presumed she was indeed after only sustenance. And her plans to leave the island would best be served after dark. He could get behind that. As he would, if she chose to leave without him. Of course he would follow her, as she had guessed.

As he intended to do now.

Minutes later, down two zigzagging streets and a covered alley, he'd tracked Kyler to the back of a bakery, where the sweet, cloying dust of powdered sugar coated the street and fogged the air. The rain hadn't touched this part of the city. Not yet. He spied the footprints marking the dust on the street. An encounter around the bakery door? Two pairs, one with petite footprints, the other wide.

"She makes everything too easy."

On the other hand, he had enjoyed her foray into control last night when she'd demanded he get down on his knees before her. He generally catered to a woman's demands, so long as they didn't annoy his sense of machismo. And oh, that bite. Didn't matter that it could never provide the sustenance he needed. He would never want to rely on such an exquisite experience for survival, only for pleasure.

He had surrendered to the bite without a second thought. After so many decades of fortitude against such a thing, Kyler had…changed him. She'd made him incautious and wanting, a man who sought to quench his desires before rational thinking held him back. He could have drunk from her endlessly.

Fool! Not once had he considered such with another vampire. He had to resolve this egg issue and brush Kyler aside before it was too late.

The scent of blood carried to him. It tasted stale on his tongue. Musty, even. Or rather, dusted with flour and sweet. He slowed his steps, not wanting to startle her or the donor. A few more minutes and she should complete her banal task.

When a raindrop splattered his nose, he smiled at the surprise and dashed out his tongue to catch the wet. Kind of how Kyler had entered his life with an equal surprise and now all he wanted to do was taste her. Any small part of her she would allow. He needed her.

Damn it, really? Did he just think that he needed a woman?

When Kyler turned the corner, wiping her lips with a finger, Dante hooked his arm with hers and strolled alongside her. She didn't tug away, but her head shake and audible huff told him she hadn't expected him to follow her and was pissed.

"Should have expected as much," he said. "We are tied at the hip, yes? Both hands on the prize. Who will emerge the victor? I believe I will. You smell like pastry and blood. Don't have to waste my time taking small sips all the time. I'd ask if you are satisfied, but I don't see how you can be. That took you but a moment."

"My drinking habits are none of your business."

"No, they're not. Unless you partake in my bed, eh?"

"Hmph."

"I worry about you, Kyler."

"I'll be fine. I took enough to tide me over for a week. And the only thing you are worried about is keeping the egg in hand. You can't fool me. The sex and the bite were great, but they meant nothing."

He was taken aback at that statement. The sex did mean something to him. And so had the bite. Yes, it had. Because he'd never have allowed it otherwise. It hurt him to hear her so callously dismiss their intimacy. He was in this…this *twosome*. Deep. And the fool who had moments ago been thinking to brush her aside and bolt? That man was out to lunch.

"It means something to me." The words spilled out before Dante could suppress them. "I adore you, Kyler."

"Wow." She tilted up her gaze to inspect his. "That's a revelation, coming from a self-professed lover of all women."

"Tuck the sarcasm back in, Kitten."

"Oh, come on! Sex means nothing to you. And I'm sure you've been bitten a million times. And don't try to convince me otherwise. I'm not that stupid."

He realized she supposed it meant nothing to him because of the game they had played. The sex did mean something. And she couldn't know how much her bite had claimed him. Because the last woman to bite him was Zara.

Why was he struggling with this? Women were designed to be admired, worshipped, fucked and then scattered in his wake like so many petals plucked from a flower. Was Kyler getting under his skin? Could he possibly be falling…

No. He would not allow it!

"Of course. As you say, it means nothing," he murmured. Yet he clenched a fist near his thigh as he forced a cool, genial tone. "Perhaps we should make plans to take the private taxi this evening. We can gain access to the Veneto with some carefully placed bribe money."

"A bribe? Why are you only thinking of this now?"

He'd thought of it immediately, when the problem had presented itself. But if he had mentioned it then, he wouldn't have had Kyler in his bed twice since then.

Nor would he have learned about King. Bless his patience.

The Council would surely like to know that the man who headed an organization dedicated to exterminating vampires was a vampire himself. Dante didn't know anyone on the Council, but he had contacts. His tribe leader would be a good start.

"Now, about that shopping you mentioned earlier…" Kyler strode ahead, and only when he stood there, watching after her, did she pause and look over her shoulder. Lush lashes fluttered and her smile reached into his chest and tickled at his confused heart. "You coming?"

He'd follow her to the ends of the earth.

That startling thought had Dante shaking his head as he marched after the lush vampiress with the fickle heart and sashaying hips.

Behind Saint Mark's square sat the Mercerie, Venice's high-end shopping area. Tourists and shoppers ranging from jeans-wearing families to silk-and-diamond-bejeweled socialites strolled the tree-lined streets. Dante had escorted Kyler into Hermès, handed over his black credit card and told her to pick out something pretty while he made a phone call. He'd strolled out, chattering away, leaving her to feel like an abandoned puppy.

That's why it was so easy for him to love women. It was all surface. He knew the right moves, the right gestures, but he never followed through on them. Probably dangerous for a man who would live for centuries to establish connections with a woman who might never live so long. To show emotion for someone who might wish to attach herself to him, when his boredom level had a very low bar.

And now with her? She could live as long as him. And once she was granted eternity? What a threat to his freedom!

With a sigh, Kyler pointed to a couple of scarves that interested her and the saleswoman with inch-long false eyelashes drew them out to display on black velvet. As the clerk arranged them artfully, Kyler glanced outside. Across the street beneath the shade of cypress trees, Dante sat on a bench. The man was actually wearing jeans. *Jeans.* Wonders did not cease. He was no longer on the phone and now spoke to an older woman. Gray hair topped her round face and a bright red dress swept to her knees, where her support hose met the dress hem. She looked like someone's sweet Italian grandmother, and she probably was.

The interesting thing was Dante's posture. He sat facing the woman, one elbow resting on the back of the bench. His body leaned forward, his head inclined, perhaps to hear her soft voice. When he spoke, he gestured kindly and smiled a lot. They both laughed. He appeared genuinely interested in her.

Kyler's heart softened. Perhaps his manner wasn't all manufactured merely to get a woman into his bed. The man did have a heart and genuine care for women.

A bright red scarf with gold chains printed along the edges caught her eye. Kyler had never spent so much money on clothes. And a silly little scarf priced at five hundred euros?

"I'll take it," she said and handed over Dante's credit card.

After the old woman left on her granddaughter's arm, Dante made another phone call. He intimated to the water taxi driver that he required discretion, and he tossed in a subtle vampiric thrall for good measure. A generous sum secured a boat ride at midnight at a dock beneath a private residence.

Kyler exited the shop with a bright orange bag dangling from her wrist and a sweep of her hair over a shoulder. A pleased woman. He would go down on his knees right now if she asked it of him.

But she did not. Stopping before him, she shoved a hand to her hip. "What was the phone call about?"

"I called my tribe leader. Wanted info about contacting the Council. I think they should be told about King being vampire."

"Who or what is the Council?"

"They are an overseeing, governing body for all paranormals in the mortal realm. They keep a close eye on what's up and have been known to act swiftly in the event of heinous goings-on."

"Hmm…well, we're still not sure that the King I am friends with is the one you know about."

"Really?" He dared her to protest, but instead she started walking down the sidewalk.

He jumped up to follow, and she handed back the credit card, which he tucked in his back pocket.

"I believe King presents a threat to you," he offered as they strode beneath the shady tree canopy. He gestured they turn right toward his palazzo.

"And since when have you designated yourself my protector? Maybe I don't need protecting? Maybe King and I are lovers, as you've guessed. I could be running home to my lover to place the egg in his hands, and then we'll turn around and stab a stake in your heart."

Dante clutched a hand over his heart. "You wound me with your nervous lies."

Because she was lying, putting up a front, a good face. She wasn't headed to a lover's arms. In fact, Dante found it hard to believe that Kyler had had an affair with the vicious, vampire-killing bastard he knew about. But she had been transformed by him, so they had shared some measure of intimacy.

"You fear him," he countered and then picked up his steps to match her sudden increased pace. "You can be honest with me, Kyler. Don't you want my help?"

"I…" She paused after they'd crossed the street before his palazzo. Her sigh was enough of an answer.

He wouldn't press. "Come on. We can save the maudlin emotional stuff for when we're safely on French ground. I've secured passage to the Veneto at midnight. You ready to do this?"

She nodded. "Lead the way."

Once safely on the Veneto, Dante helped Kyler up from the boat and paid the driver. By the time he turned around to clasp her hand, he saw her dashing across the parking lot, backpack swinging over one shoulder.

Tugging at his snugly knotted tie, he muttered, "Does she really think she can make off with it so easily as that?"

Taking off after the headstrong not-a-thief, who may have stolen more from him than he was willing to admit, Dante quickly gained on her. He grabbed her arm, swinging her around. "Really?"

She kicked his shin. A move so surprising, he took the full brunt of the pain, hissing and stumbling backward. Again, she took off in a sprint away from him.

Much as he could simply allow her to run off with the prize, he was dedicated to keeping it out of the wrong hands.

"Sorry, Kyler, but you are forcing my hand. Things are going to get rough."

He sped into a run, bypassing Kyler, then stopping abruptly right in her path. This time he watched for a sneaky kick, and when she again lifted her foot to deliver a blow, he swung upward, clocking her under the jaw.

"Had to be done," he said as he caught her falling body and swung it over his shoulder. He patted her ass, which wobbled about ear level. "You'll forgive me."

Chapter 12

Kyler woke with a start. She shook her head. The world sort of fuzzed back into motion. She didn't hear any noise, save for the soft *squidge* of her rubber-soled shoes moving on what must be a leather sofa. Muted daylight beamed through a window, and she winced. She spied Dante sitting in a chair by that window, fingers steepled before his chest, casually observing her.

This wasn't—they'd left Venice via a private water taxi. How had she…was that the top of the Eiffel Tower that she saw out the window in the distance? Why did the view look familiar?

"You kidnapped me!"

Dante shrugged. "Had to be done. You wouldn't have made it this far if I'd left you on your own in the Veneto. Wolves, you know."

"Wolves, my—" With a swear word on her tongue, she looked around and blinked. "Wait. This is *my* place!" No wonder the scenery looked familiar. "What the heck? How did you—"

"I have my ways."

"Your ways? You looked me up? I don't have my address listed anywhere. How did you…"

He nodded toward the coffee table, on which sat her cell phone. Of course her address was in the contacts. She used that to tell Siri how to get her home when she got lost in Paris. Which was often. It was a miracle the tech noob had accomplished such a search.

"Why did you bring me here?"

"Simple. You have a place in Paris. I do not." He shrugged. "Made sense. Nice digs. If a bit…sparse."

So she wasn't much for decorating. She had all the furniture a person needed; couch, table, chair, a bed. A fake ficus even stood in the corner by the window. It needed dusting, though.

"You bastard." She sat up and gave her head a good shake. "You drugged me?"

"Had to be done. The trip took a few hours and I couldn't have you waking up and attacking me before we got to Paris."

She pulled the tight blue shirt away from her chest and looked down at her bra and breasts.

"What are you doing?" he asked.

"Checking to make sure you didn't molest me."

"Please, Kyler, if I wanted to molest you, I could do that with your permission. And you'd certainly remember whether or not it happened."

She dropped her shirt. "You have an inflated sense of your mastery over women."

"Do I?"

She sighed. No, he did not. He was actually a skilled and charming master with women. With touching them, and seducing them, and licking them, and—she hated him.

Again.

"Get out." She stood and wandered into the kitchen, where she filled a glass of water under the faucet. Her mouth felt dry and tasted metallic as if she'd been sucking on a horseshoe. What kind of drug had he used on her? What could knock a vampire out for the journey from the Veneto to Paris?

"Not going anywhere, I'm afraid. I'm your guest now. No place to live, remember?"

"I hear there are plenty of hotels in Paris. I know you and your black credit card can probably find a nice, cozy bed."

"I'm here to stay, like it or not. Now, let's figure out what we're going to do about you and King."

She choked on a swallow of water. Gripping the glass tightly, she asked through a tight jaw, "Where's the egg?"

He gestured toward the coffee table. She'd not noticed the sparkling Fabergé egg sitting there when she'd gotten up in a huff and stomped in the other direction to the kitchen.

"I'm bringing it to King." She set down the glass with determination. Then she could wash her hands of this mess. "No." *On second thought.* "I can't. I…" She shivered as her heart stuttered. "I don't know what to do anymore. What if he really is a hunter?"

"He is," Dante said as he strolled into the kitchen and stood before her.

Arms crossed, peering down at her, he looked stunning in what must be a new gray suit with a subtle violet tie. *Smoldering* was a word that popped into her brain. The man was too damn sexy for her own good.

"And I'm glad you've switched to indecision about him," he continued. "Means you're starting to think for yourself."

"I always think for myself. It's not like he's got some kind of magical control over me because I'm his blood child." She pushed by the fully armored Casanova, marched out into the living room and picked up the egg. She toyed with the bottom part of the shell, wondering how it opened, but was mostly looking for a way to occupy her hands. "And I don't need your help with King."

"You do, and I won't take no for an answer. So set your bullish independence aside and allow me to play the rescuing hero, will you?"

She scoffed. "I don't see any shining armor or a sword."

"Is that what denotes a hero in your mind? I thought swords and armor went out with the medieval ages. Aren't pistols and magic more in vogue nowadays?"

"Have you either?" she asked, challenging his snark.

"Not on me, no. Just a sense of cleverness and a will

to survive. But, as well, I am compelled to protect the damsel."

Again she made a scoffing noise. "Your suits are your armor."

He tugged at the lapels of the single-breasted concoction. She bet it had cost him thousands. In her opinion? Worth every sigh-inducing euro.

"But the whole hero thing doesn't suit you as well as that fabric does," she said. "I don't think it aligns with your love-'em-and-leave-'em act. I mean, really. If you actually cared about a woman, it would throw your entire lifestyle out of whack. I'll be fine, Dante. I'm a big girl."

"A big girl who allowed herself to be kidnapped and flown to another country. And, I might note, could have had a valuable objet d'art stolen from her in the process."

"Tell me how the egg opens," she said, avoiding his obvious assessment of her less-than-skillful actions. The fact he was still here, with the egg, was remarkable. It proved he wasn't willing to simply walk away from her. Not just yet.

So she wasn't the strongest or the bravest or even the smartest. But taking help from Dante D'Arcangelo? She didn't want to be the one to ask for help. She wanted to be the one who earned it because he couldn't resist.

"I will not give you instructions on how to open the egg," he said. "I and one other person are the only vampires who know how to open it. I'm not inclined to share that responsibility."

"But if I hand it over to King, how will he open it?"

"You're not going to do that, are you? Kyler, do you really think he'll kiss you on the forehead and send you on your way with eternity in your arsenal?"

No, she now suspected King would kill her. With a stake. Because if he was as Dante said—a vampire hunter—that changed their relationship status from friends to enemies. And that freaked her out.

She plopped onto the sofa, clutching the egg like a doll to her chest. Her cell phone rang, and she picked it up. "It's him," she said. She answered with a nervous warble to her tone, "Yes?"

Of course, King would know she was in Paris. Because he was her creator, he could sense when she was near. He also knew where she lived.

She leaned forward, hoping to give Dante a clue this was a private conversation but knowing he wouldn't get the hint.

"You're back in Paris. I'm pleased." King's voice was deep and measured. It had always given her good chills. So much so, she'd wanted to have sex more than the one time, yet he'd never offered or given her a clue he was interested in anything but their initial hookup. Not even on the night he had transformed her.

Now his voice made her heart thump and her fingers curl. And not in a good way. "Have you the egg?"

Dante walked around and stood before her.

"Yes?" She couldn't lie, but it came out as a confused mix of truth and fiction anyway.

"I'll come to you."

"No, I—"

The phone clicked off.

Kyler met Dante's inquiring gaze. "He's on his way here."

"Shit." He bracketed her face with his hands. "Are you with me or against me, Kyler? Do you want me to protect you from King?"

She nodded. "Yes, I think—"

"Don't think. You either do or you don't."

In his eyes she found a glint of something he probably never shared with women. Hope. Urgency. Promise. And, bone-deep, she truly felt like the damsel who needed saving.

"I do. Please. I'm feeling less and less friendly towards King. But he'll be here soon. He doesn't live far away. How can we not give him the egg? And with you here—won't he try to stake you?"

"Most likely. We've met once before. He knows me on sight, I'm sure. Though I have recently cut off what was once very long hair."

Dante with long hair? Kyler's heart skipped a beat.

He smirked at what must have been her swooning look of desire. "Do you have any weapons?"

She shook her head. Never had any reason for a weapon. The idea of owning a gun creeped her out. She wasn't the sort who thought she'd ever need to protect herself. And since she'd become vampire, her strength and quick reaction skills allowed her to extricate herself from most iffy encounters.

"King." Dante stood in the middle of the room, glancing about, but she sensed his brain was working on overdrive. "What can you tell me about him? Who *is* he?" he insisted.

She shook her head. "I didn't even know he was a vampire slayer."

"Right. Uh, is he baptized?"

"Yes! He told me about the whole baptism thing, that vamps who were born mortal and have been baptized have to avoid religious artifacts."

"Good. You have any religious items in this place? A cross?"

She shook her head.

"No Bible, or a catechism?"

"There's a Bible in my bedside table." It used to be her mother's. "I haven't been able to remove it since being transformed."

"Excellent." He dashed into her bedroom and returned with the small, black leather-bound Bible. She'd carried it with her everywhere following her mother's death. Now she couldn't touch it because religious objects burned baptized vampires. Apparently Dante had not received that sacrament.

"It's not much. But it'll have to serve." He glanced at the egg. "Hide that in the kitchen. But make access easy, in case we have to run."

She grabbed the egg. In the kitchen she placed it in the cupboard under the sink beneath a tangle of chrome pipes. When Kyler stood, a knock on the front door prickled up the hairs on her arms.

"I'll get it." Dante tucked the Bible into his waistband. Arms crooked at his sides as if he were a gunslinger waiting for the drop of the hat, he announced, "This is going to get interesting."

Dante opened the door, and the man ready to step across the threshold paused. Of course, King had been in Kyler's home before; he didn't need an invite to again cross the private threshold.

At the sight of Dante, King's jaw dropped open momentarily, then closed. He tilted his head, cracking his neck, and assumed a calm yet imposing stature as he matched Dante's height and build. "Dante D'Arcangelo. This is interesting."

"As is the information I've gleaned about the founder of the Order of the Stake."

"Is that so?" King sneered. "It's not a secret. The Council has all the information on me."

"Oh, I doubt that very much."

"Believe what you wish." He walked in, roughly brushing shoulders with Dante. "Kyler, what is this man doing here?"

"I, uh, met him in Italy. He helped me to get out of Venice when the docks were being surveilled."

King drew a long look over Dante. He was dressed in dark suede pants and dress shirt, with a long gray canvas coat. Something a hunter would wear. "And yet he's still with you. Explain that to me."

"I sensed Kyler needs protection," Dante said. "From you."

When King took a step forward, Dante moved in front him, blocking him from getting closer to Kyler.

"I understand you've asked Kyler to obtain a rare, long-missing Fabergé egg for you?"

King took a step back and slid a hand onto his hip, pushing back his coat to reveal a holster strapped to his thigh. In the holster shone a titanium stake that Dante knew the knights of the Order used to slay vampires.

Kyler sucked in a gasp at the sight. *Good then.* She now had proof the man she claimed was a friend—her blood master—was a lying bastard.

"Where is it?" King asked, his eyes fixed on Kyler. Dante sensed the old vampire would not miss a flinch from him.

"You lied to me," Kyler said. "You never told me you slay vampires. How could you do that? Why? Do you really kill your own kind?"

"My profession has nothing to do with obtaining the egg. I'll ask you to hand it over immediately, or your dog on a leash here will take a stake to the heart."

"No," Kyler said. "I won't do it. I thought we were friends."

"You did?" King smirked. "I've never claimed friendship. Master of your creation, certainly, but never friends. You will hand over the egg. I thought you wanted to pay me back for the great gift I bestowed upon you? What about eternity?"

"Dante says the egg doesn't promise eternity."

"Does he now?" King turned his gaze on Dante. "And what do you believe it can do?"

"I didn't specify," Dante said. He wasn't sure if King had false information about the egg—the eternity-giving powers of the spell had been a rumor disseminated decades earlier—or if he'd lied to Kyler to give her incentive to actually return with the object. "But as a vampire hunter you know what it really does, don't you?"

King held his jaw so tight the muscle in it pulsed repeatedly. "This does not involve you, D'Arcangelo. You should leave."

"Or die?" Dante crossed his arms high at his chest. He noticed as King's eyes averted to the Bible tucked at his waist. "Are you going to prove to Kyler that she shouldn't have ever trusted you?"

"Kyler will obey me. She wants to do the right thing."

"Giving a vampire hunter that egg is not the right thing. It belongs to me, actually. And I intend to keep it."

"Then we have come to an impasse." King plucked the stake from the holster and spun it once before catching it smartly in his hand.

"No," Kyler said from behind Dante. "Just let him go. I'll give you the egg."

"Kyler," Dante warned calmly. "He'll stake you the moment you've handed over the prize. You know that."

"Why would I waste a perfectly good blood child?" King asked. "And for that matter, a thief? She can prove very handy to me for future endeavors." He played his thumb over the rubber grips on the stake's cylinder hilt.

There was no sharp, pointy end on it. For the moment. Dante knew from witnessing a few slayings that the hunter slammed the stake against the vampire's chest, then compressed the paddles in the grip, which released the stake end into the vamp's chest with a thumping, piercing death punch. And then? Ashes.

"If you want to start a war," King continued, "over a pretty little bit of sparkle and gold, then by all means, go ahead and deny me that treasure. But I promise you, D'Arcangelo, you won't see the pain coming. You'll turn and suddenly be ash." King sniffed disdainfully. "My favorite kind of vampire."

Dante exhaled through his nose, setting his shoulders back. "Try me."

He saw the man's arm move and reached for the Bible. Thrusting it before his chest with both hands, Dante felt the impact as the stake tip pinioned out and pierced the book. King hissed and retracted, grabbing his hand. His skin may have brushed the leather, Dante couldn't be sure. He didn't see the man's hand smoking.

"Don't forget," King said as he backed toward the open door, "you asked for this. Kyler, if you don't bring the egg to me by dawn, your lover will be ash."

Dante pulled the stake from the Bible and flipped it in the air, catching it. "You first."

The door closed behind King as he fled, the stake Dante had thrown at him embedded in the wooden frame.

Kyler clutched him from behind. "Now what?"

"Now?"

He had started something, indeed. Unwisely? Probably. But he wasn't about to let the lying vampire who would kill his own kind have the spell, whether or not it did what he thought it did.

"I'd say we get the hell out of here. You're not safe

anymore." He raised the Bible and peered through the hole at the stake jabbed into the door. "And I wager King's knights will come knocking sooner rather than later. Grab the egg."

She nodded, picking up her backpack near the couch and heading into the kitchen. She wasn't fearful or panicking, and that was good. But she should be.

Because Dante had shaken the king out of his castle.

Chapter 13

"Why do you think King gave up so easily and left?" Kyler asked as she followed Dante through the city. She lived in the fifth arrondissement, and he'd suggested they head straight for his tribe's safe house to drop off the egg. That was across the river in the eighth.

Dante stopped at the end of an alleyway, seeming to assess which direction he wanted to turn. "King didn't expect me to open the door," he said. "He thought a frightened woman whom he could manipulate would be waiting for him."

"Maybe he's scared of you?"

Dante laughed. "Don't for one moment believe that man is scared of anything. Because then he'll have you right where he wants you. No, he's taken a step back to assess and plan. And I don't believe the Bible burned him. Again, he was surprised at the prepared attack. We're being followed."

"How do you know?" She clutched his hand; his grip was firm and comforting.

"The knights move with stealth, but one of them had garlic for supper. A lot," he said. "Come on. I'm sure they're out in numbers. King isn't going to let my showing him up stand for long."

He pulled out his phone and dialed as they walked swiftly.

"Who are you calling?" Kyler asked. "You're actually carrying a phone? Won't that ruin the line of your suit?"

"Must needs, Kitten. I'm calling Christian de Baureaux. Leader of the Incroyables."

"Your tribe?"

"Yes. We're going to need backup to make it across the city all in one piece. Christian. You busy? I need a hand. Being pursued by a couple knights with garlic breath. You and Isaac? Great. We're in the fifth. Near— I don't know—that bookstore the tourists always flock to across the river from Notre Dame. Thanks."

He tucked the phone in his pants pocket. "They're close. This way."

He tugged out the titanium stake King had left behind and crossed a street. They jogged parallel to a high hedgerow that sparkled from an earlier rain. It was much later than Kyler had thought it was. She must have been out for quite some time. She'd have words with Dante about that later.

When an oncoming car's headlights forced them off

the street and onto a sidewalk, Dante suddenly ducked through a gate and into a private city park.

"Ah," he said, "I like this square. Used to be a Merovingian cemetery. And Saint Julien's stags," he said with a gesture toward the bronze sculpture in the middle of the park. "So deliciously macabre."

Surrounded by the hedges, the small park boasted a bronze water fountain in the middle of a pebbled square. The sculpture featured stag heads, and people climbing up the triangular column. Sort of looked like baby heads to Kyler, but then, she didn't think that had been the effect the artist had been going for. Benches were placed at the four compass points in the park, and the roses climbing the gateway through which they had entered bloomed sweetly.

A massive tree propped up by concrete posts caught Kyler's eye, and she veered toward it. "Wow."

"The oldest tree in Paris," Dante said. "A locust, I believe. Planted in 1601. Well *after* your creator King was born."

"That's amazing." Kyler sucked in a frightened breath as the iron gate screeched behind her. Instantly she lost all interest in the ancient tree.

Dante spun around, pulling her behind him as he did so and assuming a protective stance. Before them filed in three men, each wearing long black leather coats with high collars edged in blades. The blades were to prevent vampires from sinking in their fangs. At their thighs, chain mail lined the black leather pants. Further protection over the femoral artery from a well-placed bite. King had told Kyler this when he'd mentioned the

Order to her. It had never occurred to her he knew it from hands-on experience.

The one who wielded a stake in both hands asked, "You Dante D'Arcangelo?"

"Really? You want me to identify myself before you decide to ram in that stake? And you actually expect honesty?" Dante waggled the stake he held admonishingly. "Let's be gentlemen and leave the lady out of this, shall we? Kyler, step out of the way."

"Three against one?" one of the knights said. "Works for me. We need the woman alive anyway."

Against her better judgment, Kyler started to step back. When she'd taken two paces, suddenly her arm was grabbed and she was pushed aside by a tall man with shoulders so broad they were equal to two of the hunters.

"Ah, my seconds have arrived," Dante said.

Kyler assumed the beefy guy and his sidekick were from Dante's tribe. Now the match was even. But she couldn't begin to feel relief as one of the hunters flung a throwing star toward Dante's head. He ducked, and the vampire behind him caught it with a hiss as the sharp tip cut into his palm.

"Dipped in holy water?" the beefy guy said. He tugged the star out and shook spatters of his blood onto the pebbled walk. "Tough luck, idiots. Keep your crosses to yourself or find them shoved up your—"

"Isaac, be polite," the other said as he stepped forward. Dressed in gray wool trousers and a plaid vest with his shirt sleeves rolled to his elbows, he exuded a scholarly appeal—with rock-hard biceps. "Gentlemen, to arms!"

Dante charged a hunter with the stake. The scholarly one—Kyler guessed he was Christian, the tribe leader—pulled out a short sword. The biggest one wielded what looked like a smaller version of Thor's hammer.

Kyler's legs bumped into the concrete bench behind her, and she landed on her butt, clutching the backpack to her chest as she watched the frenzy of activity.

The opponents weren't overly talkative as swords met stakes and the remarkable hammer swung into ribs. As he took punches and dodged the swing of the stake, Dante moved like a wild animal, crouching and ducking, rolling onto his back and coming up to both feet with sinuous precision.

Kyler's heart pounded. She didn't want him to die. Much as she had convinced herself that he could never see her as anything other than "another notch," she had fallen for Dante's cool charm.

A hunter stumbled backward toward her, and the one Kyler guessed was the tribe leader managed to insinuate himself before her, kicking the hunter back and sending him flying to land sprawled on the bronze fountain.

"My lady." He bowed quickly to her, then spun to help Dante fend off a maniacal deluge of what looked like karate moves, arms swinging and boots kicking.

Kyler marveled over how the three vampires worked together without a word to one another. They instinctually seemed to know what the other was doing; whereas the knights stumbled and worked on their own.

The biggest of the tribe tumbled onto the ground after dodging a stake, but Dante soared over the man's fallen form, kicking high as he did so, connecting with the hunter who would have otherwise staked Isaac. A shout of pain accompanied the hunter falling before the old and venerated tree.

Was it wrong to feel tenser about the tree taking damage than the hunter? Not at all.

Dante offered the vampire on the ground a hand up, and the twosome went back-to-back to fend off the next barrage of swinging stakes and shouting slayers. They quickly dispatched their opponents and gave each other a high five.

Seeing Dante perform in this manner after having known only his sensual, suited-armor side made Kyler fall even harder for him. He was the knight her damsel desired. He could protect her, and she would let him.

One of the hunters lay bleeding on the ground and all three vamps stood side by side, presenting a fierce front to the remaining two who had gotten up from the ground.

"Give up yet?" Dante asked, giving his violet tie an adjusting tug. "Or do you all want to get carted out of here in body bags?"

One of them pulled a gold cross out of an inner coat pocket and held it before him.

All three of the vampires chuckled.

And then someone not a part of the standoff growled. Like a dog.

Or rather a wolf.

Kyler shuffled into the shadows at the sight of the

two new men standing inside the gate. She immediately sensed they were werewolves, and her instincts were affirmed when they began to shift.

"Really?" Christian said to Dante as they rushed toward the shifting werewolf. Best time to take out a wolf was during the shift, when it was disoriented. But the entire shift from human form to half man, half wolf took about ten seconds, so they had to move quickly.

They both charged one shifting wolf and slammed it forcefully into the other. A yelping howl was abruptly cut off with a painful whine.

Dante turned in time to dodge a stake swinging from on high. He dropped to the ground, kicked up and landed a heel in the hunter's gut, shoving him off and forcing his body hard against a metal sculpture.

Isaac picked up one of the half-shifted wolves and head-butted him with a fierce growl to match any shape-shifter's war cry. Christian swung a punch up under a hunter's jaw, knocking him out cold.

"Who invited the wolves?" Isaac shouted as he swung his hammer and brought it down on the wolf's knee, producing a painful yelp from his victim. "No one said anything about wolves!"

"They followed us from Italy," Dante said. They must have picked up the scent of one of their own, perhaps still lingering on the egg in Kyler's bag? "Take out that last hunter, and let's get the hell out of here."

Christian disarmed the hunter, gathering from inside his coat two stakes, a garrote and a blade. Isaac charged the last werewolf standing, the twosome crashing into the hedgerow where the scuffle must have alerted people walking by, judging by the surprised shouts they now heard.

Dante grabbed Kyler's hand and tugged her aside as a hunter flew over their heads and landed in the shrubbery beside the dispatched werewolf. On the other side of the shrubs, the city flashed by in headlights and tourists' flashbulbs. If they didn't move soon, the police sirens would put a damper on this unexpected party.

"The wolves won't stay down long," Isaac said as he passed Dante and Kyler and raced through the open gate. "We've a car down the street. Come on!"

They filed into a black SUV parked by the curb. Isaac took the wheel. On the passenger side Christian sorting through the booty he'd collected, while Dante and Kyler slid into the backseat.

"You okay?" Dante asked Kyler. He touched her face, searching her eyes.

She nodded, then shoved the backpack at him. "You hold on to this."

"What's that?" Christian asked from the front. He eyed Kyler, and then turned his focus to Dante. "The reason they were on you?"

"The reason the *knights* were after us. I still haven't figured out the werewolf angle."

"Knights," Isaac said with vitriol. "Why knights? You've always avoided conflict, D'Arcangelo. You're the lover—ah. Is it because of the woman?"

Dante flicked a look to Kyler. She actually blushed. *Sweet kitten.* "Partly. But no. This involved me before I even met her. We've both become entangled with King for reasons I'm also not too clear on."

"King. Don't start this war," Christian warned. "You know that bastard always wins."

"Too late." Dante patted the backpack. "Already picked up the gauntlet."

"Remember when we'd never refuse a dropped gauntlet?" Isaac asked Christian. "Those were the good ol' days."

"King is vampire," Dante said. "I told Christian that, but did you know, Isaac?"

"The leader of the Order of the Stake is vamp?" Isaac whistled lowly. "Shit. I'm with Christian. Don't get into this with him, Dante."

Christian turned and crossed his arms, not offering another word. But Kyler could feel his disapproval as a shiver over her arms. Much like the vampiric shimmer, only heavy with disappointment.

"This is getting too big for us," she whispered. "I know it—"

Dante tugged her up against his side, hugging her tightly. "Take us to the train station," he told Isaac.

"Where are we headed?" Kyler asked.

"We're going to put the wolves off our scent," he said calmly, then settled back in the seat to watch the passing traffic cruise by in ribbons of headlights and red taillights.

His sister put up her long legs on the end of his office desk. She wore supple black leather boots that stretched from her heels to her thighs, and her short black skirt probably exposed things he hadn't seen for centuries. Dark sunglasses masked her brown eyes here inside the underground headquarters for the Order of the Stake. Black leather gloves didn't allow her to wear the ruby crest ring she normally sported.

"What's kickin', bro?" she asked.

King lifted a brow at that. He hadn't seen Margot in decades, yet when they did come together it felt as if no time had passed, and only yesterday they'd been wearing medieval velvets with gold ruffs and struggling against the Protestants in the bloody wars.

"What have you been up to, Margot?"

"It's Bunny now. Been Bunny for a long time."

"Didn't Rook call you that—when? Last century?"

She nodded, which set her long, coal-black hair spilling over a shoulder. "He still around? Not that I care."

She cared. She and Rook had a love/hate thing going on. Had ever since—well, it must have been the seventeenth century, surely.

"He's living with a witch. Happily," King added. And then he sighed and flexed his fingers, which he'd been curling in and out of fists since returning to the office from Kyler's home. "What do you need?"

"Nothing. Never anything. You know that. The question is, what's eating you? You're a stressed-up mess. Girl troubles?"

He chuckled because the idea was so preposterous. He never let a woman get the upper hand with him. And romance? That was a dangerous road he rarely traveled.

"I've come from staring down Dante D'Arcangelo."

Margot had known the man. She always hit men hard and fast and was the one to walk away whistling.

"Oooh, I remember that pretty man. Long dark hair and a Bohemian thing going on?"

"He's cut his hair and taken up the task of pissing me off. He's got his hands on something I need. The bastard actually had the nerve to protect one of my blood children, to defend her. He needs to die."

"Oh, don't be so dramatic, brother dearest. Dante is too pretty to waste on anger over a female."

"It's not the woman I care about. She is disposable. But I sent her to steal a Fabergé egg that contains within it an important spell."

"Is this the spell you've been searching for for decades?"

"The very one. The one that destroys vampires for miles within range."

Margot—rather, Bunny—tapped a black-gloved finger against her bloodred lips. "You have thought about the one small complication to enacting such a spell?"

"That it would destroy me, as well?" King chuckled. "I don't intend to be the one to enact the spell. And I will be safe inside a protection circle."

"I certainly hope you give me a heads-up when you do. I'd like to live a few more centuries, at the very least. So many adventures yet to be had. So many men begging to be conquered and put out to pasture."

"What if I offered you eternity?"

Bunny scoffed. "That's the other spell you've always quested for."

"I have that spell. It's just missing a vital ingredient."

Bunny sat up. "Really? Eternity? Like, to never be killed?"

"Exactly."

"I'm in."

"Great. But it will not happen unless I can get the egg from Dante, who has taken ownership of it. I sent three knights after him and just received a report of one casualty and two serious injuries. And when the werewolves showed up things did not get any better."

"I love me a wolfie man," Bunny cooed. She sat up straight, spreading her long legs before her, then leaned onto the desktop with her elbows. "Let me talk to Dante for you. I'll get you an egg, hell, a dozen eggs. Whatever you desire, brother dearest."

King stood and walked around the desk. He stroked his sister's hair over her ear and trailed a finger down to her mouth. She kissed his fingers, then dashed out her tongue to lick them.

He gripped her under the chin and squeezed. "Watch it, little sister. Never forget who is the better in our family."

She pried away his hand. "Our family consists of but me and you now. Although I wonder about Henri some days. You changed him—I know you did. And I'd be foolish to think you'd ever come down from that self-imposed, rusting throne of yours. Of course, you are the best, Charles. Always have been, always will be. Now. Do you want me to talk to the Casanova of vampires, or are you going to send more knights after him to be hobbled and humiliated?"

He walked around behind her, threading his fingers

up through her hair as he did so. Twisting the luxurious strands about his hand, he didn't pull hard, but he tilted her head back. He bowed and kissed her red mouth. "Do it."

Chapter 14

Once dropped off at the train station, Dante thanked his friends, then strolled to a locker and locked the egg inside. Kyler questioned the security, but he said it would serve the purpose he intended and walked back outside.

"I can't believe you did that," she said as they strolled before the Gare du Nord and down the street. Dante had expressed a need for coffee, of all things. "That thing is dangerous. So many people want it. Men with stakes! Werewolves! Why the werewolves?"

"Caution, Kyler." He took her hand and squeezed as he veered toward a less crowded street. "We'll talk once we're out of the tourist shuffle and can find a few minutes of privacy under one of those striped umbrellas, yes?"

"Coffee," she muttered. "After you nearly died fighting hunters. I don't get you."

"Is there some rule that says you need to get me? Besides, you exaggerate. Nearly died?" He chuckled. "I am in one piece. And we should stay off the main streets. I much prefer maintaining a modicum of secrecy. Though, come to think of it, you know much more about me than most."

"I doubt that."

Then again, maybe she did. While Dante claimed to stand with his arms wide-open to the women of the world, Kyler had learned actually gaining access to the man behind the charming facade was another deal altogether.

"I know little about you," she said. "Only that I can't seem to walk away from you. You're like a magnet, and I am a tiny iron filing that doesn't stand a chance against your powerful pull."

"Come, Kyler. You're a strong woman." He had said that to her so often she was actually beginning to believe it. "You'll make it through this. I know you will."

She would. With him by her side.

They paused at a street corner, and Kyler reached up to swipe a smear of blood from Dante's temple where he must have been wounded during the fight. All healed now, save for some fading bruises on his jaw and knuckles. "Thanks for having faith in me."

"It comes easily. No more blood?" he asked.

"You're good. I can see the bruises fading as we stand here. Remarkable."

"Yes, but I wish the pain faded as quickly. One of

them punched my ribs through a kidney. Or so it feels that way. Either way, I'm thankful for the vampire's remarkable healing capabilities. This direction."

They filed through a scatter of iron-topped café tables and found a small nook set against the outer wall of a brasserie, shaded by a bright red-and-white-striped awning. The evening was growing long and the streetlights were already lit owing to the clouds and further promise of rain. A waitress immediately showed and grinned widely at Dante. Kyler could but smirk at her obvious swoon. Dante ordered café Americans for both of them, no cream or sugar.

That was fine with Kyler. She needed a good strong jolt to shock her out of the shock. Vampire hunters had almost killed Dante and two of his friends. And how had the werewolves found them?

Now that she sensed he'd relaxed and there was no one close by to overhear their conversation, she asked, "Do you think they were from the same pack as the wolves in Venice?"

"I suspect so. They probably scented their own pack members on the egg."

"Really?"

"The werewolves' sense of smell is remarkable. They can track prey miles away. I wonder for what reason they want the egg. They could do much with a weapon designed to kill off vampires, I guess."

"Kill off vampires? Though you've teased about it, you haven't told me the real purpose for the spell. I've been told it would grant eternity. It was the reason I risked stealing the damn thing. But now you tell me it's not? King was adamant about wanting eternity. Why would he lie to me?"

The waitress set their coffees on the table and again smiled widely at Dante. He thanked her in French and suggested she return in a bit for a refill. She eagerly nodded and toddled off.

"You want to manhandle her and get it done with?" Kyler asked.

"What?" He sipped, but behind the cup she saw his smile. "I love women."

"Right. When are you going to step beyond loving them and start getting to know them? To care about them?"

He pressed the cup to his jaw. Perhaps the warmth eased the lingering pain. "I thought we were discussing the spell in the egg?"

He avoided his truths like King avoided holy objects. Kyler decided to give him a pass. He simply wasn't the settling down and happily-ever-after kind of man. And she would do well to remember that every time she got lost in his mesmerizing gaze.

"Tell me what it really does," she said. "And why you're so eager to get your hands on it."

"As I've explained, the egg was given to me to protect. Both as an object of historical value, and as the container for the spell. A spell that, once spoken, can wipe out vast populations of vampires. All the vampires in Paris? Gone." He snapped his fingers. "Like that."

Kyler gaped at that information. She would have never purposely involved herself in stealing something so horrible. She had no reason to believe Dante would lie about such a spell.

"That's about as far from granting a vamp eternity as it gets," she said. "Yet if King were to enact such a spell, he'd be killing himself. That doesn't make any sense to me."

"Or me. Of course, he could have a proxy perform the spell while he hightails it out of town. That would make the most sense to me. What does not is *why*? Sure, he heads an organization that exists to take us out. But the Order has always been discreet and just. They only ever pursue those vamps who have proven a danger to humans. They're not staking every other vampire who strolls by. So why take us all out now? King never alluded to anything of the sort to you while you two were..."

"We were?" She sipped the coffee. It was so hot she gasped and set the cup down with a clink. "We were friends for a couple days while he gave me less than a few pointers on being vampire. I've told you I was seduced by the dream of immortality. But you know, we never got close. We did have sex. Once. The first night I met him. And as for personal conversations about life and the future and what drives us or—apparently, what our real jobs were—we didn't broach such deep chatter."

"I find it startling that he did not have sex with you more than once."

"Why?"

Dante spread his hands before him. "Look at you."

Kyler basked in the warmth of his easy admiration. It felt great. And it wasn't something she had ever felt with King. Caught up in the fantasy of a dark, eternal lover, she had thought she could fall in love with a vampire and share immortality with him. Until he'd walked away from her after the bite and said he'd see her around. And even then, she'd rushed back to him when he'd called her about the egg.

What a fool.

"So you two are still together? I mean, he sent you after the egg. I can't imagine he called you up after a few months and asked for such a favor."

"As I've told you, he called me about a week ago about the emergence of the egg. And when he said he would share eternity with me, I was in. He mentioned my mother, as well. And only now I realize he was playing on my grief. My God, I've been such a fool."

"You didn't see that he was manipulating you."

She sighed. "I did not. But I do now."

"The man is very powerful. And he doesn't care who he steps on to stay on top."

"I'm realizing that more and more as the hours pass. How could I have been so stupid?"

Dante clasped her wrist softly. "You're not stupid, Kyler. The vampire's thrall is powerful."

"But we can't enthrall one another. Can we?"

"I've never created another vampire, but I suspect your blood master might have such an ability. King wields charm as a weapon. I suspect you hadn't a chance after a few minutes with the man."

"Like you?"

"I do not wield my charm so cruelly."

She'd give him that. And yet, the man couldn't realize that his amorous attentions cut into a woman's heart and left a wanting, open scar ever after.

"Be thankful you're thinking clearly now. Yes?"

She nodded. "What about the two of us? Could you enthrall me?"

He shook his head. "We didn't bond when we bit one another. It would require a longer drink and a mutual agreement. Then? Yes, we'd be able to enthrall one another. Which wouldn't be right for me. I'd only bond with another if I felt a close connection. And then to even consider putting someone I love under thrall? Never."

"That close connection of bonding is your idea of love?"

He shrugged, and Kyler knew that his form of love was vastly different from hers.

She let him off the hook. "So do you think the werewolves want to take out a bunch of vampires?"

"Possibly. There are still some packs that harbor a ridiculous vengeance for vampires. The two species were once enemies. Wolves used our kind for vicious blood games. And some still do. And we once hunted them for sport. I'm not sure vampires participate in such hunts anymore, but anything is possible."

"Why can't we all get along?"

Dante smirked. "The world would not be such an interesting place if it was all peace, love and happiness, would it?"

"Might be a nice place to visit. For a while, at least. So, what's the plan? We could have hunters searching for us right now. You put the egg in such a vulnerable spot, so I'm assuming you have plans for it. Do you *want* the wolves to sniff it out?"

"You see? You are a very smart woman—oh."

Kyler twisted her head in the direction Dante's gaze had suddenly fixed. Approaching them from across the street with long, confident strides was a tall woman with flowing black, model-perfect hair and a lithe, sexy body clad in skintight black from gloves to thigh-high boots. She looked like every man's fantasy times ten. At the sight of them, her red lips parted in a knowing smile.

"Who's that?" Kyler asked.

Dante's coffee cup hit the saucer with a hard clink that cracked the underside. "Trouble."

Chapter 15

The woman, whom Kyler could only term a glamour slut, glided around the few café tables with the ease of an approaching black panther. Brown eyes feathered by lush black lashes fixed on Dante. She walked right up to him, straddled his lap with her long legs and leaned down to kiss him in a move so stealthy and seamless Kyler almost wanted to flip up the "10" paddle.

But she was kissing Dante. And he allowed it to happen. His hands initially shoved at the woman's hips, but now one of them actually curled around her. She moaned and twisted her head as the kiss grew deeper.

Kyler picked up her coffee cup and set it down with a clank.

Dante shoved the woman he'd called trouble off him.

She stood over him with the vainglorious smile of

a snake who'd eaten the kitten who'd stolen the cream. "It's been a long time, D'Arcangelo, but you still taste like dark, delicious things." She ran a finger along her red lips. "Another?"

"Margot, that is enough. Let me introduce you to Kyler Cole."

About time he got around to remembering she sat but two feet away from him.

"Oh. Yes." The woman didn't turn toward Kyler and barely offered her a glance. "The little mouse sitting in the serpent's shadow. So, Dante…" She pulled one of the metal chairs close and sat, crossing her legs and shoving her knee into Dante's thigh. She leaned in and trailed a finger up to his chin. "Want to get laid?"

Seriously? The woman was going to tear the man apart right before her?

"Dante." Kyler leaned forward. "Who is this *person*, and how do you know her?"

"Margot." He pushed her groping hands away from his chest. "Please, Margot. Kyler, this is Margot de Valois."

"It's Bunny now. Has been for decades."

"Bunny?" Kyler scoffed and tilted her head in scorn.

"Bunny." Dante twisted his head away. He couldn't move his chair away from the woman because it was up against a brick wall. He seemed more nervous that *Kyler* sat there. Should she leave the two of them to make out?

Not on her life.

"Interesting name choice," Dante said. "It's been what? Almost a century since we've seen one another?

You haven't changed. Still dominant and thoughtless as ever."

"Works for me," Bunny chimed in and cast a wicked eye toward Kyler. "Are you Dante's latest? Don't tell me you're actually in a relationship, Dante. He has always been known as *the lover*, you know."

Kyler felt her temperature rise and fought to keep it normal. She didn't want a blush to give the woman any triumph. The lover? She'd figured that one out on their first date and was still kicking herself for ever ignoring her heart's insistent warnings to avoid him.

"We are lovers," he offered before Kyler could be forced to actually summon a clever comeback to the Bunny bitch. "What brings you to Paris, Margot—er, Bunny?"

"Visiting Charles. You know my brother."

"He's still alive, as well? Together the two of you must prove quite the menace."

"We don't see each other all that often. He's ever busy. Though I am on an errand for him." She leaned in again and nuzzled her nose against Dante's jaw. He didn't move away from her. "You have something my brother wants, lover boy. If you give it to me, I won't damage your little mouse."

"Threats? I thought you had more class than that. Besides, she's not a mouse—"

"No." Bunny turned and looked at Kyler now. "She's my brother's blood child."

"Your brother's—" Dante grabbed Bunny's shoulder and shook her. "King is your brother? I thought his name was Charles?"

Bunny shrugged out of his tight clasp and stood. She tugged at the hem of her short skirt. "Really, Dante, I thought you were smarter. Didn't have that one figured out? Pity. The mouse has some stupid Fabergé egg. King wants it. You going to hand it over?"

Dante flashed a look to Kyler, but it said nothing; in fact, his eyes looked dark, almost black. But within a few seconds gears seemed to turn inside his brain and he suddenly nodded and said to Bunny, "Yes."

"What?" Kyler had found her voice. She didn't like that Dante intended to give something so valuable— and deadly—to the bitch with fangs. "That's not yours to give away."

"It's not yours to keep, Mouse." Bunny rapped matte violet fingernails on the café table. "My brother sent you to Venice for it, and you agreed to bring it back. You have it on you?" she asked Dante.

"No, I'll have to retrieve it from a hiding place. Can we meet, say, in a few hours? Perhaps someplace private."

"Mmm, I adore privacy." Bunny leaned forward and licked Dante's forehead. "The Jardin des Plantes. Midnight." And she turned and strode off, walking across the street and causing a car to screech to a halt. Bunny flipped off the driver.

"What the hell?" Kyler stood, wanting to run off, but not wanting to give Dante the advantage of then having the egg all to himself. As long as they stuck together, she still had a say over what happened to it. "I thought we were going to keep the dangerous vampire-killing spell out of the big bad vampire's hands?"

"She always called him Charles," Dante said. "You know, I've known Margot's brother as Charles—never met him, mind you—but have never known him as King. Which means I have met him. This is…mind blowing."

"Who cares about a stupid name?" Frustration tightening her fists, Kyler had to shake her hands at her sides to keep from grabbing him. "We are not handing over the egg to Bitch Bunny."

"Bunny," he said in wonder.

Kyler grabbed him by the shoulders. "Would you quit reminiscing about fucking her? This is serious."

"It is." He pulled her hands from his shoulders and lured her onto his lap. Softly, he kissed her mouth, intruding on her anger with sweetness and warmth. He pressed his forehead to hers. "I apologize. That kiss from Bunny was uncalled for."

Thoroughly calmed by his tender kiss, Kyler let her shoulders fall, and she dropped the urge to beat on him. "I'm angry. But more at myself than you. Trust me on that one."

"Margot de Valois is an aggressive, domineering, steel-balls bitch of a woman. She is an incredible force. And she was once queen of France."

"What?"

"That woman is Marguerite de Valois."

"Really? *The* Queen Marguerite from like…the sixteenth century? Didn't Alexandre Dumas write a story about her?"

He nodded. "And I cannot believe she'd never used her brother's moniker of King around me before. She has always called him Charles. I knew the brother was vampire. The very vampire who transformed her. But I never knew he was—and is—King. This changes things."

"How so?"

"Kyler, the founder of the Order of the Stake was once king of France."

"That's…weird. And confusing. But I still don't understand why it's important."

"Everything has changed. Maybe. The Council will want to hear about this. As well, Christian, my tribe leader, will like to be in the know, I'm sure. King was *the* king? And a vampire who hunts his own. It's hard to fathom, but I can't focus on that right now. We need to retrieve the egg."

"No. Please, I don't want to give those two such a dangerous weapon."

"The egg itself is not dangerous. It's the spell contained inside that they want. And I've never been worried that would fall into the wrong hands."

"Why not? Wait." She clutched his tie and met his dancing gaze. "Are you serious? Did you—"

He nodded. A sexy curl teased the corner of his lips.

"Of course, you would have had no other reason to put it out there for the wolves to scent. And by doing so, you intended to lure them off of our scent. You took the spell out of the egg. When? Before you put it in the safe at your palazzo? After, when we got to Paris?"

"Does it matter? Kyler, I have the spell, safe and sound. The egg, while a precious object d'art, means nothing to me beyond preserving history. And, as you've said, it has served as a red herring of sorts."

"So we can hand over the egg—but King will try to open it. He knows the spell is inside. Your subterfuge won't solve anything because when he sees the spell is missing, he'll come after us again."

"Right. But it will give us time. And right now, we need it. I have no clue where to go with this situation. Do you?"

"No." She laid her head on his shoulder. The warmth of him wafted into her being. Placing a hand over his heart, it didn't take long before their heartbeats synched. "Did you love her?"

"Margot? I did. As I love all women."

That told her a lot. Because when Dante loved a woman, Kyler had come to realize it wasn't a true and abiding love. It was surface and shallow, just fleeting admiration.

"Do you love me?"

He tilted her chin up to face him and studied her gaze. "I'm damned if I do with that question."

"I don't need an answer." She did, but she wouldn't be needy. Not when there were much more important issues literally at stake. "It was silly to ask. I just—"

He kissed her. Deeply. Abidingly. And with a commanding control that told her this kiss he wanted, and it wasn't something he thought he needed to do simply to please a woman. Dante's kiss took hold of her apprehensions and wrung them smooth, softening and caressing. The kiss entreated her to understand. To move along with him, because right now that was what worked for him.

When she pulled away he pressed his forehead to hers and kissed the tip of her nose. "I like you, Kyler."

Her heartbeat speeded up at that simple statement. That meant more than a well-practiced "I love you." It meant that the man's veneer was cracking and that she might have crept inside of him.

"I like you, too. A lot."

"Let's get the egg from the locker," he said. "We'll hand it over to Bunny, then leave for Venice where we can avoid detection, at least for a while. It'll give us a head start."

"Sounds like a poor plan, but I don't have anything better to suggest. We'll do it your way. Do you have the spell on you right now?"

"Why do you ask?"

"I'd like to see it. Just, you know, I want to take a look at what I risked my life to steal."

"It's written in Latin. It wouldn't mean anything to you."

"So you're not going to share with your kitten?" She pulled on a pouty face for effect.

With a surrendering shake of his head, and an ill-concealed smile, he reached inside his suit coat and pulled out a folded piece of paper. Just like that. Carrying it around on him as if it were a grocery list or some other insignificant writing. Kyler sat up on his lap, turning to settle against his chest, and he handed her the paper.

"It's very old, so be careful. It was torn from the bottom of a page in *The Vampire Codex*, though I'm not sure what that greater page was. More spells?"

"This little piece of paper will kill thousands?" Kyler carefully unfolded it and studied the words, but he was right—the Latin looked like scribbles to her. A runic language, for all she knew. *The Vampire Codex* sounded mysterious yet intriguing. This paranormal realm of which she'd only recently become a member would ever fascinate—yet also frighten. "What's this drawing here?"

"I've never been sure."

She traced what looked like the bottom half of a circle, drawn with fading red ink. It was a spotted tube of sorts and on the right side, where the paper was frayed from the tear, the narrow tube expanded in a sort of head shape.

"An ouroboros," she said in an excited whisper.

"What?"

"It looks like the bottom half of an ouroboros. You know, the symbol of a snake swallowing its own tail."

"He who eats his own tail," Dante recited. "Yes, a symbol of eternity. What could that mean? King is killing his own kind for…"

"He really does want eternity," Kyler guessed. "And maybe this spell is part of a larger eternity spell. It makes sense. Why else would such a symbol be on this paper?"

"That's assuming your guess about the symbol is correct. Though it does make a weird sense. So he really is after eternity? Perhaps the page from *The Vam-*

pire Codex that he holds is the actual eternity spell, and this is merely an ingredient to it."

"Killing thousands of vampires an ingredient? That makes me sick. And what's *The Vampire Codex*?"

"It's book of spells, history and foretellings for the vampire nation. A valuable and singular item that is under some kind of magical protection. It's similar to the witches' Book of All Spells. Like the master bible of the species. Something like that. I've never seen it. But I am aware King owns a page from it, because my creator, Zara, told me. I hadn't thought to put the two together—the Codex page and this spell—until right now."

He hugged her against him, and she tucked the spell back in his pocket. "Can't we destroy that paper so no one will ever have such power?"

"We could." He kissed the crown of his head. "But then we'd have nothing with which to bargain. And I sense we're going to need such a chip sooner rather than later. Come along with me, Kitten. Let's head back to the train station."

Fifteen minutes later they rounded a corner and headed toward the Gare de Nord. Dante still couldn't get Kyler's question out of his brain, and his lacking answer. *Do you love me?* His usual response was to answer with a few kisses and say, "Of course I love you, darling. I adore you." Kiss, kiss. Fuck, fuck. Goodbye. It's how his love life was structured.

Love was his veneer, his armor. A false kind of emotion he used as a shield to placate and appease.

So why hadn't he reeled off the usual reply to Kyler?

She was different. She didn't deserve the indifferent dismissal. She deserved—well, he knew what she deserved but also knew he wasn't the man to give it to her. Real love. Trust. Honor. All that admirable stuff. It wasn't in his nature. Hell, he'd been raised in a brothel. An understanding of love and monogamy did not run in his veins. He was unchangeable.

Though something inside him was beginning to shift. To soften, perhaps? It confused him. He wanted to shove it away, yet at the same time he simply wanted to surrender and say, "Have at me!"

But in the absence of any solid assertions of his current emotional state, he could offer few comforting words.

"You're quiet," he said as they walked by touristy storefronts that were closing for the evening. "You have every right to be angry over the scene at the café."

"I can't remain mad over some chick kissing you. I know she was doing it to get a rise out of me. Besides, you're not mine and I'm not yours. You can kiss whomever you like."

"Is that so? But I thought you liked me?"

This woman was so maddening in her ever-shifting alliances to his heart!

"I do. But that doesn't give me any sort of ownership over your heart. You, Casanova, are a free man." She strode ahead of him.

Dante's heart did something strange. It stopped for a moment or two. And in those moments he felt the empty ache for something more. He wanted her to care. He wanted…to be hers.

She glanced over her shoulder. "You coming?"

And because he would follow her everywhere, he said, "Yes."

Once inside the Gare du Nord, they both came to an abrupt stop before the shocking appearance of the rental locker. Dante tilted his head and closed his eyes, opening his senses to the cluttered surroundings. Scent of dog lingered in the air. They'd just missed the culprits.

"Now what?" Kyler asked, a touch of franticness in her tone.

He ran a fingertip along the metal locker door that had been sheared open to look like a curling rooster tail by what could have only been a werewolf claw. He noticed a traveler standing not twenty feet away, staring at them, and shrugged as if to say, "Guess I'll never get this one locked again." Inside the locker sat a manila envelope that contained some legal documents related to his estate. He'd placed it in there years earlier. The envelope hadn't been touched.

The egg was not inside.

He'd thought to get here before the wolves had tracked it down.

"The wolves don't know how to open the egg," Kyler said. "Not that it matters with the spell in your pocket. But now there's King and the Bunny bitch. What do we do about them?"

Dante's jaw pulsed. He turned and marched toward the exit doors.

Time for plan B. And they hadn't even had a decent plan A.

Chapter 16

They walked across the Pont de Sully to the Left Bank, Kyler trailing behind Dante at times because his pace was relentless. At other times, she picked up her pace and paralleled him, as she did now. He hadn't spoken much since they'd left the train station, and the walk had been long. He was fuming, and yet she couldn't understand why. If he already had the spell, then who cared about the egg beyond the fact it was valuable? Dante wasn't a man who cared about material things. Other than a bespoke suit.

"We don't have to meet her now," Kyler offered, swinging her arms to keep up the pace. "Bunny."

His pace slowed a little. "Yes, we still have to see Bunny. Bunny! That name is ridiculous."

It was. "Does the name bother you because it's childish and immature or because you actually slept with a woman who calls herself Bunny?"

He cast her a glance, and it wasn't so heavy with anger any more. *Good.* She didn't like serious Dante. She preferred him suave and amiable.

"You have me there," he replied. "But trust me—I've slept with some oddly named women over the decades."

"I've had a few strange names in my bed, as well." She wasn't about to let him have this one. And she felt the need to bring the tension down to a more manageable level.

"Name one," he asked.

"How about...Crawford?"

"Doesn't sound so terrible."

"It is when every time he leans in to kiss you all you can think about is crawfish."

Dante laughed and clasped her hand. They slowed to wait for a few cars before crossing the Rue Cuvier and heading down a tree-lined sidewalk.

"Well, I have slept with a Gladys," he stated.

Kyler chuckled. "I suppose all the Gladyses of the world were once young at some point, eh?"

"She was lovely, as I recall. And the name, at the time, was equally as lovely. Your turn."

"Okay, how about Ruby?"

"A man?"

"Yep. Kind of weird, right? He had red hair, too. I don't even want to go there. That may have been my first, and only, walk of shame. Messy hair and heels hooked on my fingers. Oh yeah!"

"Ruby. Ha! Let's see...how about Anastasia?"

"That's a pretty name."

"Yes, but it must be said with an uppity, nasal intonation and an inflated sense of entitlement."

"Okay, I'll give you that one. But I've got one more."

"Fine, but I don't think you'll top mine."

They paused at the entrance to the Jardin des Plantes and Kyler said, "King."

Dante nodded in acknowledgment of defeat. "You win."

Dante and Kyler strolled down the moonlight-sprinkled allées in the Jardin des Plantes. Rose scent mingled with jasmine and pine. Fruiting citrus trees promised tangy bursts of summer. And everywhere the greenery blossomed with abundant life.

No tourists this late, though he almost wished there were. He was uptight and pissed at how everything had gone down lately. He needed a good long draft of blood. And he wanted nothing more than to take Kyler in his arms, strip off her clothes and make love to her while he fed on her blood.

He shook off the thought and put Bunny in his brain. *Bunny.* Talk about the past springing up to haunt a man. Not that he'd ever cared for the woman. Theirs had been a brief encounter, a week or more, perhaps. All sex. No blood, despite her pouting insistence on the exchange. She had exhausted him. He'd come away with an appreciation for a strong woman, as well as a dislike for a demanding woman. And he knew Bunny was wicked and would do whatever necessary to get what she wanted.

"You and Bunny," Kyler said. "Tell me about that."

Should he answer it truthfully or embellish their history? Kyler deserved only the truth.

"We had a fling," he responded to her avid curiosity. "Toward the end of the nineteenth century, if I recall my dates correctly. It was during the World's Fair Expo when the Eiffel Tower had been newly erected. We climbed to the top one night and fucked up there."

"Wow. I have no words. That's got to take some daring, if not careful, acrobatics."

He laughed at her easy acceptance of that stark truth. "Margot—er, Bunny has always been aggressive. She tells you what she wants. You can either comply or walk away."

"I imagine not too many men walk away from all that."

Dante chuckled again. "She is a sex bomb, for sure. But she's dangerous. I'm not so stupid as to be attracted to the wickedness beneath the outer flash and glamour."

"What about mice?"

"Mice?" *Ah.* "Seriously, Kyler? You are not a mouse. Don't let that bitch get into your head." He clasped her hand to reassure her. From the pulse beats at her wrists, he'd noticed their heartbeats synched much faster now. That was cool. Must be a result of their sharing blood. "You have nothing to fear regarding my ever again hooking up with that woman."

"Then why are we here? The egg is gone. You have the spell in a safe place. Well—not so safe, but at least you know where it is." She patted his chest right over the pocket where he'd tucked the spell. "Why come here to tell her that? Let her and her lying brother stumble about looking for it on their own."

"If we didn't show, they'd know something was up. By meeting tonight we're showing the Valois siblings that we were duped, too. Now it's in their hands to go after the wolves and leave us alone. Yes?"

"Maybe. I think King is too smart for that."

"Yes, well, fortunately, Bunny is not. She puts on a good show. But beneath the bravado she's a woman desperate for love and attention. Allow me to work my charm."

"Oh, brother. Do I have to stand by and watch?"

Dante batted at a bee that buzzed near his head. "I promise it won't get out of hand."

"I don't get it," Kyler said as their stroll angled them toward the insectarium. "Wasn't Marguerite de Valois like sixty years old when she died? The chick who sucked on your tonsils at the café was still in her twenties."

"A clever imposter, the queen most read about in the history books," Dante provided, having heard the whole detailed story from Marguerite over truffles and wine one evening. "The real Margot de Valois only reigned about ten years. Her brother Charles was instrumental in making sure history was ever unaware that the royal family had turned to vampirism. He transformed their brother, Henri, as well, though Margot is unsure whether or not he still lives. Damn. I had never put it together after all these years. That the leader of a band of vampire hunters was possibly a real king *and* he was also a vampire."

"But you wouldn't have believed he could kill his own kind."

"Knowing now that King is Charles IX, former Valois, and king of France? Oh, yes, I believe he could

commit genocide. The man comes from Catherine de
Médici's womb. The entire family was bloodthirsty and
vile. Bunny!"

A simmer of buzzing insects lured Dante to the edge
of the pebbled walkway, and he eyed a hemp rope bee
skep. Leaning against the massive conical thing, one
elbow propped on the skep and bees buzzing around
her like the queen she was, stood Marguerite de Valois,
former queen of France and Navarre—aka Bunny.

The vampiress, still clad in the sexy black dress and
thigh-high boots, flipped her long hair over a shoulder
and approached. A halo of bees orbited above her head.
None of them seemed eager to sting or touch down on
her pale, moon-showered skin.

"I see you brought along the mouse." Bunny sighed
dramatically. "You've really got to watch out for your
reputation, Dante."

"The only thing that may tarnish my reputation's
shine is a certain leather-clad rabbit."

"And what fun such tarnish would bring." She fluttered her lashes and licked her upper lip.

"I don't have the egg," Dante announced bluntly. At
Bunny's dropped jaw, he explained about finding the
locker at the train station ripped open. "It was obvious
who committed such vandalism. The wolves have it.
I'm not sure which pack they were from, though. We
encountered them on a few occasions while in Venice."

"So that's that?" Bunny asked. "You can't find the
thing—now you're just going to walk away?'

"What do you want me to do? Help you find something that will give your brother the power to destroy

not only Kyler and myself but all the vampires in Paris? I think I'm good with stepping back and letting you handle this one now. You have all the information I have. Wolves have the Nécessaire egg. You can go to the Gare du Nord and scent them out yourself. As for Kyler and I…" He clasped her hand. "We're done with you. And your brother is done with Kyler. She has performed the task he asked of her. It isn't her fault it was stolen from her."

Bunny stepped up and shook a fist at them. "She fucked it all up is what she did. I should take her out right—"

Dante slammed a hand around Bunny's tiny fist. "Stop. Step back. Think this one through. I know things about your brother now that I'm sure he would like to keep a secret from the Council. If you so much as disturb the air about Kyler, I will retaliate. You and King back off. Got it?"

Bunny drew a pouting gaze over Kyler and lifted her nose in mockery. "She's not worth it, Dante." And she strode off, heels crunching the loose gravel at the edge of the sidewalk, a spin of bees still dancing above her head. "This isn't over!" she called over a shoulder. "Not until we have that damned egg."

"Your charm was sorely lacking," Kyler commented. "Good show."

Dante exhaled and pulled her into an embrace. He knew it wasn't over. He'd never expected Bunny would walk away and let them go on living their lives in peace. He'd threatened King. And he'd meant it. And Bunny knew that.

"We're not safe, are we?" Kyler asked.

He kissed the crown of her head. "You're always safe with me, Kitten. I give you my word. Let's go back to your place. I want to make love to you."

"Why? Because you need to work off the horny vibes from Bunny?"

"No, because I want to feel you against my skin. And taste you in my mouth."

She tugged him to a stop. The look on her face was doubtful.

"You are jealous of Bunny?"

She sighed. "She was right. I'm not worth it. I got you into this mess, but I really should try—"

He grabbed her, pulling her against him and pressing a hard, bruising kiss to her mouth. She initially struggled but quickly relented, grasping his shirt and melding her curves to his hard structure. She fit him like no other. He wasn't sure why she still felt she had to struggle against him. Didn't she understand what she meant to him?

No, she could not, because he'd yet to speak it in words.

"You are worth so much more to me than you can ever imagine, Kyler. Remember...I like you."

Her lashes fluttered. Her eyes looked from one of his to the other. She didn't speak but instead nodded. And he was glad she didn't question him. Even if only a few simple words, he'd spoken from his heart. And he meant it. Because he wanted to make her his. For longer than he, a self-professed Casanova who might never settle down with one woman, could feasibly imagine.

Chapter 17

Bunny strode down the limestone-walled hallway toward her brother's office. She had been given access to the Order's headquarters centuries earlier, and despite Charles changing the access code on her many times, she still managed to get in. Because no one was going to keep her out of anything.

She did not enjoy walking these weirdly cold stone hallways beneath a Catholic church. They still, apparently, held services on Sundays. She had been baptized, and while there was no need to go through the actual church to access the Order headquarters, being this close gave her a shiver.

That she could no longer kneel before the cross and worship the God who had given her life disturbed her. She'd never come to terms with that. And while her family had a history of using religion in the most wicked and foul ways possible, she still believed. She was a good Catholic girl.

Who liked to bite.

And she was also the girl who was so over trying to help her brother destroy vampires. He could have his little boy's club and poke the occasional vampire with a pointy stick. But lay flat an entire population? It reeked of the St. Bartholomew's Day massacre that had destroyed her wedding party in the sixteenth century (not to mention a few thousand Huguenots; no loss there).

Yet Bunny wasn't taking any credit for that.

She knocked on the office door and entered before her brother could invite her in. She'd been in here before. Didn't need an invitation.

Charles moved swiftly to stand before his desk, hands behind him. An oddly suspicious look brightened into a rare smile and she paused before him, hands on her hips. "What's up, brother dearest?"

"Nothing," he said. Which meant everything.

"I wasn't able to get—"

"This." He moved aside. He'd never been able to keep a secret from her for long. On the desktop sat a gold egg embellished with sparkling gemstones. It was about the size of a human skull.

"What the hell?" Bunny lunged for it, but her brother caught her wrist. "Where did that come from? Dante said wolves stole it from the train station locker—wait. Do you have werewolves working for you? Did you even need my help?" She shoved him away from her and stalked behind the desk. "I am done with this undermining bullshit! You're always second-guessing me and sending in the cavalry."

"If I recall correctly, you've been in need of just such bullshit over the centuries."

Ignoring his statement of the obvious, she grabbed the egg and shook it. It clattered as if there were a hidden surprise inside.

"How do you open this thing?"

"I have no idea." Charles put up a leg on the corner of the desk and watched her play with it. "I suspect D'Arcangelo is one of the very few who has that knowledge."

"Why would he know?"

"Because he owned the thing for decades. It was given to him by Zara Destry for safe keeping. *After* she stole the spell from me while I had *The Vampire Codex* in possession."

"Zara Destry," Bunny said with all the vitriol she held for the fruity piece of sunshine and murder.

That vampire bitch had been transforming males against their wills for centuries, biting them and running off. She'd changed Dante, leaving him with little knowledge of what to do about his sudden craving for blood. And a broken heart. Of course, he had asked for it. Poor little boy who'd lost his courtesan mother because she couldn't handle growing old. Fortunately Bunny had come along to teach Dante a few things. Whether or not those *things* had anything to do with vampirism was something she couldn't recall or care about.

"How did D'Arcangelo know werewolves had taken it?" Charles asked. "Careful with that, Margot."

She set the thing down with a clunk, then sat on the plush leather office chair with an equal lack of grace. Crossing her arms, she hiked the heels of her boots up onto the desk corner. "He said it was obvious by the claw marks torn through the steel locker where he'd stashed this thing at the train station. Your thugs were indiscreet."

"They got the job done."

"You sent me after Dante, knowing you had already sent out the wolves. And since when do you work with fucking werewolves? I thought that Remington asshole almost burned you recently?"

"Remington Caufield is a minor annoyance. Besides, I've relegated him to the States. Out of sight, out of mind."

Bunny knew differently. Caufield was in possession of some very damning letters sent from Charles to a particular werewolf female. Postmarked mid-nineteenth century. Proof of some illegitimate half-wolf/half-vamp children? That was one secret with which Charles would never trust her.

Her brother didn't notice her annoyance. "And if I do something kind for a pack, I expect returned kindness."

Bunny scoffed. "Since when does *the king* hand out kindnesses?"

"Sister dearest, why are you so down on me? Have I ever harmed you, taken a hand to you or otherwise done anything to frighten you?"

The man seemed to forget their early years, the mortal years when her brothers had loved her—too intimately. And roughly. She'd welcomed the liaisons, not knowing any better at the time, and finding a sexual alliance with a brother had always been useful for court intrigues. They had saved her ass on more than a few occasions when her mother would have fed her to the human wolves to secure a political alliance. The woman had been infamous for ordering her enemies' deaths by her favorite weapon: poison.

Charles had transformed Margot to vampire, much to her protestations. She'd wanted to reign as queen, not be replaced by some idiot lookalike to sit the throne in her absence. That woman had gone on to write *her* memoirs as if she really were the actual queen of France! Ridiculous. Of course, she'd gotten fat. Served the bitch right. On the other hand, it was those puffy-faced illustrations of her that had been preserved in history books. So wrong.

And yet Bunny had come to embrace vampirism, and could never be sorry for such a gift. As well, she was thankful for being saved the indignity of sharing a bed with the insipid Henri de Navarre.

"Yes, well…" She flipped her hair over a shoulder. "Dante didn't seem all that upset that the egg was gone. Told me to run along, that the matter was our concern now."

"Really?" Charles leaned forward, pressing his knuckles onto the desk. His intense brown gaze both attracted and horrified her. He had grown hard over the centuries. Adamant. There was no hope for his wretched soul. "Tell me truthfully—you don't think he'll continue to search for it?"

She shrugged. "I think he gave up. Seemed kind of relieved to have the thing out of hand. Truthfully. He took his mousy girlfriend's hand and walked away. And I don't feel as though it was an act. I do know when a man lies to me."

"Damn it!" Charles smashed a fist onto the table.

The egg wobbled, and Bunny reached to catch it with both hands. "What is it?"

"There's no spell inside that egg. D'Arcangelo has taken it out. The physical egg is of no value to either of us. It's always been what is inside. The spell, damn it, the spell!"

Bunny rapped her fingernails on the desktop. So Dante had gotten one over on her. And for some reason, she didn't mind tossing him the point. "Maybe that's a good thing. I can't say I'm behind you destroying an entire city of vampires, Charles—"

"It is King," he said through a tight jaw. "And the spell is merely the catalyst to what I really desire."

Bunny tilted her head, stuck out her tongue and rolled it along her upper lip. "Of course, it can't be as easy as that for you. What are you after, brother dearest?"

"Super immortality."

"What?" She laughed. "I don't even know what that means. Wait. Is this the eternity stuff you wanted me on board with? This is getting complicated."

"It's actually very simple." Charles strode around the side of the desk, opened the top drawer and pulled out a yellowed piece of paper about the size of a notebook sheet with the bottom torn away. It was nearly brown with age and featured tiny black scrawls in a language Bunny couldn't interpret.

"This is from *The Vampire Codex*," he said. "I managed to briefly get the book, stolen from a retriever in the nineteenth century. It is a spell to grant me eternity. The missing part on the bottom? It was torn away by Zara fucking Destry. She hid it away, or perhaps she gave it to Dante immediately to get me off her scent. I only later learned he'd been its keeper. No matter. It is the key part to the spell which, I'm told, requires the ashes of a thousand vampires. See this?"

He traced a small red half circle at the bottom of the page where the spell had been torn away. Bunny thought it looked like a snake. And then she realized it was a snake eating its tail, a symbol of eternity.

Yet while it sounded good in theory, she still didn't understand. "Charles, you have immortality. What more is there?"

"A guarantee to never die, not by stake, beheading or holy object. I would be immune to holy objects, Margot! Can you imagine? *We* could be immune! Never again to have to flee because a simple Bible has been thrust before me." He rubbed his hand, studying the side of it briefly.

"Yes, that sounds awesome. But—I don't know. Killing so many to achieve something you can only give to one or two vampires? That's not right."

He gaped at her.

"I know." She felt the need to continue. "Our family

has committed horrible crimes over the years. Well, I have not. I mean, I try not to. Charles. Please. You're depressed, yes? Maybe you need a vacation? To step down from heading this stupid little club of yours and go off and…have a real life. Take a wife. Make a family. Don't you want to hear the patter of little feet as they gnash out and test their fangs?"

He slammed his hand on the desk before her. His fangs lowered, indicating not that he would lunge for her, only that she had pushed him to anger. "I will have this! I deserve this peace. No one has suffered more for the common people. And even now, I protect them from the dangerous and deranged vampires who would mark them as their dinner target."

Her brother had never lost the pompous entitlement of royalty. Not that there was anything wrong with that. She kept her crown in a safe-deposit box, and occasionally stopped by to try it on. But their reigns had ended centuries ago. And Charles could not rule over the vampires while also executing them.

Bunny pulled her feet down and leaned forward, meeting her brother's gaze. "You would sacrifice thousands for one?"

"I will. With the spell enacted by the warlock I have engaged to assist me and the ash of a thousand vampires. I will collect that ash."

"A warlock, eh? Ian Grim?"

King drew a breath through his nose, pacing a few steps toward the door and pressing a hand to the wall near it. He looked over his shoulder at her. "I won't involve Grim. That man…he's—you do know who he is?"

She shrugged. "A fucking warlock. Been around since—hell, long as I can remember."

King shrugged. "He's…almost family to me."

"I don't get that. I've never been introduced to him. He's not *my* family."

"Rook is also like a brother to me."

"Yes, I know that."

Rook was King's second hand, his ally; they had been friends since the early seventeenth century. They stood side by side, slaying vampires in the name of Charles's twisted sense of vengeance for being turned into a vampire himself. Who would ever expect a vampire behind the Order of the Stake? Not even the Council.

"What Grim means to me is not your concern," he said. "Instead, I've hired the warlock Boa to enact the spell."

Bunny swore. She'd heard that name only once. And it had been muttered as a vile welcome to all that was truly evil and malicious. And while she did enjoy living on the edge and pushing life to the limits—she was ever wary immortality did come with an asterisk that detailed "avoid stakes"—if Charles were bringing in the warlock, she preferred to leave the immediate vicinity.

She stepped toward the door and put up her palms in staunch refusal. "I'm out."

"I thought you'd say that. And I respect your decision. Much as I could probably use your help to soften up D'Arcangelo and tease the spell out of him, I won't involve you further. You should probably get as far away from Paris as you can. The spell can't discriminate from one vampire to the next."

"I'm headed for Russia."

"Should I ask?"

He needn't, because he already knew she was on yet another trip seeking adventure, good times and as many handsome and virile men as she could manage.

She took his hand and hugged him. "Charles, are you sure about this?"

He nodded. "I've been searching for the missing piece from the eternity spell since the middle of the last century. I am more than ready."

"Even if it means ending the lives of so many?"

"You should go now." He kissed her and then held his mouth against the corner of her lips for the longest time. "Don't hate me."

"I hate you." She kissed him back quickly. "I love you. We will always be family, good, bad and evil."

While he should be more concerned werewolves believed they had their hands on a device that could destroy hundreds, perhaps even thousands, of vampires, Dante was currently focused on the curve of Kyler's neck where it segued into her shoulder. She smelled like softness and the roses pinking the Jardin des Plantes.

He'd pulled off her shirt and tossed it aside the moment they'd stepped inside her place. Pushing her against the wall by the door, he hiked up her leg along his hip and dove along her skin, tasting, kissing and nipping the heat of her salted perfume. The pulse of her heartbeat was so close. Just a tilt of his head to the left.

"You're hungry," she cooed and slid her hands down his shirt, unbuttoning it with an ease he appreciated.

"For a bite," he murmured. He quickly loosened his tie, but before he could pull it off he kissed her right over the vein. She didn't tense, and he took that as a sign that she was ready and willing to give blood.

He would take it because she was his. And only his.

Dante lifted Kyler and carried her into the bedroom. Moonlight danced across the gray bedspread and painted hardwood floor. The room looked cold, but holding Kyler warmed him soul deep. He laid her on the bed and tugged down her pants. She wore no panties, and with a flick of his fingers he quickly relegated the lacy bra to the floor. He took a few moments to glide his gaze over her moon-dappled skin. The pale luxuriousness of her stomach, the sweet rises of her hips. Her breasts sat high, and the nipples were so tight he had to kiss each one in turn. He loved how the areola tightened under his tongue.

She curled her finger and enticed him up to again kiss her neck. "Come here, lover boy. Don't you want another bite?"

"Kitten," he murmured. "You are something I never wish to resist. But you must know that I've never allowed another vampire to bite me before you. Save for my transformation."

"I suspected that." She held him away to meet her eyes. Lush black lashes, highlighted with a line of kohl, fluttered. "I don't know how you've been able to resist. You've been vampire so long…"

"Truth?" It was getting easier to share his deepest secrets with her for reasons that baffled him, but with which he wouldn't struggle. "I've never wanted a woman to have that much of me."

"I get that. Especially knowing the conditions in which you were raised. So why me? Aren't I the last woman you'd ever trust? I think, at times, I hate you more than I like you."

"Your hate feels remarkably exquisite in those moments. It seems I don't mind so much giving myself to you. I had thought to resist the shared bite, but..." He patted his chest right over his heart. "It's something I can't put into words."

"You don't need to. But if you want to take things more slowly, I do understand."

"I don't think it's possible to go slow with you. That's another thing I like about you. You don't stand back and wait for my direction. If I'm at a loss, you simply take the lead and dive in. You challenge me, Kyler."

"I do like a good challenge." She brushed a forefinger over his mouth and teased it open to tap his fang. "These are so sexy."

He allowed his jaw to drop open, giving her better access to his fangs. The stroke of her fingers against them was equal to that when she stroked his cock. It shuddered through his system as if his fangs were directly connected to his genitals. *Mercy.* She wasn't afraid of anything.

Not even the unknown longing she'd opened up in his heart.

"I've no intention of going slow with you, Kitten."

He laved his tongue over her finger, then grazed a fang tip along the length of it. "Ask of me what you wish."

Her playful grin revealed her lowering fangs. "May I have some more, pretty please?"

"Always. Take what you will and know that I trust only you."

Her fangs pierced his skin with ease and a sweet promising pain. Every touch from Kyler held such promise. As she licked and sucked at his blood, Dante pulled her on top of him. The orgasmic sensation of his blood leaving his body was indescribable, yet to increase the high he pumped his erection against her thigh, rubbing it harder and faster.

Finally he could resist no longer, and he dove to sink his fangs into her neck. *Mmm, utter bliss.* Hot blood filled his mouth and caressed his throat as if it was a liquid hug from Kyler. He clasped her across the back and lifted her breasts against his chest, thumbing a nipple as she sucked at his life and he at hers. The shared feeding went beyond satisfying a hunger for sustenance. It fed his soul.

And when they'd slaked that rapturous thirst, Kyler kissed the puncture wounds on his neck. He felt them heal with a pulling tightness. "When we share blood," she whispered in his ear, "it goes deep."

"Yes, I know. All inside me."

"No, Dante, like I feel it in my soul. It's hard to explain, and…I know you won't get it, but I'm not afraid to tell you this means so much to me."

"Yes." He spoke his thoughts. "I can understand that kind of soul deep." And he did. Because she touched him in a way no other woman had. Dare he allow her to love him? Could he love her in return? A part of him wanted to grasp that hope. Perhaps he already had. "As I've said, I trust you, Kyler. You own me. My soul."

"I'll take it. Now." She kissed him and glided a finger down between her breasts and to the top of her mons. "Blood was a treat, but now I want you to make your kitten purr."

"I can do that."

Chapter 18

Dante placed the toothbrush back in the medicine cabinet where he'd gotten it. He wasn't sure why Kyler stocked five extra toothbrushes, but he couldn't knock having the option the morning following a night of sex. Actually, afternoon. It must be after one, he figured. It was pouring rain, so it was difficult to determine the time from the sky, and he couldn't find his cell phone to check. Probably lying under a blanket or a piece of abandoned clothing.

He stretched a palm over his tight, hard abs and then turned to the side, almost glancing in the mirror. Lately he assessed his appeal in Kyler's eyes.

He needed that admiration. Or he had, until very recently. He released a breath, and his gut relaxed. Still firm, as it would remain, for vampirism tended to preserve a person's shape, whatever that may have been at the time of their transformation.

Did it matter how he dressed or the looks he gave a woman? He'd picked up mannerisms and ways to seduce and attract from his mother and her collection of prostitutes. They had moved to appeal to a man's eyes. He moved to attract a woman's eye. They had spoken to enhance a man's self-esteem and make him feel powerful. He spoke to capture a woman's interest and instill confidence. They had touched to grant pleasure, while harboring power in that touch. He touched to instill a wanting desire, while maintaining his control and power.

He bit into the vein to please himself. That was something his mother could have never taught him.

He glanced at the closed bathroom door. Kyler was still lazing in bed. With her he didn't feel compelled to put on the act of the rogue, the Casanova. He wasn't that man around her. Or at least, he couldn't find that man when lying beside her, enjoying her warmth and the acceptance she gave him. What was that about?

She was falling in love with him. And it didn't bother him as much as he thought it should. He wasn't about to consider if he, in turn, were falling in love with her. He wasn't ready to face that truth.

He rubbed a brow with his thumb. By now he would have bitten the woman—only once—fucked her more than enough times to ensure she never forgot his name and then sent her on her way. On to the next amorous adventure.

Was it because Kyler needed his help? A knight

adorned in Armani and bespoke leather shoes to protect the lush damsel? With hope, he'd solved that dilemma by giving Bunny the endgame handoff. Yet still he wanted Kyler to stay with him. To not leave him alone. Because he now felt that the next woman could never be as interesting as this one. And that had always been the reason for his quest. To learn the next one's secrets, to examine what differences they all had. To, indeed, add another notch.

To form a blood bond with Kyler, or not to bond? It meant taking a lot of blood, more than he normally would when he slaked his hunger with a human. It was a commitment akin to marriage. To confessing love. He adored Kyler, but he wasn't sure he was ready to plunge in so deeply.

But what was he afraid of? The bonding did not require them to live together and date only the other. It merely made them two of a kind, intimate on a level most others could never dream to share. It would open him to her completely and expose him at an emotional level.

That was it. He didn't know how to do that. Sure, he'd exposed himself by confessing to her his past growing up in a brothel with the relative removal of a bystander. Such memories were distant enough that he could view it that way and not feel the emotional exposure. And he'd learned to leave the past where it belonged. Mostly. Zara still haunted him. She was the only woman who had ever broken his heart.

If he told Kyler he loved her, he then risked her

breaking his heart. He wasn't sure he'd know how to patch up the thing a second time around.

He closed his eyes and drew in the scents of lingering tea tree shampoo steamed to a heady brew by the hot water. Beyond that, he moved his senses through the wood door and into the bedroom, thick with sensual musk and the crisp lavender that clung to the sheets. And Kyler's hair, silken and teased with a hint of rose and citrus from the gardens. Her skin, hot and salty-sweet. And her blood.

Fangs descending in his mouth, Dante parted his lips, allowing the tease of the sharp teeth over his skin to shiver desire through his system. He wanted more of her blood. To feel it running down his throat, coiling into him, becoming a part of his very being.

She thought him the rogue, a man who would simply play with her until he tired. He had to prove to her he could be more.

"I want her," he whispered his sudden revelation, "to want me."

To ask for the bonding. To prove that she could devote herself to him. To become the one person he could trust completely with his fragile heart.

Yet, hadn't she said the same of him? That she'd wanted him on his knees, wanting her?

"Dante?"

Opening his eyes, his senses returned to the bathroom and the dripping showerhead and the taste of toothpaste in his mouth.

"Come to bed," she coaxed from the other side of the door. "I miss you."

Pushing open the door, he padded across the room and stood before the bed.

Kyler eyed his erection. "I can take care of that for you. The fellow looks in need of a kiss."

"If you think so?"

She patted the bed, and he crawled between the sheets and nuzzled up beside her irresistible warmth. Who ever said vampires were cold?

Her fingers wrapped around his cock, and she squeezed and pulled and stretched and played with an expertise she'd gained over but a few days. Touching the head of him against her mons, she slicked her own wetness onto him, and he groaned and buried his face in her hair. Her touch mastered him in ways he couldn't comprehend. Because it wasn't as though other women had not done the same to him. Only with Kyler, he wanted to fall into the feeling and simply…surrender.

"You make me…" he whispered.

But he couldn't put into words how he felt right now. Close to her. Surrounded by her. Desired and wanted. And somehow, in his place.

"You don't have to say it. I'm slowly figuring you out. Love doesn't mean the same thing to you as it does to most."

"Perhaps."

"But you did love that one woman who transformed you?"

"Zara. Yes."

"The only woman you ever loved gave you that egg to protect." Her hand stopped moving, which he silently cursed. Why the urge for conversation when they should only be breathing heavily? "So you went after the egg because if you got it back, you might have gotten her back," she posited.

"No, it's not like that at all. I don't want her back." He meant that. And he believed that. Maybe? "She's moved on. Zara had a tendency to love them and leave them."

"The female Casanova?" She tilted a knowing look at him. Gave his cock a teasing squeeze.

So that was it? Why had he never thought of Zara in that way? And he'd become the thing he'd once loved in an attempt to—what? Carry Zara's memory with him forever? To punish all women as he'd been punished when Zara had left him? He'd been thankful for the gift of vampirism, but when she'd refused to stay and teach him how to adjust to his new condition, only then had Dante realized how little he had ever meant to the callous vampiress.

So why had he kept the egg for her?

That was obvious. Because when she'd asked him he'd felt hope, as if they had another chance. And really, it had been an immense show of trust and he'd felt honored knowing that in his care was something an entire population of vampires would appreciate him protecting.

Kyler had confessed much the same; she'd run back to King with hopes of rekindling what she'd wanted to be a real relationship.

They truly were two of a kind. He understood her. He *trusted* her. And he knew that she could understand him.

"Kyler." He clasped her free hand and kissed it. His

heartbeat thundered, warning him not to do what he felt compelled to express. He had to. He must. It felt as necessary as breathing. "All I've ever wanted is to be loved. I know that's stupid."

"Oh, Dante." She nuzzled her head onto his shoulder and kissed him softly. Another tender squeeze of his cock held him securely. "That's not stupid. In fact, that's the most honest thing you've said since I've met you." She hugged him. Bright blue eyes flashed at him. "You can have love if you learn to recognize it."

The gentle stroking of her thumb against his penis calmed him. Recognizing love? Was it akin to lying quietly in a bed with a woman who had somehow put into words that she understood him? And she did, even if he hadn't put it all together until she'd said it.

"I love you," she said softly. She lazily stroked his cock. "Whether or not you like it, it's the truth. I admire the man you are, and the vampire. You've shown me that I am beautiful and that I'm pretty skilled when it comes to surviving intense life situations. And you are dedicated to keeping a harmful spell out of a monster's hands, thus protecting so many. I aspire to be like you." He looked down at her, and she met his gaze, asking, "Let me love you?"

Such a simple request, and yet he didn't know what to do with it. It felt welcome and vile at the same time. Those very words he had given Zara so many decades ago, thinking, finally, he had found love. And Zara had laughed, even as he'd clutched the Fabergé egg to his heart. A gift from one he'd admired.

He only wished for Kyler to want him. Were they one

and the same, love and wanting? No, he knew they were not. Wanting was superficial and callous. Love, well, it seemed as though the attachment delved to a soul level.

Behind them on the nightstand, a cell phone rang. It was Kyler's ringtone that sounded like chimes. He hoped she would ignore it, and then realized that with everything they had going on right now she had better not.

He clasped a hand about hers, stopping her ministrations, and said through a clenched jaw, "Get it. Please."

She kissed him, then rolled over and checked the phone. "It's him."

"Let me answer it." He took the phone and the immense sexual high crashed and his cock wilted too quickly. *Fuck the bastard vampire hunter.* "King," he said with forced cheeriness. "How's Bunny?"

"She's off to Russia."

"Interesting. I guess she found the egg for you, and now everyone is pleased as punch."

"You're the only one who knows how to open the egg."

"Well, yes, there is that. Need a bit of help?"

"There is no spell inside the egg. You have it. Don't deny it."

Of course, he should have expected King would come to such a conclusion when he hadn't fought Bunny to get the egg back. Poor planning on his part.

"I'll need that spell," King said. "You can bring it to me at ten. I'll be waiting in the aqueducts beneath the Louvre."

"I'm sure I'll be otherwise occupied at the time. So sorry."

"Then you'd better keep a sharp eye on Kyler today. One moment of inattention, and she'll be gone. When that occurs—and it will—you'll know how to get her back. Ten o'clock," he said and hung up.

Dante handed the phone to Kyler, and she spread a hand across his chest. "What did he say?"

"He wants the spell, of course."

"So how do we avoid giving him that? Leave the city? Why can't we just tear it up?"

"I'm not sure. Give me a few minutes to consider this, will you?"

She propped up on her elbows and tried to meet his gaze, but he dodged it. She wanted more, but he wasn't willing to tell her about the threat to her life. Because it was a real threat. One he had best take seriously. But how to *not* give the spell to King *and* keep Kyler safe?

"I'll take a shower," she said.

He nodded and couldn't even distract himself with the sight of her naked body padding out of the bedroom, for his mind spun with how to hide a vampiress from a vampire who would kill his own kind.

After the shower, Kyler dressed, then took to blow drying her hair. And her thoughts wandered as the appliance noise filled the tiny bathroom.

He wasn't in top form. While normally Dante was two steps ahead of her and already planning the next day's moves, Kyler sensed he was out of sorts. For good reason. They'd both been through a lot the past few days.

But she trusted he would know what to do about King wanting the spell. The best thing they could probably do was to leave town. Head to Venice, as initially planned. It wouldn't get King off their asses, but it would give them a head start.

If only there was something she could do to help. Bonding would bring them closer. Maybe make them both stronger. And she wanted that. Yes, even if Dante was going to toss her aside when this was all over. It was in his genes. He didn't do relationships. And she, well, she'd wanted eternity. With all hopes for that dashed, perhaps bonding could be the next best thing.

Should she have admitted she'd fallen in love with him? It was the truth. And she didn't want to dance around it. Nor did she want to accept the brush-off when he did try to walk away from her.

She wanted Dante D'Arcangelo for herself. And fuck all the other women. Especially the Bunny bitch. Because Dante made her want to be the sensual vampire she, at times, felt she was. And he was good to her and for her. If only he could be so good to himself and realize the veneer of lover to all women was simply that, and beneath the sheen of charm, he was a wanting man.

He had admitted that to her—he wanted love. Did he believe it or had he simply been speaking another line from his seductive arsenal?

"I want him to love me," she said as she clicked off the blow-dryer and flipped her hair down over her shoulders. "But I don't want to push him. And I'll take bonding if that's all he's willing to offer."

Dante stood out in the living room, fully dressed.

He buttoned the cuffs of his shirt. Kyler rushed over to help him. He wore no shoes and the casual sexiness of him was something she could never get over.

"No cuff links?" she asked.

"I haven't had a chance to dress properly since my last suit went for a swim in the canal."

"This suit and tie is lovely."

"Yes, and it's Armani. Though not bespoke. You like the violet tie?" He preened the silk in question with his fingers.

"I do. It's an excellent addition to your armor."

"Bespoke armor. I suppose that is the best kind. A knight in armor, shining or otherwise, should always be fitted properly for his raiment. But I'll need to get back home to Venice to speak with my tailor before I feel one hundred percent."

"We should go there now."

"You've the same idea I considered. But do you actually think running away from the problem is going to stop it? He'll find you. And I suspect with our evening deadline looming, he'll make it difficult for us to leave the city."

"What do you mean he'll find me? Did King threaten me? You didn't say anything about that."

Dante winced and bowed his head.

"He *did* threaten me," she guessed. "What? Like if you don't bring him the spell, he'll kill me? You're not going to let him get away with that, are you?"

"Absolutely not. But, Kyler, the man hunts vampires for a living. I'm a little out of my element here. I need… weapons. Crossbows and even bullets. Some religious items. And—the stake." He sniffed the air and looked at her. "You smell that?"

She sniffed and noticed only the rainy air and the usual burned-sugar scent that wafted up from a nearby patisserie.

"Werewolves. Down on the street. I'm sure of it," he said. "I think that bastard is working with a pack. Or they are working for him. That's the only way to explain the wolves taking the egg and King telling me he had it. Is there a way out of here via the roof?"

"Yes. Down the hall is the roof access. You're sure it's wolves?"

"Positive. Put on your shoes. We're going for a stroll. I lost the silver blade I picked up in Venice during our scuffle in the park. Any weapons you might suddenly remember owning?"

"The Bible was it. Unless you count the mace I carry in my purse."

"Might come in handy. Grab it. Stick it in your pocket." He opened the front door as she retrieved her purse. The mace fit in a back pocket, and she emptied out her cash from the purse she rarely carried. Seventy dollars and some change.

"Leave it," he said hastily. "I've got credit. And I think the wolves have entered the building."

They filed down the hallway and took the stairs to the rooftop. Rain pummeled their shoulders as Dante escorted her along the slippery red-tiled roof to the edge, where, two stories below, another rooftop offered a flat, pebbled landing.

"You ready?" he asked.

"With you? Always."

He kissed her then, his mouth cool with rain. And he pulled her head closer as he deepened the kiss. Hungry and greedy, he took from her. She gave back. Everything about Dante felt right to her. Even if they were running away from something—even each other—most of the time.

He wrapped an arm across her back and said, "I've got you," before leaping into the sky.

Chapter 19

Dante landed on the lower rooftop with both feet, Kyler secure in his arms. The impact barely registered in his bones. He didn't pause and rushed to the roof door. He kicked it in and hustled her down the staircase to the ground floor.

Once out on the street, he grasped her hand and they raced toward the river. If the wolves spent any amount of time in Kyler's apartment, they'd have her scent and his, as well. He hoped the rain would keep them off their scent.

"Where are we headed?" she asked as they passed down a street narrower than a car could navigate.

"The Incroyables have a safe house in the eighth. It's a few stories underground but nice." He intended to leave Kyler there and go to King himself. But he wouldn't tell her that. "You like wine?"

"Uh, yes?"

"We've a vast wine cellar at the safe house. A great way to pass the time."

"Sounds like something only vampires from centuries past could have designed."

"Indeed. This way."

Ten minutes later, rain had soaked them to the skin, and he had to adjust his body temperature to shake off the chill. Kyler shivered subtly, and he didn't remind her how to do the same. Instead he hugged her against his side as they wove through the chestnut and elm trees paralleling the Champs-élysées. He didn't smell the wolves. But to be safe, he took a zigzagging path to make their trail more difficult to track. Finally they stood before the digital entry box for a private courtyard nestled between five-story buildings, mere blocks away from the Arc de Triomphe.

"I'm going to need another shower to warm up," Kyler said as she followed him into the open courtyard, which featured a square garden in the middle replete with tiny box shrubs, blooming violets and white roses.

The entrance to the safe house was through an empty apartment labeled "Private." Inside the small foyer Dante turned left, pressed his hand to the wall, paused and then pushed again. The wall opened to a dark hallway. At a back wall, Dante pressed the paneling to reveal a digital keypad. Deceptive in that it was a retinal scan. Christian liked all the latest technology. Dante leaned forward and opened his eye wide. A confirming beep sounded. The airlock huffed open, and the wall slid to the side to reveal a staircase lit by blue LEDs.

"Very James Bond," Kyler noted as they started down the stairs. "Totally unexpected from the technology noob."

"Christian is the tech nerd in the tribe. He's also the oldest, clocking in with a seventeenth-century birth date."

"Are all the vamps in your tribe created?"

"No, Kindred was born to Lark and Domingos La-Roque. He is dhampir; half vampire, half human. And Damian, well, he was transformed by his sister in the eighteenth century. We don't discriminate."

"Unless you're a woman."

"We've got to uphold some sanctum from all the frills and fripperies."

He led Kyler into the front apartment, which, decorated in steel and ice blue, was as frill-less as it got. Blue neon glowed from under the steel bar and at the cornices at each corner of the ceiling. Dante had only ever used this place as a bachelor pad. He'd never *needed* it before now.

He pulled off his wet suit coat and tossed it across the back of the couch as he passed by. Kyler followed as he veered down the hallway lit with more blue LEDs to the armory. This time the entry was digital, and he punched in an eight-digit code. The armory lit up with too-bright white lights that always made him blink. The narrow room stretched twenty feet, and both long walls were hung with weapons of all sorts that the tribe had occasion to use over the centuries. The high-tech stuff hung closest to the door because Christian liked quick, easy access to the articles he used the most. Pistols and standard knives were farther back. And at the very back, where Dante headed, the medieval stuff had been carefully preserved and kept well-oiled or sharpened to stay in working condition.

"This is cool."

He swung a look over his shoulder. Kyler held the ring-size pistol he'd once nicked from a woman's vanity just before the turn of the previous century. It had only the one bullet in it at the time, and he'd never found more to fit it. But it was a collectible, so he'd hung on to it. And Isaac did like to marvel over it even though the behemoth of a vampire couldn't fit it onto his ring finger.

"And look at this!" She set down the pistol and touched the wavy blade of a kris dagger.

"Careful," he cautioned. "That one can split hairs in two."

She nodded in appreciation, then touched the silver hilt of a rapier set with rubies. "Are all these from your tribe's collection over the ages?"

"Yes."

"You do prefer the old-timey stuff."

"Is there any other way?" he asked as he selected a silver-bladed dagger from the wall. It was much sharper than the one he'd purchased and lost in Venice. This one fit at his hip nicely with a holster clip. And he still had the titanium stake that he'd claimed from King earlier. He took that out and set it on the counter below the hung weapons and replaced it with a standard wooden stake.

"Really?" Kyler said as she hugged up against his arm and patted the stake. "Old tech is cool, but don't you want the advantage? I'm pretty sure any opponents we have to face from here on in will wield the fast, precise stuff."

"You'd be surprised what finesse and perfect aim can do." Satisfied he had what he needed, he turned to stride out, but Kyler tugged him back at the threshold.

"Which ones do I get to use?"

"For now?" He pushed back a fall of her wet hair over her shoulder. "None. You've the mace, yes?"

"Yes, but—"

He kissed her for good measure. "Good for now, Kitten." He smirked at her heavy sigh as she followed him back toward the main room.

Once there he pushed aside an original Olivia De Berardinis painting that featured a kittenish blonde crawling forward on a bed, wearing a black tail and ears and nothing else to cover her ample cleavage. Set in the wall behind the painting was a safe. Digital. He entered the code and opened it to reveal an assortment of files and even a few velvet jewelry boxes. He wasn't concerned about what the boxed contents were. None belonged to him.

He tugged out the spell paper from his pocket and placed it inside.

"Do I get the code for that one?" Kyler asked from behind him.

"Do you want it?"

She shrugged. "Nah. I'm good. So now what?"

He closed the safe and returned the painting to a level hang. "The wine cellar is down the hall and to the right," he said. "Bedrooms to the left. A bathroom, as well. The kitchen is stocked with water and I'm not sure what else. There are movies and books in here. You have your cell phone?"

She pulled it out. "Why? Oh, wait. You're not going to leave me here—"

He grabbed her by the shoulders and kissed her hard. Always that initial struggle, like she didn't want this but then quickly realized how much she did. It bothered him a little. And yet she'd told him she loved him.

Pulling away from the kiss, he said, "I have to do it like this. I won't put you in harm's way. I'll call."

And he shoved her onto the couch and turned and raced up the stairs. Once at the top, he heard her yell, "Bastard!" and his heart cracked open. He paused before closing the door. He was being cruel. But it was a necessary cruelty to keep her safe.

Kyler stomped on the floor in frustration. Because stomping felt appropriate right now. And so did screaming and shaking her fists at nothing more than the stupid picture of the naked cat woman on the wall.

"I hate him!"

She plopped onto the couch, not caring that her wet clothing would probably soak into the suede, and grabbed an ugly gray pillow to punch. A few punches did no more to disturb the pillow's existence than it did to calm her. The sneaky bastard had done it again. He'd been planning to abandon her well before they'd arrived at the safe house.

He deserved so much of her hate. And yet…

She tilted her head against the back of the couch and exhaled. "I love him."

* * *

As far as dramatic meeting places went, this one rated a three on a scale of one to ten. The aqueducts beneath Paris were only as fascinating as bricks and water could get. And, having consorted in these very tunnels many a time in his younger, pre-vampire years, Dante could only wonder when the city would get better security to keep the unsavory people—which included evil vampire hunters plotting to destroy many—out.

He wasn't surprised to see that only King stood waiting for him. Of course, there were doors set into the limestone walls unseen from his vantage point, so Dante wouldn't let down his guard for a moment. He wielded the wooden stake as well, he'd tucked the silver blade in a back pocket. He would not overlook the sudden appearance of werewolves.

King, dressed in leather pants and a long black leather knight's jacket with a bladed collar, also wielded a stake. Titanium, spring-loaded, deadly. Dante knew from experience the knights' jackets were packed with inner pockets that contained more stakes, garrotes, blades, holy water—all the necessities when fighting vamps. Though he doubted King packed holy water.

It gave him a chill to know that King was vampire. He'd neglected to notify the Council. He would, when he could find a moment to think.

"Do you really want to do this, D'Arcangelo?"

Dante stepped forward, putting his distance from King at about twenty feet. The Seine burbled beside them. The cobblestone walkway was about eight feet wide.

"I really want to do this," he replied and spun the stake a few times.

"You didn't bring the spell."

Dante splayed out his hand as if to state the obvious.

"I didn't believe you would. That's why I came alone," King said. "No need to go all hunter on you if you've still got what I need."

"I appreciate the restraint. Make me understand," Dante said, "why you need to kill so many. Doesn't your little murder club take down enough vampires to satisfy your twisted need for genocide?"

"It's simple. I hate vampires. Always have. Just because I was transformed into one during my early vamp-fighting efforts didn't mean I had to suddenly embrace them all as my brothers. But that's not ultimately what I'm after."

"You could have fooled me. The only thing that spell will do is destroy vampires. And if you think I'll hand it over and then stand back and let you end my life, along with the lives of all my friends, you need to think again."

"What if I gave you a day to leave the city? Alert all your friends?"

Dante chuckled. "You're insane. I still don't get it."

"The spell you hold will produce the ashes of a thousand vampires," King said firmly.

"At the very least. Paris is rife with vampires." Dante still wasn't following, but he figured if he let the guy talk, he'd eventually spill.

"It is a requirement for the real spell. The one I told

Kyler about. The page that the death spell was torn from in *The Vampire Codex*."

The one he'd told Kyler about? Dante winced. "Eternity? So that's *not* bullshit? But that's basically the same as the immortality you've already got."

King crossed his arms, the stake glinting by his shoulder. "I slay 'immortal' vampires. You tell me how to define such a word."

True. Immortality only lasted so long as the vampire avoided the stake.

"With the eternity spell invoked, I will become immune to death," King said. "The stake?" He thumped his chest with a fist. "Right through and yank it back out. Instant healing. And I need never fear something so ordinary as a leather-bound Bible."

Dante schooled his expression. But he had gotten the upper hand with that book. *Amen.*

"Bring me the spell and I won't harm Kyler."

"No deal," Dante said with conviction. "I've never been one to mark myself as overly sensitive and caring for my fellow vampire, but I'd be a bastard to allow such a slaughter to occur. The spell remains with me. And if you should slay me? You'll never touch that dream of eternity."

"Of course, I knew it wouldn't be simple. But there are measures I have taken to ensure you will hand it over."

Dante tapped the stake against his thigh. "Like what?"

"By now my wolves should have extracted Kyler from your safe house."

Dante chuckled. "It's called a safe house for a reason. You don't even know where it is."

"Please. You think the Order hasn't been aware of the Incroyables' safe house for decades? It's our job to know that kind of stuff. It was built in 1920 by Christian de Baureaux. I believe you did a little remodeling and expansion project on it with the turn of the twenty-first century. The Order has simply never had reason to approach it. Your tribe has never presented a threat to humans. But now, well, it's proven handy to have such information."

"The security is impenetrable. I'm not worried."

"You should be. We tortured Damian Desrues for hours before he finally gave us the entrance codes. That vampire is insane but not without a pain threshold. And, of course, an eyeball was required."

Dante clenched the stake. They'd taken out the weakest of the tribe and tortured him. Damian would have been no match for such evil because truly, that vampire was insane. He'd suffered insanity by trying to wait out the moon when he'd initially been transformed. On his good days, he was barely lucid.

Dante would make King pay for that cruelty.

The possibility that Kyler had been taken was suddenly very real.

"You harm her, and you will never have the spell," Dante said.

"Oh, she's safe. For now. But you know how this blackmail business works."

"You want me to trade the lives of a thousand vampires for one?"

King shrugged. "It's entirely your choice."

"I choose neither. I think I'll take my chances with one fanatic instead."

Rushing forward, Dante leaped and landed a kick to King's shoulder before the man could get the stake out from his holster. He stumbled backward, toeing the edge of the sidewalk, while Dante landed on both feet, spun around and delivered a right hook. King caught his fist before it connected with his ear and dropped, pulling Dante down with him. He lodged his hard combat boot against Dante's jaw and shoved him roughly off.

Both men were at their optimal performance as they lunged, dodged and swung stakes. A few times Dante dodged the stake just in the nick of time, and once he almost toppled into the Seine. But as his body leaned forward, King grabbed his arm and whipped him back on balance. They could go at each other all night, yet Dante knew King would not kill him.

This was getting him nowhere fast. King wasn't about to give up. Nor was he. In a moment of quick thought, Dante, instead of returning an uppercut after King had swung away from his high kick, stood there a second too long. King collided with him, shoving him back to land on the cobblestones. Dante spat blood with the hard impact but didn't move as the round hard base of the titanium stake slammed against his chest.

King's smile wasn't so much triumphant as disappointed. "You win for now. But I've got the girl." He pushed the stake against Dante's chest but didn't compress the paddles to release the deadly tip. "You know where the Order's headquarters are. She's being held in the cathedral. I have Boa setting up the sanctuary for the spell right now. It's best performed at midnight." He checked his watch. "That gives you a little over an hour. The sooner you comply, the sooner you'll have your precious Kyler back."

Pushing up, the slayer strode off, wobbling once, likely from the kick to his kidney.

Dante closed his eyes. The cold water from the Seine soaked through his clothes, chilling his skin.

Boa was setting up the spell? He'd heard that name before. Boa was a warlock. One of the darkest and vilest of them all. The warlock hailed from Viking times, or so the rumors held. Hell, a warlock of any sort was out of Dante's league.

They already had her. This had merely been a lure to get him away so they could take her. Not only had a valued tribe member been tortured because of Dante's neglect, but he'd let Kyler down.

Could he trade the lives of so many for one?

Chapter 20

Kyler woke in a fog and sat up in the middle of what looked like a church sanctuary. Wooden pews had been pushed against the wall, and overhead moonlight shimmered in cool streams of blue, green and red through the stained glass.

She shook her head and touched her temple where it ached. She'd taken a punch from…a werewolf? She remembered now, scenting the wolf and turning around only to spy his meaty fist aimed straight for her face.

She'd been taken out of the safe house? What kind of safe house was it that werewolves had been able to breach the retinal scan? Such access would involve— she didn't want to know. She really didn't.

Twice now she'd been kidnapped and taken to a new

location. Something wrong with that. As a vampire she should be on her toes. Able to avoid kidnapping.

"I've a lot to learn," she muttered and then shivered.

She sat on the cool stone floor of a church. And everything she knew about vampires and holy symbols— she had been baptized as a baby—meant she could be in a lot of trouble.

Gathering her legs up to her chest, she clasped her arms around them and took in the room. Her eyes moved inward from the pews and stone flooring to the ring of something white that surrounded her in a circle about twenty feet in diameter. Tiny crystals of something—

"Salt?" she whispered.

And then she knew. She didn't even have to talk to King to get answers. He'd had her kidnapped. And somehow, she was a part of his plan to either gain eternity or wipe out hordes of her own kind.

Including her?

"Dante?" she whispered. "Where are you?"

She'd didn't want him to come after her and risk his life. Better that he couldn't find her, and King never got the spell to work his evil.

The door of the safe house was open, and Dante rushed inside and down the stairs, knowing he wouldn't find Kyler. His heart dropped when he entered the first room and smelled werewolves. But they were long gone, with her.

He swore and kicked aside a sofa cushion that must have been tossed to the floor in a struggle. They had better not have harmed her. He prayed she had gone along peacefully with her captors.

"Her captors," he spat. "Damn it, D'Arcangelo, you've failed her." He swore loudly and punched the air. More swearing burst from him, but he wouldn't wallow.

At the wall, he tore away the pinup painting and opened the safe. He pulled out the paper on which the spell had been written and tapped the half symbol of the ouroboros that Kyler had easily recognized. A fitting symbol, the snake eating its own tail, for the vampire slayer who would kill his own to gain eternity.

"The bastard didn't lie to Kyler. But he didn't tell her the complete truth, either."

Kyler had believed King would share eternity with her. Dante knew that would never happen. And she had not been aware of the cost of vampire lives required to complete the spell, else he knew she would have never agreed to obtain the egg for King. She was too good to commit such an atrocity.

And now she would be involved in just that unless he rescued her.

After tucking the spell into the suit coat he'd left across the back of the couch, Dante threaded his arms through it and rushed back down the hallway. He suddenly stopped, slapping a hand to the wall. "Boa," he said. "Warlocks are witches and…witches and vampires? Yes!"

He turned and dashed into the armory, looking around until he found what had just occurred to him could be an excellent weapon. A hypodermic syringe.

Stuffing that in his suit pocket, he then rushed up to the front room and called Christian on his cell phone.

"I have to talk quickly," Dante started right in. "The situation with King has come to a head. I'm meeting him. I don't need your help. I can get Kyler out. But it's Damian."

"Desrues?" Christian asked.

"They tortured him. King and his werewolf henchmen. They gained access to the safe house and kidnapped Kyler. I'm not sure where Damian is right now, but you need to find him."

"Yes, right away. You sure you don't need backup, D'Arcangelo?"

"I'm good. Thanks. Tell Damian I'm sorry."

"You'll do that yourself when we've found him. Check in with me."

"Yes. Soon. Wish me luck."

"Luck."

He raced up the stairs and out into the night. It took him all of fifteen minutes to cross the river and gain the fifth arrondissement where the Order's headquarters were situated.

Dante walked around the building that looked to unknowing eyes like just another Gothic cathedral tucked within the tight confines of Paris central. The limestone walls traveled up four stories and the stained glass windows did not catch the moonlight on this dark side of the building.

He assumed the place would have peripheral security, probably cameras, so King would know he'd arrived. And although the advantage of surprise had been taken from him, Dante decided to act as if he had it anyway. He climbed up the side of the building, fitting his fingertips between the stone bricks, until he reached a stained glass window two stories up. Fortunately, it was a latch window and not set permanently into the sill. He jiggled the window with his fingers, and eventually the latch loosened. He focused on lifting the latch and had the window open within a minute.

Making sure that the stake was at his hip and the syringe was still in his pocket, he then checked the spell with a confirming pat against his coat. Crouching on the windowsill, he took in the scene below. The wide and long nave had been cleared of pews, with most pushed into the ambulatory. Thin moonlight beamed through half the windows, illuminating the floors, where myriad colors stained the dull stones.

He assumed the church had been unblessed, otherwise how could a baptized vampire possibly pass through it? Unless King had his own access from a different entry point. That made sense. The Order would want to keep their headquarters as vampire-free as possible. Fortunately, Dante had never been baptized; bless his mother. She had never believed there existed an all-powerful God who would punish wrongdoers and those who sinned. She had meted such cruel punishment against herself.

As for Dante's beliefs, if there was a God, wasn't his ministry all about love?

Love. That insistent feeling that kept creeping up on him. He couldn't shake it. And it was completely different from the one other time he'd felt love for a woman. He had, indeed, fallen in love with Kyler.

Now to prove to her he was worthy of her love in return.

Down below in the middle of the sanctuary, looking up at him, stood Kyler. His curvaceous kitten, his accidental thief, his utter and complete downfall. It was a fall he had not intended to take. But really? He didn't mind it so much anymore. For he belonged before her, on his knees, looking up into her beautiful blue eyes. She would not break his heart. She mustn't.

She wasn't bound or tied up, simply contained within the middle of a large salt circle. Salt wasn't known to keep back vampires, but if it was a spelled circle, then he understood when she shook her head at him and didn't call out. She then made a concerted show of turning to look toward a door on the north wall, which was open. It likely led to the place where King waited, along with his warlock lackey.

Warlocks were witches who had committed a grave crime against their own species. And vampires and witches had this nasty *thing* between them. Witch blood was once known to vamps as a death cocktail. Get a few drops of that in the bloodstream? Bye, bye, vampire. Of course, that was before the Great Protection spell had been destroyed, and now, apparently, witch blood no longer had such an effect on vamps. But Dante did know that a witch or warlock who had been around since the induction of such a spell might still possess that deadliness in their blood.

He'd brought along the syringe, with hope.

Dante leaped and landed on the limestone-tiled floor with quiet grace. He approached the salt circle and strode around it. Kyler turned as he circled her. Fear watered her eyes. He would stab the stake through King's heart simply for that.

He clutched the stake tightly and stopped before the salt line, which was spread about five inches wide on the floor. He could draw a foot over the line, opening it and releasing Kyler. But what else would he release? Or let inside? Warlock magic was malefic and vile. Perhaps for now she was safest inside.

He pointed toward the open door, and Kyler nodded confirmation. How far could he get if he grabbed the girl and ran? Perhaps to the street? He could send Kyler on her way and—she'd never be free. Not unless Dante could destroy both of the men behind this foul venture.

"Get out of here," she suddenly said in a tight whisper. "I don't want you here."

"It's okay to be frightened, Kyler. I'm not going to leave you."

"You don't understand. I *want* this to happen. King has promised me eternity."

At that statement he dropped his arms to his sides. She couldn't mean it. Not after all they'd been through, the confessions they'd made to each other...

"It was a great few days," she continued, "but I can't keep this up. If given a choice between eternity and you? Well." She shrugged and looked aside.

Dante beat a fist into his opposite palm. "Kyler?" She was lying. She had to be. To protect him? Didn't she realize he had her back?

"You promised you'd protect me," she said. "So why am I here? I can't love a man whose word lacks integrity. I just…can't. So leave, will you? Get the hell out of Paris before it's too late for you."

"No." Even as his heart cracked open and the pain of heartbreak threatened to force him to his knees, Dante stood firm before her. She wouldn't meet his eyes. She couldn't. It had to be a lie. He needed it to be a lie.

And yet her words held truth. He hadn't protected her. It should have never come to this, him standing here, unable to help her out of the circle. And her, having been manhandled and taken into custody—who knew what the warlock had already done to her? And King.

He had promised her eternity?

"He won't give it to you," Dante tried. "He's not that generous. He'll stake you as soon as he's gotten what he wants. If you don't love me, then…" He squeezed his eyelids shut tightly, fighting the crazy need to scream. "I'll get you out of here, then you can walk away from me. But I won't leave. I…"

He had to tell her that he loved her. He had to reveal his heart, even as the broken muscle was bleeding into his soul. He'd been afraid that she would break his heart. Had so idiotically protected it from harm for all these decades. And now, when he'd finally relented to love, he'd once again lost.

"Kyler, listen to me." He would tell her and let her have that part of him. It was all he had left. And if she couldn't love him, then he didn't want that part inside him to linger.

"You bring the spell?" King called.

Just as Dante had been about to confess, the founder of the Order of the Stake stepped out into the cathedral. He wore no shirt and the wide belt that topped his black leather pants was stocked with stakes, blades and a pistol. He strode up to the edge of the salt circle, opposite where Dante stood.

He would make good on his promise to rescue Kyler. No matter what she wanted—or did not want—from him. He must remain true to his word.

"It's right here." Dante tapped his coat pocket and the paper within crinkled. "It's the real spell. Promise."

"I know it is. Boa can feel its energy."

"Where is your pet warlock?"

"Preparing." King nodded over his shoulder to indicate the hallway from which he'd appeared.

"You can have the spell," Dante said, "if you give me Kyler. I'll walk out of here with her—" Or she would push him away and run for freedom; she had to do what her heart demanded of her. "And you can do whatever it is you need to satisfy your bloodlust."

"Okay." King held out his hand. "Give the spell to Kyler, and then she can hand it to me."

"You have to release her *before* I hand it over."

"That's not how this works, D'Arcangelo. I don't need you running off with both the girl and the spell. She's safe within the circle."

Dante considered his options. Though he hadn't tried to broach the circle, he suspected access would be impossible if a warlock had laid it down. And he couldn't leave Kyler behind. No matter what. His life would not be the same without her in it.

Yet she didn't want him anymore.

Please let it be a lie. He believed in her. He had to believe she wouldn't do this to him.

"As soon as the spell hits your hands," Dante said, "you open up the circle and let her out."

"Fair enough." King gestured with a nod of his head to Kyler. "Get the spell from him. Hand it to me."

Kyler walked over to Dante, and now he saw a teardrop spill down her cheek. She closed her eyes and shook her head subtly. King was not going to let her go. They both knew that. So Dante would instead rely on his strength and quickness. And pray the warlock took his sweet time with the preparation.

He handed the spell over, and the paper bent and curled downward right above the salt line.

"Right," King said. *"Pervius,"* he announced in Latin. "Now you can do it. But don't touch her."

Dante placed the paper on Kyler's palm, and the shimmer of their touch sparkled through his being. She felt it, too, and her sigh hushed across his skin as if a beckoning summer breeze.

"I've got you," he said quietly. And his soul shivered. "No matter what."

She again shook her head subtly, but with another Latin word from King the salt circle suddenly *whooshed* up as an invisible wall. Kyler inhaled sharply and stepped back. Dante shook the sting from his fingers. He felt like he'd been burned and could smell burned flesh even though his skin looked unscathed. But Dante did not step back from the impermeable circle.

Kyler turned and strode over to King. The man took the spell and looked at it, nodding.

At that moment the warlock stepped into the cathedral. Dante felt the air grow heavy and colder. Fists formed at his sides, Boa marched forward with bare feet and head held high, eyes focused on Kyler. He had a Mohawk streaked with red, green and violet within the black hair, tied high in the back where heavy dreadlocks spilled down past his shoulders. The sides of his head revealed intricate black tattoos that Dante assumed were spell tats. Silver rings laddered down both ears, and two such rings had found their way through his lower lip. A high-waisted, belted leather girdle contained his lean yet muscled torso. Rings on his fingers glinted in the moonlight beaming through the stained glass windows. And what looked like crimson *blood* dripped from his fingertips.

Dante scented the foul odor and recognized it as human—or paranormal? He had to act now or lose all chance at rescuing Kyler. He'd handed over the spell; she should be free to go. Lunging forward in an attempt to step across the circle, his foot and hands were repulsed, and he toppled backward, barely catching himself.

"That's the thing," King said as he stepped over to join Kyler. "I lied. We need her as the vessel."

"The vessel?" Dante kept an eye on the warlock, who stood solidly at circle's edge, eyes now going white as he began to hum in a low tone. Kyler did not protest

King's suggestion. Hadn't he promised her eternity? Shouldn't she be more upset to know he'd lied to her? Unless he had not. Was this all part of the gift King had promised her?

"You don't need her!" Dante shouted. "Let me take her away."

"I need something to contain the spell ingredients. She will collect the ashes of a thousand vampires," King said. "And then I will bite her and have my eternity."

"Kyler, come to me." Dante tried to reach across the salt circle, but it was as if an invisible wall blocked him.

"I can't cross it," Kyler said. "It's my fault and I got myself into this mess. I don't love you, Dante! Run! Get out of here! Get out of Paris before the spell is enacted."

"I don't need you to love me. And I'm not leaving you."

"I wouldn't want you to," King said. "You'll miss all the fun. And you'll provide the final pile of ash as the spell moves toward completion and focuses back toward the point of origination. Boa!"

Still chanting, the warlock crossed his arms high over his chest and stepped over the salt line to insinuate himself into the circle. As he crossed the salt, the invisible wall crackled as if white lightning had just arced across the curve.

At that moment, Dante stabbed a foot at the salt in an attempt to open the circle, but the salt acted as if it had been epoxied to the floor. It wouldn't move. He pushed his toe against the line without feeling the electrical zap; then a twinge traveled through his muscles and he was again repulsed.

King presented the spell paper to Boa, who, pausing from his chanting, read it carefully and nodded. "You are sure?" the warlock asked. "It does not discriminate."

"Of course," King said. "I've been waiting for centuries for this. You'll protect me, yes?"

The warlock smiled then, as if he knew something no one else did. "I have seen the egg in which this spell was contained. Of course, this is a favor I perform for you."

Dante sensed the warlock's sudden disgust. *A favor?* Did he not want to do this? Or maybe he wasn't getting anything in return? He had smiled as he'd read the spell. There was something wrong with the spell. Had to be.

Boa lifted his bloodied hand and traced a symbol onto King's forehead while chanting some mumbo jumbo Dante did not understand. It could be voodoo, for all he knew. But he sensed the malefic presence growing in the room, radiating out from the circle like a wicked fog. A shiver traced his shoulders and up the back of his skull. He'd never before felt evil so tangibly. It clutched at his soul and warned him to run.

King grabbed Kyler and jerked her over to stand before Boa.

"Don't hurt her!" Dante shouted.

Ignoring the instinct to flee, he beat against the impenetrable wall. He needed to break it somehow. He looked around and eyed the pews lined up along the wall. He might use one of them as a battering ram.

Boa drew the same symbol on Kyler's forehead, then shoved her away as if she were discarded trash. She hit the invisible wall, palms out to stop her momentum, and Dante pressed his fingers against the wall, hoping to touch her. He could feel her fear, and when she turned to him he wanted to brush away her tears. To make it so that they'd never even left her eyes in the first place.

"Wipe the symbol off," he hissed, quietly enough that the warlock and King, who were conversing over the spell, would not hear.

"Just let this happen," she said. Blood dripped down onto her cheek. "You can't get me out of here. And…" Choking gasps betrayed her forced bravery. "I'm scared."

"What can I do to make you feel safe? I'll die here with you, Kyler," he said. "But today doesn't feel like my last day."

"My knight in a well-tailored suit." She smiled, and tears again spilled down her cheeks.

"I love you, Kitten."

"Y-you do?"

He nodded. "Not like my usual love. What I feel for you is different."

"I know that. You're a complicated man. Your love could never be simple. Oh."

"I know you lied to get me to leave. You don't need to explain. I would have done the same. It doesn't matter. I will always love you."

"Dante…I wish I could touch you."

"Feel me in your blood."

She nodded. "If only we had bonded."

"We've taken one another's blood, which connected us in a small way. You can feel me if you focus. It might help—"

"Bring the vampiress to the center!" Boa announced with ceremony.

If they had bonded, would he be able to reach across the salt circle and pull her out? Or perhaps together they'd possess some powerful thrall that they could work against the warlock? He didn't know, and it was too late to wonder and wish.

"I'll figure something out," Dante said. "We're walking out of here together. I promise."

King grabbed Kyler's hand and sneered at Dante. "You're not running yet? You are a disposable fool."

Yes, he was a fool. In love. And if he was going to leave this world, it would be with Kyler in his arms. He wouldn't let her die alone. She didn't deserve any of this. She was an innocent caught in a web. He hated that he could not stop the spell—so many vampires would die—but as soon as he felt a rift, anything, he'd be on the warlock and King.

Boa's arms were outstretched to encompass the sanctuary. The blood on his fingertips continued to drip. Odd. It should have stopped—and then Dante realized the blood was dripping from his wrists. He'd cut his wrists to perform a blood spell? Wasn't that…deadly? He eyed the doorway from which King and Boa had emerged and then noted the blood drops on the floor. So much of it, and it was the *warlock's* blood.

"Vamps and witches," he muttered. It was an opportunity he'd hoped would arise. "Worth a shot."

The warlock began a deep, canorous incantation. Witches used verse and rhythm and chanting to invoke spells, a divine connection to the universe. It sounded like Latin to Dante. He knew it wasn't the recipe for a love spell; that was for sure. And then it seemed to hum like the bees that had swarmed about the former French queen's head. But too quickly that swarm segued into a babble of animal sounds and human voices that defied his understanding of how it was all coming from one person.

Dante shook his head. He mustn't lose focus and risk Kyler's life. And yet, the warlock's blood was on her. *Please don't let it enter her bloodstream.*

Beneath his palms he felt the invisible wall quiver, and then it cracked as if a rock had hit glass. Not ten feet away around the curve, something dark and wispy seeped through that crack. Aware the three inside the circle were not focused on him, Dante stepped around to study the crack where the entry had occurred. He touched it. It wasn't open, but he could feel the sharp-edged fissure. The shadow that had moved through it— it had to have been vampire ash.

The spell had begun to seek victims. Somewhere out in Paris, vampires were dying. But would it occur so slowly that they would enter one by one? He could hope. And when the ash entered the circle…the protection spell weakened to allow that deceased entity through the warded wall.

Stepping quickly, he noted King's eyes were closed, as were the warlock's. Kyler followed Dante's movements as he bent and tapped the syringe tip to a large puddle of blood on the floor. A few more drops sucked into the plastic syringe and… *That should do.*

Another wavering black cloud spilled in through the open window above. It glided mournfully toward the center of the nave where the dark spell was chanted.

The moment the wall cracked and the dark ash moved through it, Dante placed his hand on the invisible wall, and it moved to the other side of the salt line. And just as quickly something sealed about his wrist, making it impossible to move in farther or tug his hand out.

He eyed Boa and King, who stood beside Kyler. Slowly, she inched herself away from the two of them. No one had noticed Dante's position, stuck partly in the circle. The warlock continued his babble of a thousand voices.

The next shadow arrived. Another crack in the protective circle. Dante's arm slid in up to his elbow. He stepped up and fitted his body beside the wall, holding the syringe at the ready with his other hand. The next crack allowed him more access. He dropped the arm that was inside the circle so as not to draw attention to himself. Just a few more shadows—ashes from dead vampires—and he'd be completely inside.

The warlock's chants filled the cathedral with a droning, dreadful song. King tilted back his head, eyes closed and chest heaving as he spread his arms wide as if to accept whatever came to him. The blood symbol on his forehead spilled back into his hair and down his cheeks. It hadn't dried; it remained liquid and flowing. If it entered his bloodstream, bye bye vamp. Or so Dante hoped.

Dante had counted only seven or eight shadows so far. If they needed the ash from a thousand vamps, this was going to take all night.

Not on his watch.

The next shadow slipped through. As it did, so did

Dante. Completely inside, he slid his hand down to clasp the stake. The syringe he tucked at his waist. If he killed King immediately, that wouldn't stop the warlock, and he was the one he needed to worry about most. He had but one chance at surprising Boa. Then he'd have to pray to a god he'd never believed in for strength.

Charging Boa from behind, he leaped onto the man, landing high on his back with his knees and wrapping an arm about his neck. He stabbed with the stake, feeling the sharp tip enter his chest with a powerful *thump*. He wasn't sure if he had hit heart, but it didn't matter. Any wound might slow the warlock down; yet all wounds may never kill him.

The warlock bucked and spun, trying to shake off Dante. And the chanting was silenced abruptly, causing the walls rising up from the salt to shiver erratically.

"No! It's not finished!" King yelled.

Dante noticed Kyler run to the wall and press her back up against it. A swipe of her hand took the blood from her forehead. *Good.* She needed to stay out of the way. And if she could slip over the salt line when the next shadow crossed, then all the better.

Crushed up against the wall by Boa's force, Dante's shoulder and head suddenly moved through it, and he had the forethought to grab Boa's head. Two newly arrived shadows moved through the wall, pushing him completely out, save for one leg. But Boa's head was also out while the rest of his body was still inside the circle. Suspended in the awkward clutch, Dante pummeled the warlock's head with punches as he struggled within the circle to release himself. He did not relent, focusing all his strength toward bruising, beating and ultimately knocking the warlock out cold.

With the warlock's slip into unconsciousness, the spell shattered. Dante saw the wall shimmer and begin to dissipate, and then his body was completely released. He and Boa dropped to the floor in a sprawl. He kicked the warlock aside and stood.

King landed on top of Dante's shoulders. A swing of his arm brought down the titanium stake, which pierced his upper shoulder.

Dante yelped and managed to fling King from his back to collide with the breaking wall. He landed on the last foot of failing wall, and his spine bent awkwardly backward. Then he rolled to his stomach on the floor as the protection circle vanished.

The warlock lay unconscious from the beating he'd taken. But for how long?

Dante pushed up and groped for the stake in his shoulder but couldn't reach it. He gave up on it and instead wielded the syringe before him. "You don't get it, do you?"

"What's that?" King asked, now holding another stake at the ready. He jumped to his feet. His eyes flickered over to Kyler, but as quickly he resumed deadly focus on Dante.

"You're not going to win this one," Dante said, surprised that he had to explain this to the slayer. He thrust the syringe before the man's greedy, power-obsessed dark eyes. "This is the warlock's blood. I believe ancient witch's blood might supersede any protective purposes of the broken Great Protection spell between vampires and witches. You want a taste?"

"You're bluffing."

"Maybe. Maybe not."

King pointed to his forehead. "Same stuff, idiot!"

"Yeah? Then take a taste."

King's jaw pulsed.

"You still on the warlock's side?" Dante asked. "You were going to end up as ash, too. And he knew it."

"That's not true. Boa owes me." King thumped a fist against his blood-spattered chest.

"Yeah? How much did you pay him?"

King scoffed. As Dante had guessed, he hadn't paid the warlock anything. The warlock may have owed him for some past deed, but he sensed the man preferred cash. And if he wasn't going to get any? Then who was he to ally himself to a cheapskate?

"I saw the truth in his eyes when he read the spell," Dante said. "The spell is indiscriminate. It will take out any and all vampires within its range."

"This protects me!" King pointed to the smeared symbol on his forehead, then lunged for Dante, colliding head to chest. Both fell to the stone floor in a struggle that scattered the salt out in a spray.

A fist to his rib cage did little but annoy Dante. He matched King's strength and was able to pull out a stake from the hunter's weapon belt. King smashed his wrist to the floor, releasing the stake to roll away. So Dante swung up his other hand, wielding the syringe. King caught his elbow, barely stopping the needle from jabbing into his temple.

And then Dante felt the minute intrusion into his will. A thrall? Impossible. And yet…his fingers loosened around the plastic syringe. He couldn't drop it. It was his only weapon. Yet he wanted to. Some part of him that had tasted Kyler's blood—that of King's blood child—wanted to relent. So he did.

The syringe rattled across the floor and landed at Kyler's feet. Dante swore. King's intrusion into his brain dissipated, but his smirk said it all. He'd won that one.

Kyler picked up the syringe.

"Stay back, Kyler!" Dante shouted. "Get out of the church. Just go!"

She shook her head. Had he favored her stubborn need for challenge before?

Boa jumped to his feet. With a flicking gesture of his bloodied hand, he sent Dante flying away from King. His shoulders hit the wall behind him, slamming the stake through his flesh until the point of it emerged four inches out of his chest before him. The vampire hunter's aim had missed his heart. That's all that mattered. He gripped the stake tip but realized he couldn't pull it out. The handle at his back was thicker and the tip was slick with his blood.

King rushed over to Boa and shook him by the shoulders. "Start the spell again! Where is that bitch? Kyler!"

Boa gestured defiantly. "I cannot begin it again! And the other vampire is right. You would have died."

"What? Me? Killed, as well?"

"The spell does not honor my malefic symbology."

"Then why did you even speak it?"

A flick of Boa's fingers sent blood droplets spattering through the air and King dodged them. "I like to kill vampires. And that gold egg in your office is worth millions. Once you were dead? Heh, heh."

"You bastard, we had an agreement. We've—I've done things for you!"

"Ah? Is that so? Who is the one who has watched over Ian Grim all these years? What have you given me in return?"

"I gave you an opportunity to kill a hell of a lot of vampires!"

While the two argued, Dante signaled to Kyler. Now would be a good time to get the hell out. But she shook her head, ignoring his insisting gesture toward the door. She had a vendetta with King.

The stake in his shoulder hurt, but it wasn't going to drop him. When he reached Kyler and she clasped his hand, the massive wood and iron door behind them shook as if a hurricane rattled it from the other side. More warlock magic.

Boa realized they were attempting escape and with a flick of his fingers drew Dante and Kyler across the floor to him and King, their shoes skidding on the stones.

"Stay put," the warlock said to the two of them. "You want eternity without fear of death?" he asked King. "There must be dozens of dead vampires within the vessel. You can give it a go."

"Give it a go? Sounds not very professional to me. He wants to kill vamps," Dante said to King. "All of us."

Boa bristled proudly. The blood at his wrists had

ceased to drip, but his abdomen and arms were smeared with it.

Dante stepped before Kyler. "You touch her and you die," he said to King.

"Kill him," King commanded Boa.

"No!" Kyler pleaded from behind Dante. "Accept that you are what you are, King. You've had a long life. It can continue!"

"Bitch," King spat.

She lunged around Dante's protective stance, and with a swing of her arm landed the syringe against King's neck. The point of it pierced his carotid.

Boa whistled in appreciation of her daring.

"I'll do it," she threatened. "But I don't want to."

Cautiously raising his hands near his shoulders, King hissed and eyed Boa. The warlock crossed his arms high over his chest, inordinately pleased at the turn of events. His expression indicated he wanted to see if the vampiress would play her hand.

"That stuff won't kill me," King said.

"My blood?" Boa leaned forward in query and Dante nodded confirmation. "If it enters your bloodstream, it will. Any witch who was alive before the Great Protection spell? Oh yeah, our blood is powerful shit. And I am torn between allowing the pretty vampiress to have her triumph and protecting a man who does not appreciate all I have done for him."

"It was your choice to continue to watch Grim," King said through a tight jaw. He did not move. Dante kept an eye on his hands, neither of which gripped a stake. "If you kill both of them, you can write your own check. Take the egg!"

Boa scoffed. "It's already mine. And I choose the woman. She wins this time."

With that announcement, Boa clapped his hands together high above his head. In a golden flash the bejeweled Fabergé Nécessaire egg appeared in his hands. A triumphant chuckle erupted from the warlock. With a wink to Kyler, he then disappeared in a thunderclap of white light.

King said sharply, "Do it then!"

Without depressing the plunger, Kyler pulled the syringe away from his neck and tossed it to Dante.

King fell to his knees, defeated, head bowing until it touched the salted floor. "It is all I have wanted! I cannot continue always having to beware such mockery from a Bible." He beat a fist on the floor.

Kyler stepped back to Dante and inspected the stake in his shoulder. "I did lie," she said softly. "I didn't mean any of those cruel words. You've always been there for me. I'm sorry if the things I said hurt you."

"I'm tough," he managed. But it had been close. He'd believed her and had felt his heart weep. "We'll talk later. Pull the stake out," he said. "Please?"

Wincing, she stepped behind him and gripped the stake. She put up a foot at his hip to create tension as she began to twist it out. It came out slowly and felt as though she were tugging out his skeletal structure along with it, but finally it came free and she stumbled backward. The stake hit the floor with a metallic clank. Dante clamped a hand over the bleeding wound. It would heal.

"Get out of here," King huffed at them. "Go!"

"It was never meant to be," Kyler said to the fallen vampire as Dante embraced her and turned her toward the door. "Be happy with the forever you have, King. Try love for once."

King straightened with a hint of his imperious pride. A swipe of his hand wiped the blood from his forehead.

"He doesn't want that," Dante said. "He prefers drama and suffering. Just as he always has. You're no longer a king, Charles de Valois. Accept that, and start living a real life."

And with that, Dante and Kyler walked out, leaving the failed hunter kneeling in the middle of the destroyed salt circle. Death would have proven easier for him than the humiliation of failure.

Chapter 21

A week later...

Kyler strode across the vast marble floor in the fourth-floor apartment that Dante was considering buying. Located on the Île Saint-Louis in Paris, it sat directly behind Notre Dame cathedral. A strange view for a vampire to have, she thought. While Dante inspected the closet in the bedroom, she had wandered out to check the windows, to see if they were easy to open to let in the fresh air.

It mattered to her because they would share this place as a couple. After escaping King's ridiculous quest for eternity, Dante had asked her to stay in his life. For as long as she desired.

That could be a very long time. But she would take

each day as it came. With Dante in her life, she foresaw a wondrous and adventurous future.

"What do you think?" Dante asked as he strolled across the floor toward her. He wore his standard armor, bespoke gray Zegna accessorized with a summery mint-green tie. His leather scent filled her senses as he wrapped his arms around her waist from behind and leaned in to kiss her neck. His hand moved up to possessively squeeze one of her breasts.

"I like it. The location is central. The view is—hmm, a bit religious, but I can deal if you can. And the space is massive for a Paris apartment."

"Have you looked in the closet? You'll never be able to fill it with all the dresses and shoes you could buy over the decades."

That he spoke in decades of their relationship meant the man's walls had really been felled.

"I'll give it a try," she said. "But I suspect you'll have as many suits and shoes yourself."

"Nothing wrong with a well-tailored suit, Kitten."

"So you're really in, aren't you?"

"In what?" He turned her around and tapped her nose with a finger. "Oh. You mean love?" He nodded and cracked a silly grin. Very different from his Casanova smirk. This smile was genuine and true. "I am. And I'm not afraid of it, either. I know I can trust you with my heart."

"Oh, you can." She slid a palm inside the suit coat to press against his chest. "You feel that?"

He nodded. "Our heartbeats synch much faster now. If we were bonded, our hearts would always beat the same pace. We'd know when the other was upset or even excited."

"I'm excited right now. Can you feel that?" she asked, with a flutter of lashes.

He placed his hand at her breast and squeezed again promisingly.

"My heartbeats, silly," she chided.

"Oh, I thought you wanted some excitement. A well-pleasured kitten is my one and only desire right now."

"You want to do it here? What if the Realtor shows up?"

"She won't be here until much later. Contract in hand and dollar signs in her eyes. I'm hungry for you. I want you on my tongue. Your skin, your lips, your blood."

She turned into his embrace, and he bowed his head to kiss the top of her breast. And the prick of his fang teased at her skin. With a sigh of desire, Kyler said, "Yes, my love."

He pierced her deeply, drawing up an unbidden moan from her. Drawing out his fangs, he smiled up at her. A few droplets of blood dripped from his fangs to land on the hardwood floor. The Casanova grin returned.

"Let's mark our new home in body and blood."

* * * * *

I hope you enjoyed Dante and Kyler's story! I've been wanting to tell Dante's story since mentioning him in THE DARK'S MISTRESS. If you are interested in reading the stories about the other characters in this book, here's what titles to look for at your favorite online retailer:

Rook is the hero of BEYOND THE MOON.
King has showed up in many stories, but mainly in BEYOND THE MOON.
Ian Grim also pops up in many stories.

Be sure to visit my website at michelehauf.com, and if you want to see the Pinterest boards I've created for each hero-heroine couple, stop by pinterest.com/toastfaery.

MILLS & BOON®

n o c t u r n e™

AN EXHILARATING UNDERWORLD OF DARK DESIRES

A sneak peek at next month's titles...

In stores from 12th January 2017:

- **Twilight Crossing** – Susan Krinard
- **Brimstone Bride** – Barbara J. Hancock

Just can't wait?
Buy our books online a month before they hit the shops!
www.millsandboon.co.uk

Also available as eBooks.

Give a 12 month subscription to a friend today!

Call Customer Services
0844 844 1358*

or visit
millsandboon.co.uk/subscription

MILLS & BOON®

Why shop at millsandboon.co.uk?

Each year, thousands of romance readers find their perfect read at millsandboon.co.uk. That's because we're passionate about bringing you the very best romantic fiction. Here are some of the advantages of shopping at www.millsandboon.co.uk:

* **Get new books first**—you'll be able to buy your favourite books one month before they hit the shops

* **Get exclusive discounts**—you'll also be able to buy our specially created monthly collections, with up to 50% off the RRP

* **Find your favourite authors**—latest news, interviews and new releases for all your favourite authors and series on our website, plus ideas for what to try next

* **Join in**—once you've bought your favourite books, don't forget to register with us to rate, review and join in the discussions

Visit **www.millsandboon.co.uk**
for all this and more today!